SPACE MOVIES II

INCLUDING STORIES BY:

TERRY PRATCHETT
EVAN HUNTER
NIGEL KNEALE
JOHN WYNDHAM
ISAAC ASIMOV
RAY BRADBURY

Further Titles In This Series From Severn House

SPACE MOVIES II

Famous Science Fiction Television Series

Including stories by:

TERRY PRATCHETT
EVAN HUNTER
NIGEL KNEALE
JOHN WYNDHAM
ISAAC ASIMOV
RAY BRADBURY

Collected & Edited by

PETER HAINING

SEVERN
SH
HOUSE

This first world edition published in Great Britain 1996 by
SEVERN HOUSE PUBLISHERS LTD of
9–15 High Street, Sutton, Surrey SM1 1DF.
First published in the USA 1996 by
SEVERN HOUSE PUBLISHERS INC. of
595 Madison Avenue, New York, NY 10022.

British Library Cataloguing in Publication Data

Space Movies II
    1. Science fiction television programs 2. Science fiction
    I. Haining, Peter, 1940–
808.8′3′8762 [FS]

    ISBN 0-7278-4897-6

Typeset by Palimpsest Book Production Limited,
Polmont, Stirlingshire, Scotland.
Printed and bound in Great Britain by
Hartnolls Ltd, Bodmin, Cornwall.

PROGRAMME

Note: This is a list of film titles. The original works on which these films were based may have had different titles from those listed above. The original title for each story is given in its introduction.

CREDITS

The editor and publishers are grateful to the following authors and their publishers or agents fc permission to include copyright material in this collection: Random House Group for 'The Adventures of Superman' by George Lowther; King Size Publications Inc for 'What Price Venus?' by Evan Hunter; HarperCollins Publishers Ltd for 'Enderby and the Sleeping Beauty' by Nigel Kneale; Bantam Books for 'The Monsters Are Due on Maple Street' by Rod Serling; Michael Joseph Ltd for 'Dumb Martian' by John Wyndham; BBC Enterprises for 'The Lair of the Zarbi' by Bill Strutton; Greenleaf Publishing Company for 'The Invisible Enemy' by Jerry Sohl; *Astounding Science Fiction* for 'Liar!' by Isaac Asimov; Abner Stein Ltd for 'I'll Not Look For Wine' by Ray Bradbury; Colin Smythe Ltd for 'Final Reward' by Terry Pratchett. While every care has been taken in securing copyright permissions for this collection, in case of any accidental infringement interested parties are asked to contact the Editor in care of the publishers.

PROLOGUE

'Worlds of Space in the Living Room'

Orson Welles' notorious radio broadcast of H.G. Wells' *War of the Worlds* which was transmitted on the night of Hallowe'en in 1938 and convinced thousands of American listeners that Martians were landing in New Jersey and even panicked hundreds into fleeing from their homes, has a parallel occurrence in the annals of British television. This was a programme called *Alternative 3* which Anglia Television networked on May 13, 1977.

A former newscaster, Tim Brinton, played a similar role to that of Orson Welles as the straight-faced front man who informed viewers that a number of high IQ citizens had gone missing in recent months and there were various theories as to *why* they had disappeared. One of these theories was the subject of *Alternative 3*, Brinton announced earnestly, and would prove that the missing people had actually being 'recruited' to form the nucleus of a standby civilization on Mars against the possibility of the end of the World resulting from a nuclear disaster.

The documentary-style programme, which had been written by David Ambrose and directed with breathless pace by Chris Miles, cleverly utilized NASA footage of the surface of Mars along with photographs of the 'missing' people to baffle and enthral its nine million viewers. Although unquestionably a clever spoof intended to satirize some of the fashionable conspiracy theories of the time – just as Orson Welles' radio play had done forty years earlier – there were still a number of viewers who

1

believed that it was all *true*. Even assurances from Anglia that *Alternative 3* was pure fiction and had originally been scheduled for screening on April 1 could do nothing to shake the conviction of these people – and as a result the programme has now joined *War of the Worlds* and a handful of other similar SF hoax broadcasts in becoming a legend.

That any viewers would accept the premise of *Alternative 3* as possible let alone probable says much for the power of television. Indeed, although Science Fiction stories have been around almost as long as the medium itself and have had to make use of the most rudimentary special effects until recent years, the genre has thrown up a number of classic productions whose very titles are instantly recognizable: *Superman, Quatermass, The Twilight Zone, Doctor Who* and *High-Hiker's Guide to the Galaxy*, to name just five. All the evidence points to the conclusion that SF is every bit as popular on TV as it is in the cinema, and over the years virtually all space movies made for the big screen have sooner or later turned up on television.

Archive records show that the first SF programme was *Captain Video* (1949–1953) a 'live' American series for youngsters about an intrepid spaceman (played by Richard Coogan) who battled various threats from outer space aided by his Video Rangers. Despite all the shortcomings of being confined to a small New York studio – although the early scriptwriters included such important names as Damon Knight, C.M. Kornbluth and Robert Sheckley – the five nights a week serial enjoyed great popularity and it was not long before other superheroes of space were joining the Captain including *Buck Rogers* (starring Ken Dibbs, 1950), *Tom Corbett, Space Cadet* (with Frankie Thomas, 1950), *Space Patrol* (with Ed Kermer, Lynn Osborn and Ken Mayer, 1954), *Commando Cody – Sky Marshal of the Universe* (starring Judd Holdren, 1955) and, most famous of all, *Superman* with George Reeves (1953), of which more later.

Prologue

Despite the often wooden acting and crude attempts at portraying space flight and the terrains of distant planets, the success of these programmes lead to the still highly-regarded 'anthology' shows such as *Tales of Tomorrow* (1952), *Out Of This World* (1952) and *Science Fiction Theatre* (1955) which drew the material for their weekly, half-hour episodes from the short stories of a number of leading SF authors.

It was in the Fifties with *The Quatermass Experiment* in Britain and *The Twilight Zone* in America that Science Fiction really came of age on television. And once the TV programme makers on both sides of the Atlantic had realized that the genre was not just fantasy fare for children but had much to say to adult audiences about the probabilites of space travel and the possibilites of life on other worlds – as well as entertaining and exciting them – it has never looked back as the selections in this collection which span the past half century will make very evident. For herein are representative stories from some of the best Science Fiction television shows written by some of the genre's most famous writers.

Space may well be a thousand miles away in reality, but thanks to television and space movies it is only the distance to the other side of the living room . . .

PETER HAINING

SUPERMAN

(ABC TV, 1953–)
Starring: George Reeves, Phyllis Coates &
John Hamilton
Directed by Thomas Carr
Adapted from the screenplay by George Lowther

Superman is undoubtedly the most enduring television series hero of all, having first made his small screen debut in the days of black and white TV in 1953, and today, forty years later, is the star of a multi-million dollar production which benefits from all the advances in special effects and film-making technology. Now the famous 'Man of Steel' really does seem to fly on the screen! Superman actually made his debut as a strip cartoon character in 1938 in *Action Comics*, and two years later had his own animated cartoon series directed by Dave Fleischer for Paramount. In 1948 a serial for cinema audiences was made with Kirk Alyn (1948), and then in 1953 he finally reached the television screen with George Reeve in the title role. The original concept of this man who, as a child, had escaped from a cataclysm which overwhelmed his home planet of Krypton and come to live on Earth in the dual role of self-effacing newspaperman, Clark Kent, and indestructable caped crime fighter, had been jointly devised by writer Jerome Siegel and artist Joseph Shuster. Within a matter of years of their first strip cartoons, Superman had become the most influential Science Fiction comic hero as well as an icon in contemporary culture. Such indeed is the character's fame that a copy of the issue of *Action*

Comics in which he made his debut sold recently at auction for over £14,000! The original ABC TV series was produced for much of its five-year run by the versatile Whitney Ellsworth who part-scripted the opening episode, 'Superman on Earth' with Robert Maxwell. The impact on viewers of the early 25-minute episodes was instantaneous, and even Thol Thomson's special effects – crude by today's standards – still held audiences spellbound when George Reeves appeared to leap over skyscrapers and halt speeding trains with his bare hands. Reeves, who had actually made his screen debut in *Gone With The Wind*, unfortunately became hopelessly typecast in the role and when the series ended in 1957 he was unable to find other work and tragically committed suicide in 1959, aged just 45. Nothing, however, could diminish the appeal of Superman: and comic books, radio series and the constant use of his image in advertising and promotion ensured world-wide popularity. In 1978 he returned to the cinema again in a blockbuster movie starring Christopher Reeve and Marlon Brando; and then in 1984 he was back on TV once more in 'The New Adventures of Superman', played by former American football player, Dean Cain, with Teri Hatcher as Lois Lane. This latest version has, in fact, made the 'Man of Steel' a rather more 'realistic' figure, while the stories themselves contain cynical remarks about his prowess and moments of irony that would never have been possible in the original. Nonetheless, it has proved a ratings winner with audiences on both sides of the Atlantic. The following adaptation by American television writer George Lowther (1914–) is based on the original script by Ellsworth and Maxwell and relates how the legend of the unique crime-fighter began half a century ago. As a result of the success of Superman, the era of Science Fiction on TV had effectively begun . . .

1

The Great Hall of Krypton's magnificent Temple of Wisdom was a blaze of light. Countless chandeliers of purest crystal reflected the myriad lights into a dome of glass where they were shattered into a million fragments and fell dazzling over the Great Hall.

Below the brilliant dome the Council of One Hundred waited. Attired in togas of scarlet and blue, they looked impatiently for the arrival of Jor-el, Krypton's celebrated scientist. They had been summoned from the length and breadth of the planet to hear a message Jor-el would deliver. What the message was they did not know. They knew only that when Jor-el spoke all men listened.

Now they waited, curious as to the nature of Jor-el's message. Rarely did the brilliant young scientist leave the mysterious regions of his laboratory. Whatever he had to say tonight they knew would be of great importance to Krypton and its people.

There was a sudden movement and a murmuring wave of voices rose and fell, echoing in the Great Hall.

Jor-el had arrived at last.

All eyes centered on the tall, thin figure that moved forward on the raised platform and took the hand of white-bearded Ro-zan, supreme leader of the Council. There were those who noticed at once that the handsome face of Jor-el was drawn and haggard. Something, they knew, was wrong. The Council of One Hundred waited in hushed suspense.

Wearily, the young scientist turned to the gathering. Standing tall in the yellow and purple robes of his calling, he drew a deep breath. There was a moment's pause and then his voice filled the vast Hall.

"Krypton is doomed!"

Had a thunderbolt crashed through the crystal dome of the Temple at that moment it could not have produced a more startling effect!

Ro-zan rapped heavily for order, and in time the tumult aroused by Jor-el's startling words died down. Silence reigned as the two men, one the aged supreme leader of the Council, the other Krypton's foremost scientist, faced each other. Ro-zan's kindly face was grim as he strove to keep his voice steady.

"Say on, Jor-el."

Jor-el nodded and again faced his audience. He spoke slowly now, carefully, choosing his words.

"Members of the Council, I repeat – Krypton is doomed!"

A gathering wave of protest began, but Jor-el stilled it with a lifted hand. The wide yellow sleeve of the gown he wore fell away from his upraised arm and showed the gauntness of it, accentuating the thin boniness of his fingers. Whether the Councilmen believed him or not, they could see that long hard weeks of toil had aged this man. They listened respectfully as he went on.

"Would that I could bring you good news, but I cannot. Week upon week, pausing for little sleep and less food, I have worked in my laboratory, striving to understand the signs which have come to us from outer space. You, my friends, for months past have seen the sudden showers of stars that have fallen upon our planet. Comets of great magnitude have appeared from nowhere, whirling dangerously close to Krypton. Not many weeks ago a monstrous tidal wave rose from the sea and roared toward our city. Good fortune was with us, for the wave died before it reached our shores. It was then I first realized there might be something wrong and I set myself to discover the meaning of these phenomena. I have found out. Krypton is doomed to destruction."

Again a murmur of protest rose among the Councilmen and again Ro-zan was forced to rap for order. When quiet had been restored, he said, "Jor-el, how explain you this?"

The young scientist shook his head.

"Would that I might answer you, Ro-zan, but even the

learned men of science who work under me cannot fully comprehend my equations and formulae. I will be as clear as I can. The Planet Krypton may be likened to a volcano – a volcano that for years has slumbered peacefully. Now it begins to come awake. Soon it will erupt! Whether that eruption will be slow or sudden, I cannot tell. *But it will come!* And when it does, the mightly Planet Krypton will burst into a million molten fragments!"

The glowing eyes set deep in the haggard face of the young scientist held everyone in the Chamber spellbound as he added, "Time is short! I bid you prepare!"

The spell, however, lasted only for a moment. Then, with a mighty surge, a roar of anger and protest burst forth. Jor-el had lost his mind, some cried; others that he had made a mistake in his calculations. He was overwearied with too much work and needed rest. In brief, they could not and would not believe him.

His arms half raised, the scientist turned beseechingly toward Ro-zan, a tragic, almost helpless figure.

"Make them understand," he pleaded. "You, Ro-zan, can make them believe!"

Ro-zan's smile was filled with pity. He spoke in a kindly voice.

"Come, Jor-el," he said softly, "surely you have made a mistake. Surely—'

"I have made no mistake! Ro-zan, you must believe—'

Ro-zan's upraised hand commanded silence.

"I understand well what faith you must have in your deductions, Jor-el. But certainly it is difficult to believe the thing you tell us. Krypton doomed? Krypton fated to destruction? Impossible! You yourself must realize that, Jor-el, in your – er – saner moments."

The scientist stiffened, as if Ro-zan had struck him across the face. He waited a moment to master himself before replying. "You think me out of my mind?"

Ro-zan shook his head slowly, smiling patiently as he did so.

"No, Jor-el. I think that not at all. A mind as lordly

as yours knows not destruction. But certain it is, friend, that you are weary. You have toiled long and well in the service of the people of Krypton, and you need rest."

"I tell you—" Jor-el began, but again Ro-zan stayed him with an upraised hand. There was now a slight trace of annoyance in the older man's voice.

"Please, Jor-el, this is unlike you! What if your strange deductions are correct? What if your scientific equations and astronomical formulae are true? What can we do about it? Where can we go?"

With desperate eagerness Jor-el seized the opportunity to answer Ro-zan's question.

"I have not come here with this tragic news," he said hastily, "without bringing with me a solution for it. You ask me where we can go? My answer is – to the Planet Earth!"

There was a pause before the Councilmen realized what Jor-el had said. Then the Great Hall racked with laughter.

"Listen to me! Listen to me!" Jor-el cried over and over again. But his voice was drowned in the thunderous laughter. Even Ro-zan did not rap for order this time, but turned away to hide the sudden smile that came to his lips. Only when the laughter had worn itself out did he again address Jor-el.

"Dear friend," he said, "you see how right we are? You see how badly you do need rest? No – please – speak not till I have finished. You say if Krypton is destroyed we can escape to the Planet Earth. How could we live there, Jor-el? You yourself – you who have studied the Earth for years through the great telescope – have told us how inferior to ourselves are the Earth People. They are thousands of years behind us in everything, mental and physical. Their cities are as nothing compared to the cities that have existed here on Krypton for centuries. Their minds are so far beneath the capacity of our own that actually, in comparison, they have no intellect at all! As for their bodies, you yourself have said that they are weaklings. It takes a hundred Earth People together to do what one man on Krypton can do alone! They have not the power to fly, but must walk at snail's pace on the Earth's surface! They cannot breathe beneath the sea!"

Ro-zan shook his head slowly from side to side.

"Would you send us to live among such a people, Jor-el? Nay, I think not! Death is preferable to life in a world of such inferior people."

"I have studied the problem with the utmost care, Ro-zan," Jor-el persisted. "The atmosphere that surrounds the Earth is the only one that can sustain us. There is no other planet to which we can go, no other—"

"Stop! Don't say another word!"

Ro-zan's voice was harsh and his face had become stern.

"I would not be angry with you, Jor-el, but you drive me beyond patience. The Council of One Hundred and I have heard enough. What you tell us is sheer nonsense. Krypton is not doomed, nor will it ever be! You are weary and need rest – I hope it is no more than that. Now, until you have recovered your senses, please come to us no more."

Again Jor-el stiffened, for again it was as if Ro-zan had struck him. After a moment's pause he turned to go, then stopped and faced the Council.

"I will go," he said, bitterly, "but before I do, I would have you know one thing." He paused, letting his eyes rove over the assembly. "I am right. I know this. You must learn it. When you do learn it, I trust it will not be too late. I am at work on a model of a Space Ship—" A titter ran through the audience, but Jor-el did not stop. "– a Space Ship that I had hoped would carry us all to the Earth! I shall continue with my work, for only in that way may I still save you from yourselves when this tragedy comes upon us. And now – I leave you."

Not a word was spoken as Jor-el turned and moved slowly out of sight through the high arched doorway – a tragic, beaten figure.

2

A long Silver rocket – the model of Jor-el's Space Ship – gleamed under the powerful lights of the scientist's laboratory, amidst a clutter of scientific instruments. Jor-el, the sleeves of his robe rolled back, worked over the model with feverish haste. So deep was his concentration that he did not hear a panel in one of the walls slide back, and did not see his wife, Lara, as she entered with their child in her arms. She waited until Jor-el looked up and noticed her.

"I heard you at work," she said. "I knew you had returned. What did the Council say?"

Jor-el shook his head sadly. "As you warned me, Lara, they refused to believe me."

"But you intend to continue your work on the Space Ship?"

Jor-el fitted a valve into place before he answered. "Of course! Whatever they think, Lara, I am right – I know it! And if there is still time, I will save them!" He gave the valve a final twist. "I shall start constructing the Space Ship itself as soon as this model is finished."

Lara nodded, understanding. The child in her arms whimpered and she began to rock it back and forth. "Little Kal-el has been strangely restless these past few days," she said. "He has scarcely slept at all. Jor-el, do you think he feels the approach of this thing you have foretold?"

"It may be," said Jor-el. "He has always been sensitive to the elements."

The scientist continued his work, his thin hands moving swiftly and surely over the intricate mechanism of the model Space Ship. Lara sat and watched, rocking the child in her arms. Finally she gave voice to the question that troubled her. "Is there much time, Jor-el?"

"No," he answered, "there is little time. That is why I

11

hasten to finish the model. It is almost ready. I have only to install the Atomic Pressure Valve and—"

Whatever he was about to say froze in his throat as an ear-shattering crash burst over Krypton! He clutched the model Space Ship to steady himself, for the entire room was rocking. Things were falling and splintering all about. A tall cabinet filled with tubes and measuring glasses fell with a mighty crash. Gaping cracks appeared in the walls and the cement floor surged underfoot like an awakening monster. The high arched window broke into a thousand fragments. And through the yawning hole where the window had stood, Jor-el saw a seething fan of flame spread upward and envelop the sky.

"It has come, Lara!" he cried. "It has come!"

And come it had! In seconds, night was turned into flaming day. Across the sky, countless comets whirled screaming through brilliant space. The stars began to fall, showering upon Krypton a rain of liquid fire. Asteroids of every color careened across the heavens. Lights of every size and hue, dazzling and eye-searing, scattered over Krypton.

The elements, as Jor-el had predicted, had gone mad!

Jor-el, a man of science, remained calm in the face of this sudden cataclysm. As the sky fell, as the ground seethed, his mind teemed with the possibilities of the moment. The Space Ship was not ready. It was too late to save the people of Krypton. Too late to save Lara and himself. But the child—

"Lara!" his voice commanded. "We can do naught for ourselves or the others. But there is hope for Kal-el!"

"Jor-el— ?"

He answered her question before she asked it.

"The model of the Space Ship!" he cried. "I have only to install the Atomic Pressure Valve. A few moments will do it! And then, Lara, if it works—"

Even as he spoke he was collecting the tools he would need. And as he worked, Lara stood with the child in her arms, gazing out at a crumbling world.

12

Flames of every color roared from great fissures in the land. Against the frightful glow could be seen the majestic spires of Krypton shattering into dust. And under all this was a strange rumbling, as if some mighty force were stirring fitfully and gathering its strength for one great and final upheaval. Lara knew that when that upheaval came it would be the end.

"It is ready!"

She turned at Jor-el's words to see him standing beside the gleaming silver model.

"Give me the child," he said, "and pray the model works! For in it we shall send him to the Earth and to safety!"

Lara said not a word but placed the tiny form of Kal-el in his father's arms. She watched silently as Jor-el placed it, whimpering, into the model of the Space Ship and closed the steel door. When he was certain the door was sealed securely, he quickly threw a lever.

Together they waited. And, waiting, they heard the strange rumble gathering under them for the final upheaving surge that would spell the end of Krypton. As the rumbling increased, the flaming sky grew brighter, the comets whirled faster, the stars fell in greater showers!

They heard but saw none of this, for their eyes were fixed on the needle of the gauge that marked the atomic pressure of the model. Something seemed to be wrong. The needle had not moved. The pressure necessary to send the steel bullet hurtling into space was not increasing. But the ominous rumble beneath *was* increasing, building toward that final cataclysm that would burst the Planet Krypton!

Jor-el clutched at the lever, working it back and forth. He stared at Lara with wild eyes, and beads of sweat stood out on his forehead. Seconds, literally, stood between the infant Kalel and safety. The moment of Doom had come! A monstrous crash in the distance marked the end of Krypton! The fissures in the ground opened into yawning chasms. The laboratory began to fall about them! And the atomic pressure of the tiny, futile Space Ship—

The needle moved. There was a hissing, as of some tremendous skyrocket. Jor-el had only time to let go the lever as the model strained and trembled and, rending loose, shrieked into flaming space, bearing toward Earth its tiny passenger.

3

Eben Kent reined his horse to a stop, leaned on the worn handle of his plow, and looked off across the rolling land he had just tilled, to the point where hill met sky. There was something strange about that sky. He knew the weather, as well as any farmer born to the soil, and off-hand he would have said a storm was brewing. Yet he was not quite sure. It seemed to him there was the feeling of something more than just a storm in the air. He had seen that same slate sky before, had felt the same heaviness in the air, had seen the thunderheads rising in the west. And yet—

Eben reflected for a moment, shook his head in a puzzled way, clucked to the horse, and set about finishing the South Forty before night closed in.

He heard thunder rumble in the distance, and thought vaguely that there was something peculiar even about that. Unlike the thunder he had ever heard before, it did not die away but was continuous, increasing in volume. He clucked again to the horse, for the animal had stopped in its tracks with the first rumbling sound, its ears flattened against its head.

As Eben continued his plowing, the sun broke through the heavy slate sky. At least he thought it was the sun, for there was a sudden blaze of light in the heavens, a light that grew larger as he watched it. In the next instant he became alive to the fact that it was not the sun!

The plow was wrenched from his strong hands as the

horse reared, screamed in fright, and bolted across the fields, dragging the plow after it. As Eben stood in mute amazement at the animal's singular behavior, he heard a strange whine in the air, and then a distant roar that changed to a series of thunderous explosions. Dizziness overcame the old farmer as the whining filled his ears. He almost cried out for help as, reaching out with his hands, he sought to steady himself. It was then, as he stood tottering and afraid, that the growing blaze he had thought to be the sun struck the earth not far from him. Blinded and afraid, he threw himself to the ground, burying his face in the new-turned loam, his fingers clutching the good brown earth for safety. Then, trying feebly to crawl away on his hands and knees, he fainted.

The crackling of flames was the first sound he heard as consciousness returned to him. The air was unbearably hot, but not so hot that he could not stand it. The thunderous explosions had stopped and the strange whine in the air had died away. Eben raised his head and looked about him.

Not a hundred yards away was a strange, bullet-shaped object, almost completely enveloped in flames. Hesitating only a moment, Eben ran toward it, a conviction growing within him that someone might be inside that flaming silver shell.

Peering through the flames, he saw a child lying helpless behind the thick glass window of the door that sealed the rocket. Already Eben had come as close as the wall of heat would let him. He realized instantly that unless he broke through that searing wall the child would die.

He made up his mind quickly, took a deep breath, and plunged through to the rocket. When he emerged again from the flame and smoke, agony stood in his eyes, for he had been severely burned. But in his blackened arms he held the child!

Eben Kent and his wife, Sarah, never knew where the

child had come from, never pierced the mystery that surrounded his strange appearance on earth. Destiny perhaps played a part in directing the rocket to the Kent farm, for the Kents were childless and desired a child above anything else on earth. And here, like a gift from Heaven, was the infant Kal-el. The old couple took him into their home and raised him as their own.

They called him Clark, because that was Sarah Kent's family name. The circumstances surrounding his peculiar arrival were almost forgotten as year ran into year and the infant grew to be a strong and handsome boy, helping Eben with the chores about the farm, listening to stories at Sarah's knee in the long winter evenings. He seemed no different from other boys of his age. He attended the little country school, played games, went fishing in the hot summer afternoons, and worked and studied as all boys do.

It was not until his thirteenth year that the incident occurred that was to set him apart from ordinary humans, and was to give him his first glimpse of the powers he possessed, beyond those of the earth people who were his companions.

It happened on the last day of school. The pupils of the eighth grade, young Clark's class, waited with great expectations for the arrival of Mr Jellicoe, the principal. It was Mr Jellicoe's custom to award personally any prizes that had been won by the pupils during the year – prizes for excellence in composition, mathematics, spelling and so on.

Miss Lang, Clark's teacher, had taken the prizes from the drawer of her desk and placed them on a small table, where the children's eyes could feast on them while waiting for Mr Jellicoe. There were books of all descriptions, medals, and ribbons. Hearts beat faster as each child wondered which of these he would receive.

At last Mr Jellicoe arrived, a short, bald, and immensely stout man who was much given to laughter. There was great excitement as he began to award the prizes – a book for one, a medal for another, a blue or gold ribbon for a third. Young Clark himself was awarded a copy of Shakespeare's plays. He had shown remarkable talent in composition and had the highest marks in English Literature. He had even begun to have thoughts of making his living later on as a writer – a novelist, perhaps, or a playwright, or what was even more exciting, a reporter.

As he returned to his desk, carrying the book Mr Jellicoe had just given him, he heard Miss Lang say, "That's strange, Mr Jellicoe. I'm sure it was here."

"I don't see it," Mr Jellicoe said.

"Then it must still be in the desk," Miss Lang answered. "I'll get it."

She opened the drawer of her desk and began searching for something. Mr Jellicoe went on handing out the awards, occasionally casting an anxious glance in Miss Lang's direction.

It was at this moment that the strange thing happened.

Clark watched the teacher as she poked about in the desk drawer, and as he did so he became slowly aware that he was also looking at the inside of the desk, that his eyes had pierced the wood, and that the interior of the desk was quite plain to him. Caught behind the top drawer where Miss Lang could not see it was a blue ribbon.

"Are you looking for a blue ribbon?" Clark asked.

Miss Lang looked up in surprise. "Yes, Clark," she said.

"It's a ribbon for General Excellence," said Mr Jellicoe. "It's for Lucy Russell. But it doesn't appear to be on the table here. Do you know where it is, Clark?"

"Why, yes," Clark answered. "It's caught behind the top drawer of Miss Lang's desk. If you'll pull the drawer out, you'll – you'll—" He paused and began to falter. The eyes of everyone were upon him, eyes filled with a growing amazement. He realized suddenly that what had seemed to him a natural and ordinary thing was actually most remarkable.

Miss Lang lost no time in pulling out the top drawer of

her desk. A moment later she was holding the blue ribbon in her hand. She looked at Mr Jellicoe, then at Clark, and then back to Mr Jellicoe again.

The silence that filled the classroom was almost more than Clark could bear, and he was relieved when Miss Lang said, finally, "How did you know the ribbon was at the back of that drawer, Clark?"

Clark tried to answer but the words would not come. He was as startled as anyone else at what had happened. The simple truth was that he *had looked through the desk* as though the wood were transparent. He was about to say as much when he realized that he would not be believed.

"I – I just knew," he said at last. "I had a – a feeling that – that was the only place the ribbon *could* be."

There were another few moments of silence in which everyone looked at him queerly. Then Mr Jellicoe frowned and cleared his throat.

"Very strange," he said. "*Very* strange."

The cold, unfriendly tone of Mr Jellicoe's voice could mean only one thing. Clark looked at Miss Lang. Her mouth was set in a hard, thin line. Even his classmates seemed to shrink away from him. All at once he realized what they were thinking – that he had rummaged through Miss Lang's desk – that he had done a dishonest thing. And there was no way of clearing himself.

When he arrived home puzzled and confused he found a surprise waiting for him. Greeting Eben and Sarah as he came in, he showed them the book he had won.

Eben rose from his chair and put an arm around the boy.

"Son," said old Eben, "ye've done a fine job – a mighty fine job. That book – that book of plays – why, shucks, boy, that's one o' the finest things that's ever happened to yer ma and me. We're proud o' ye!"

Clark looked up at them and felt everything going soft inside him. He loved these two, loved them as nothing else on earth.

Old Eben cleared his throat.

"Yer ma's got a – well, a kinda present fer ye, son. Ye know the masquerade thet's bein' given up to Judge Marlow's place tonight—"

"Yes, I know," said young Clark. "But we decided I couldn't go."

"'Course ye kin!" cried Eben, slapping him on the back. "It's bein' given in honor of all them young students that won prizes! Ye got t' go!"

"But we talked this all over, Dad!" said Clark. "You said we couldn't afford to rent a costume from the city—"

"That's right, son," Sarah Kent said. "We couldn't afford to rent a costume, but there was nothin' stoppin' me from makin' one – now was there?"

"Get the costume, ma, and let him see it," Eben said.

When Sarah Kent returned with the costume and draped it over Clark's arm, he felt he had never seen anything quite so exciting. There was a tight-fitting suit of blue, a wide belt of leather, knee-length boots, and – most thrilling of all – a scarlet cape. He could hardly wait till he reached his room to try it on.

It took him but a few moments to slip out of his clothes and into the costume. Arrayed in the blue suit, with the scarlet cape draped from his shoulders, he stood before the mirror and surveyed himself. It was a wonderful costume! And to think that he had not expected to go to the party at all—! He whooped suddenly with delight and leaped into the air, spreading the cape for effect.

The shock of what happened next was almost more than he could bear. He had merely started to jump up and down in his boyish happiness over the costume. When his feet touched the floor again, he was standing *at the other end of the room!*

He stood motionless, staring about him in utter amazement. He could not believe that he had actually flown across the room, and yet—. He decided to try it again.

He bent his knees and pushed upward. And then – he was in the air, flying about the room!

He was frightened at first and his heart beat like a triphammer. Just as his eyes could pierce the wood of Miss Lang's desk, so he could fly. What was the answer? How could he do these things when other boys, he knew, could not? Was he different from other boys? He had never thought so before and he didn't want to think so now. He had a feeling that to be different would set him apart, and he saw himself as a queer and lonely figure, shunned by all.

He tried in the months that followed to forget the strange powers he had discovered in himself. Yet as time wore on he would begin to wonder whether he still possessed them, and the temptation would be too great. At such times he would look at whatever was nearest and, using his remarkable vision, see straight through it. At others, when he was sure no one could see him, he would leap lightly into the air and fly about. And after a time, when his fear of these odd things wore off, he came to like them and found joy in practicing them.

As months became years, a superhuman strength was growing in him as well, but he was not aware of it. It was not until he was seventeen that he had his first knowledge of it. It came about in an unexpected way.

The Kent farm had never been successful. Old Eben was a good farmer and a hard worker, but as far back as Clark could remember, bad luck always struck at the very moment when it seemed the Kents were about to find some small measure of success. About the time Clark reached his seventeenth birthday old Eben found himself heavily in debt. He told the boy about it on the eve of the State Fair.

They were standing in the field together. Eben had finished haying for the day and was unhitching the old horse in the light of the setting sun. Clark, having completed his chores about the house, had come to help him put the horse in the barn.

"Looks like a mighty fine day for the Fair tomorrow," Eben said, gazing off across the fields to where the sun was dropping behind the hills.

"Yes, Dad, it does," Clark said.

Eben seemed thoughtful and moody, and Clark knew he had something on his mind. He would speak of it in his own good time. He did. He said, finally, "Son, what would ye say if I was t' tell ye I was thinkin' o' enterin' the Anvil Contest tomorrow?"

Clark straightened up and looked at Eben in surprise. He could not believe the old man meant it.

"I know it sounds silly to ye, lad," Eben went on, "but we need the money bad! I won the contest once. 'Twas many a year ago when I was a younger man. Still mebbe I might have a chance. If I can win the prize—"

But how could he hope to win it? Only young men – yes, and only those noted for their strength in the county – ever thought of entering the Anvil Contest. To compete, a man had to grasp an anvil in his arms and lift it from the ground; whoever lifted it highest won $500. The prize had been won the year before by a farmer who, because of his tremendous strength, was locally known as 'The Bull'. A close second had been Fred Hornbach, whose powerful muscles had made him the champion wrestler of the state. Both were young men, and both would undoubtedly enter the Anvil Contest this year, yet here was Eben Kent, an aging man, proposing to pit himself against two such adversaries. The need for money must be desperate indeed.

It was, as Clark now learned. For the first time, Eben unburdened himself to the boy, told him of the unsuccessful struggles of the past years, and of the inability to make both ends meet. As the two walked toward the barn, Clark listened and found growing within him an overwhelming desire to help Eben Kent.

How he was to do it only time could tell.

4

The day of the State Fair dawned bright and clear, but there was little happiness in Clark Kent's heart. He had slept poorly during the night, his active mind trying vainly to invent some method, to find some way, of helping the aging farmer. He found none, and as dawn broke he sat at his window, looking out across the misty fields, vaguely troubled at thoughts of what the day might bring.

After a hearty breakfast, old Eben and Clark started for the Fair Grounds. Sarah Kent remained at home. The misfortunes of the past years had been harder on her than on her husband, and she had aged, it seemed, much more than he. Fair-going days were over for her, and she preferred now to sit at home.

The Fair Grounds presented a lively sight. Hordes of farmers and their wives and children milled about the various exhibits, and as the sun rose higher and hotter in the heavens the scene became even more hectic. There were competitions of all sorts, prizes given for the finest cows, the best hogs, the sturdiest bulls, the plumpest chickens. There were horse-shoe contests, potato-sack races, all sorts of tests of skill and strength. People filled themselves with hotdogs and ice-cream and pickles and a hundred other good things to eat. And everywhere there were laughter and gleeful shouts and the happy din of people who have come to celebrate.

Somehow young Clark and Eben bore the suspense of waiting through the day, for the Anvil Contest was not held until late in the afternoon. At last, as the shadows lengthened across the Fair Grounds, the crowd began to move toward the platform on which stood the mighty anvil.

The platform itself was decked out gaily with red-white-and-blue bunting. Toward the rear was a bench reserved for the three judges, and to the side another bench where the contestants were to sit. The anvil, newly polished, stood in the very center for all to see.

Clark's eyes roved over the crowd, sought and found what he most feared – the faces of 'The Bull' and Fred Hornbach. Throughout the day he had hoped they would not be there, that something might happen to keep them away. He was not disappointed when he saw them, however, for he had felt from the outset that his hopes would be in vain.

Old Eben looked at his son. Clark did not like what he saw in the farmer's face, for one glance was enough to convince him that Eben regretted having come. The old man realized, perhaps for the first time, the impossibility of his winning against such heavy odds. It was too late for him to back down now, however, for his name had been entered on the list, and already one of the judges was beckoning to him to come up on the platform.

"Well, son," he said, "wish me luck!"

"Good luck, Dad!" Clark said, and as he said it he felt empty inside. If only he could help, if only *he* could mount that platform in Eben's place. But how futile that would be! Even now, Fred Hornbach and 'The Bull' were taking their places on the side bench, and there was no mistaking the power of their muscles, the strength of their broad backs. Instinctively he felt the muscles of his own arms. Yes, they were strong arms, but they could hardly compare with those of the other two. His heart sank as old Eben mounted the steps.

A ripple of laughter went through the crowd as it caught sight of Eben. Beside the other two he looked indeed a futile, piteous figure. The crowd could not know the desperation that had brought the aged farmer here, could not know the dire need for money that had spurred him to take his chances against impossible odds. It knew only that he looked ridiculous in comparison with the other two.

Clark looked about at the laughing faces and felt a rage smoldering within him. Jeers and cat-calls were heard as the old man's name was called, and he took his place beside Hornbach and 'The Bull'. Clark, watching Eben, saw his face flush.

"There's no fool like an old fool," a voice said close to Clark. The owner of the voice was a middle-aged man with graying hair and a face as sour as a lemon. He wore rimless glasses and squinted through them as if he found difficulty in seeing anything even with their aid. He was well dressed, and it needed but a glance to tell that he was from the city.

Clark glared at the man, who returned the unfriendly stare. He was about to say something, when one of the judges was heard announcing that the contest was about to begin.

The first name called was that of a man who had mounted the platform after Eben. He was not a young man but his strength was apparent. He walked to the anvil and stood over it a moment. Then, amidst encouraging shouts from his friends, he took the anvil in his arms and tried to lift it. Strain and struggle as he might, the anvil would not budge, and he was forced at length to give up.

Fred Hornbach's name was called next. Standing beside the anvil, he spat upon his hands, tightened his broad leather belt about his waist, and waited for the crowd to quiet down. Then he braced himself, his arms about the anvil, and lifted. His face grew dark with the effort it cost him, and the muscles bulged on his arms and neck and shoulders. A roar of approval burst from the crowd as the anvil left the floor. Hornbach held it as the judges quickly measured the distance. One inch. The relief on Hornbach's face was evident as he sat the anvil back in its place.

Now came 'The Bull' – huge in body, with sturdy legs and a broad muscular back. He was stripped to the waist, and as he approached the anvil the crowd, noting his deep chest, his powerful stomach muscles, the strength of his mighty arms, cheered their champion.

This was 'The Bull's' moment, and he did not intend

to let it pass quickly. He clasped his hands above his head in the manner of a prize fighter and turned to all corners of the platform, acknowledging the plaudits of his admirers. As his gaze moved over the crowd it fell upon young Clark. Their eyes met, and the boy disliked the man instantly. There was a smugness in 'The Bull's' smile, an arrogance in the curve of his lips, that brought a flush to Clark's face and stirred his heart to anger.

Having given his followers time to admire him, 'The Bull' now prepared to lift the anvil. His legs spread wide, his feet firmly planted, he put his arms around the anvil and lifted it from the floor. He seemed to accomplish the feat almost without effort, holding the anvil a good three inches above the boards. He waited till the judges had accurately marked the distance, and then slowly lowered the anvil. Strutting a bit, he returned to his seat amid deafening applause.

Now the name of Eben Kent was called and again a ripple of laughter was heard. Jeers and derisive shouts filled the air as Eben moved toward the anvil in the center of the platform.

"Ye ain't got a chance now, Bull!" somebody called, and the crowd rocked with mirth.

Eben Kent was not a man to be stopped by the unfriendliness of others. He braced himself, gripped the anvil and, gathering all his strength, heaved mightily. Slowly the laughter died and the cat-calls ceased, for Eben Kent had succeeded in lifting the anvil off the floor and was now straining to win the contest! One inch – two inches – Clark, watching the old man's face, saw it slowly redden, saw the veins standing out like whipcords on his neck. He felt like screaming, "Put it down, Dad! You'll never make it! You'll kill yourself!" But he could do nothing except stand in the crowd and watch, as Eben Kent refused to own himself beaten and strained in vain to raise the anvil more than three inches from the floor!

A spasm of agonizing pain suddenly shattered the old man's face. He gasped and dropped the anvil. He staggered for a moment – but only for a moment. In the next instant he had straightened up and was smiling gallantly but painfully at the crowd.

Many laughed, for now that Eben had failed he again became for them a ridiculous figure. He was something to laugh at, and the crowd wanted to be amused. Again jeers and cat-calls and derisive remarks were thrown his way. As Eben sat down on the contestants' bench, 'The Bull' made a dumb show of being afraid of him, throwing up his arms in mock fear. This was what the crowd wanted and they encouraged 'The Bull' to continue. This he obligingly did, to their great delight.

Clark could stand it no longer. Blinded by hot, unreasoning anger he fought his way through the crowd and onto the platform. He stood before 'The Bull' with tears of rage streaming down his cheeks.

"Let my father alone!" he shouted. "Let him alone – you hear?"

'The Bull' looked at him in mild astonishment and amusement. He reached out a powerful arm to push Clark away.

"Go 'way, kid, or I'll—"

He never finished what he started to say. As his hand reached out for Clark, the boy stepped aside and swung his fist against the other's jaw. 'The Bull' shuddered and sank limply to the floor.

Hardly realizing what he had done, white-hot anger still seething within him, Clark turned toward the anvil, his eyes blazing. Laugh at his father, would they? He'd show them! He reached down, gripped the anvil in both hands, and lifted. He was almost thrown off balance at the ease with which he raised it and held it aloft, high above his head!

Not a sound, not a breath, came from the astounded onlookers. Clark stood there, looking into the amazed faces of a silent, gaping crowd. And then slowly the wonderment of what he had done came over him. He raised his eyes to the anvil, held aloft in his hands. He shifted it a little to feel its weight. There was no weight. The anvil was like a feather.

He looked toward the other end of the platform. Three of the four contestants, Eben amongst them, were staring at him dumbly. The fourth, 'The Bull', lay stretched full-length on the floor. He turned his head still further to where the judges sat. Three pairs of startled eyes were looking at him.

He lowered the anvil to the floor.

And then the crowd went wild!

Shouting and cheering, they surged toward the platform and onto it, milling about the boy. Hands clapped him on the shoulders approvingly and fingers reached out to feel the muscles of his arms.

Questions came from all sides. How had he managed to do it? Had he practiced a long time? What was the secret of such amazing strength?

A middle-aged man with graying hair pushed his way through the crowd to where Clark stood. It was the man with rimless spectacles and the city clothes who had stood beside him not so long ago and called Eben an old fool. He took hold of Clark's arm.

"Young man," he said, "you're what I've been looking for! You're a scoop! I represent the *Daily Planet* in Metropolis. I want the full story of how you developed your amazing strength!"

Clark gulped and seemed unable to find his voice.

"Out with it!" snapped the reporter. "No false modesty now! Give me the story – all of it!"

Clark tried to speak but the words would not come.

"All right, all right, have it your way!" the man barked. "I'll write the story *my* way! But I'm in your debt, anyway, young man. You've given me the beat I've been looking for all day. If you ever need anything, look me up at the *Daily Planet!*"

He shook the boy's hand and started off through the crowd.

"I don't know your name," Clark called after him.

"Eh?" He paused, squinting back at the boy. "Oh yes. Couldn't very well find me without knowing my name, could you? Well, son, if you ever come to the *Daily Planet* just ask for Perry White. That's all. Just Perry White!"

A moment later he was gone in the crowd.

5

Clark Kent never forgot that day, nor the night that followed. When the wonder of what he had done abated somewhat and the crowd began to move off and leave him, he found his way to Eben who still sat on the contestants' bench. In his hand Clark held five new one hundred dollar bills, which the judges had awarded him, and he was anxious to give these to the old farmer, happy that a kind, though rather strange, fortune had given him the chance to help.

Eben Kent looked up at the boy and tried to smile, but his face was ashen with pain.

"I – I've done somethin' – inside – here," he faltered, pressing his hand against his chest. "We'd – we'd best be gettin' on for home."

Supporting the tired old man, Clark broke a way through the crowd. Five miles or more lay between them and home. They had walked the distance that morning, but Clark knew Eben would never be able to walk it now. How right he was he did not know until they reached the narrow wagonroad that led to the Kent farm. Here Eben suddenly went limp in the boy's arms, and Clark knew he had collapsed.

Clark looked about him. There was no one in sight. Speed was vital. He must get to the farm quickly and call a doctor. There was no time to waste. And so now he did what he had never attempted before. He lifted Eben Kent in his arms as easily as if he were a child and, like a bird, left the ground.

Sweeping through the air, with the old man cradled

in his arms, the full realization of his powers dawned on him. Up to now this curious ability of his to fly, to see through things – this wondrous strength discovered only that afternoon – all these had seemed like strange playthings, not to be taken seriously. But now, as he sped through the air, he knew suddenly that he was a man apart, that he was not like ordinary men, that he was a super-being. He understood more than this. He understood that these miraculous powers could be harnessed and put to use. If a man could fly, if his eyes were gifted with X-ray vision, if he possessed the strength of countless men – what could he not do? He turned these things over in his mind as he flew toward home.

Once arrived at the farm, he quickly summoned the local doctor. Clark and Sarah Kent waited anxiously while the doctor completed his examination of Eben. At last he finished and joined them in the parlor.

"Well?" Clark questioned anxiously. "What is it, doctor?"

The gray-haired physician placed his instrument bag on the table.

"It isn't easy to tell you this, Sarah, or you, son, but lifting that anvil, I'm afraid, was too much for Eben's heart – more than it could stand. I could put it into scientific language for you, but – well – the simplest way to say it is that he used up all his strength. I – well, frankly – I don't expect him to last the night."

When the doctor had left, Sarah Kent went into the room where Eben lay. She was with him a long time. When she came out, Clark saw that she had been crying, even though now her eyes were dry.

"He wants to see you," she said.

Clark nodded and entered the room.

Eben lay propped up in bed. Against the white pillows his face was haggard and drawn with pain. He smiled wanly as Clark entered the room. He motioned the boy to a chair near the window through which a setting sun was sending its last, weak rays.

"Dad—" Clark began, but the old man raised a restraining hand.

"There's not much time, lad," he said, "so I'll do the talkin'."

He leaned back against the pillows and regarded Clark with a sad smile. For some moments he lay thus without saying a word. Then he began to talk. As he talked the shadows deepened in the room as the sun sank lower behind the hills. The western sky became a blazing flood of color. Then the colors began to fade, melting into each other, blending at last into a somber gray. And the old man talked on, telling the boy the story of how he had been found and adopted, of his early years, of the mystery that surrounded his life before the arrival of the miniature Space Ship on earth.

"And now ye know," he said at length. "Lad, ye have within ye powers there's no explainin'. Ye're a – a modern miracle, that's what ye be. 'Tis not for you nor me to question the ways of God." He raised himself against the pillows. "But these powers ye have, lad, and it rests with you whether ye'll put them to good use or to bad!"

Clark said nothing. He sat looking out at the western hills, tears burning his eyes. Old Eben went on.

"Let me guide ye, son, as I have these seventeen years. There's great work t' be done in this world, and you can do it. Ye must use these powers of yours to help all mankind. There are men in this world who prey on decent folk – theives, murderers, criminals of every sort. Fight such men, son! Pit your miraculous powers against them! With you on the side of law and order, crime and oppression and in justice must perish in the end!"

Clark sat and said nothing and the shadows deepened in the room.

"One thing more—" Old Eben's voice came feebly out of the growing darkness.

"One thing more. Men are strange. They believe the wrong things, say the wrong things, do the wrong things. 'Tisn't that they want to, but, somehow, they do. They'd not understand ye, lad. 'Tis not given me t'say how they'd act toward ye, but I know it would not be in the right way."

He took a deep breath before going on.

"So ye must hide your true self from them. They must never know that you're a – a superman. Aye, ye must hide yerself from 'em—"

His voice trailed off oddly.

"Ye must hide yerself – from – 'em—"

Clark leaped from the chair to the bedside, and his arms were around the old man in an instant.

"Dad—" he choked.

"Listen to me, son." Clark could barely hear the words and bent his ear close to old Eben's mouth. "It strikes me now. I called ye a – a superman, and that's what ye be. Remember that. You're *Superman!*"

Once again, for the second time that day, Eben Kent went limp in Clark's arms. But this time was the last. No need for words now. Clark left the room. Sarah Kent was waiting outside. Their eyes met. Without a word she stepped into the room and closed the door behind her.

Clark walked to the front door, opened it, and went out into the cool, night air. Stars were twinkling now in the blue vault of the heavens. He started across the fresh-turned fields, the smell of the earth in his nostrils, the damp air against his cheeks. He never knew how long or how far he walked. He only knew that when finally he sat down on the brow of a lonely hill, with nothing about him but the quiet moonlit land, he had decided definitely what he must do, what course his life must take.

TALES OF TOMORROW

(ABC TV, 1952–3)
Starring: Leslie Nielsen, William Redfield &
Robert Keith, Jr
Directed by Don Medford
Story 'What Price Venus?' by S.A. Lombino
(Evan Hunter)

Tales of Tomorrow has the distinction of being the first Science Fiction anthology series to be shown on television. Planned from as early as 1951 by ABC TV in co-operation with the The Science Fiction League of America, the show not only adapted several of the classic SF writers like Jules Verne and H.G.Wells, but also introduced a number of new magazine writers including Julian C. May, Robert Lewine and Frank De Felitta. The show was the brainchild of producer George Foley and Richard H. Gordon, a rising young TV executive who would later make several successful horror movies such as *Grip of the Strangler* and *Corridors of Blood*. Anxious to portray SF as accurately as possible, the pair recruited the expertise of the Science Fiction League of America. Founded in 1934 in the pages of *Wonder Stories* by the editor Hugo Gernsback and his friend, Charles D.Hornig, the League's purpose was to bring together all those with an interest in the genre. The success of the group lead to the formation of local 'chapters' in England and countries as far away as Australia and New Zealand. It was, therefore, very appropriate that the League – the first professional sponsored SF organization in the world – should have been instrumental in the making of television's first SF anthology series.

Surviving kinescope copies of the episodes of *Tales of Tomorrow* make it plain that Foley and Gordon had ambitious plans for the series, but like so many productions of the time it had to be screened live with all the technical problems inherent in such broadcasts. The first two half-hour episodes were an adaptation of Jules Verne's *Twenty Thousand Leagues Under The Sea*, starring Thomas Mitchell, and with the TV cameras apparently positioned behind water tanks to simulate underwater scenes! This was followed by a version of H.G.Well's story, 'The Crytal Egg' with Thomas Mitchell once again the star. Richard Gordon's penchant for horror was obvious in at least two of the episodes, 'Momento' and 'Past Tense' both of which starred Boris Karloff; while his ability to spot stars of the future can be judged by his casting of the young Rod Steiger and even younger Paul Newman in leading roles. The titles of the most popular stories indicate the variety of themes and locations used in the ground-breaking series: 'The Dune Roller', 'The Lost Planet', 'Ice From Space' and 'Appointment on Mars'. This last story is perhaps the most interesting of all because it was written by one Salvatore A. Lombino (1926–) a New York teacher and SF fan who would soon afterwards write a novel around his experiences in a violent local school, change his name, and alter the entire course of his life. The book was *The Blackboard Jungle* (1954) and the author's name appeared as Evan Hunter. Lombino had actually begun writing SF as early as 1951, with a series of magazine stories and two pseudonymous novels, *Rocket to Luna* (as by Richard Marsten) and *Tomorrow and Tomorrow* (as Hunt Collins). Today, of course, he is best known of all as the thriller writer, Ed McBain. Hunter's contribution to *Tales of Tomorrow* was inspired by 'What Price Venus?' a story he had written for

Fantastic Universe **magazine and it was brought to the small screen with the same characters but a change of planet – Mars being considered more familiar to the show's viewers. Starring in 'Appointment on Mars' was the ubiquitous Leslie Nielsen, and even in 1953 some of the wry humour and off-beat acting skills which he has employed in making himself a major star after a lifetime in secondary roles was evident as he stomped around a curious alien landscape which had been recreated in one of ABC's tiny New York studios . . .**

1

Tod Bellew balanced on the tip of the diving board. His was a tall figure against the blue of the sky. His body was muscular, compact and lithe. His hair was blond and close cropped, his eyes narrow and pale blue.

He leaped suddenly into space, down into the shimmering pool below. His world became a cloudy blue, swirling before his eyes. He thought, *It's good to be away from people.*

Silence, dead silence, except for the pounding of blood in his veins. A blue silence that shifted and shimmered. No people. No fools.

His blond head popped up above the surface. The sunlight blinded him momentarily. He shook his head and swam toward the side of the pool with bold easy strokes.

He clambered out, shook himself, walked to a drying chamber. Methodically he adjusted the dials and waited patiently while the warm gusts of air covered his body. In two minutes, fully dried, he stepped out into the sunlight again.

A short man in a tight tunic, much too tight for the stomach that preceded him, smiled at Tod. "Mr Bellew?" he asked.

"Yes," Tod replied, thinking, *What can this fool want? Why can't they all leave me alone?*

"A message for you, sir." The man handed him an official-looking blue envelope. Tod glanced at it briefly. The man waited.

"Well?" Tod asked.

The man grinned sheepishly and said, "Nothing, sir. I . . ."

"Nothing is exactly right," Tod said drily. "I don't carry credits in my swimming trunks."

The balding man looked embarrassed. He bowed obsequiously and turned away.

Tod dropped into a foam chair by the side of the pool. The palm trees whispered softly in the mild breeze. A few clouds, gauzy and white, tiptoed aimlessly across the Neopolitan blue of the sky

It was all very pleasant – easily one of the nicest areas on Earth, Tod thought. He wondered idly if it could be bought. It would be nice to get rid of the tourists. The Earth, Tod thought, would be a wonderful place if it weren't for people. Perhaps a few – carefully chosen and skillfully disposed of as soon as they began to show signs of wearing around the edges. They would have to be perfect specimens of . . .

The letter.

Tod glanced idly at the blue envelope. Behind the cellophane window were his name and the address of the hotel. In the upper left hand corner, in bold black letters, were the words OFFICE OF THE MILITARY. Below that was the seal of Earth Seven.

Earth Seven – the entire area extending through what had been Canada, the United States, Mexico, South America, the Atlantic Ocean and England.

Tod tore open the flap of the envelope and unfolded the letter that had been inside.

S.A. Lombino

'Mr Tod Bellew
Hotel Crestshore
Miami Beach, Florida
   You are requested to report immediately to the Office
of the Military, New York, New York. ETA 2100 Tuesday,
March 29, 1989.
(signed)
Leonard Altz

Commander, Earth Seven.'

Tod looked at the brief message again. Estimated time
of arrival was 2100 Tuesday, March . . . Why, that was
today! His eyes swept rapidly to the large clock in the
face of the bath-house wall. He had exactly four hours
to dress, pack, eat and get to New York. True, he could
probably make it in less than an hour by fast ship, but it
was still damned inconsiderate.

   Just what did the military want of him? He considered
ignoring the message, then thought better of it. *A sad
commentary on society*, he thought wryly, *when a citizen
can be ordered to be someplace he doesn't want to be.* The
worst part of it was that the order had to be obeyed.

Fred Trupa, tall, gangling, his thick brown hair matted on
his skull, glanced briefly at the scattered garbage cans in
front of the building. He hitched up his pants and started
up the steps.

   A tall girl, redheaded, with a nose too long for the
small oval of her face, glanced up from a magazine she
was reading. "Hi, Trooper."

   "Hi," Trooper said.

   The girl wore a tight tunic, molded firmly to the curves
of her body, ending abruptly above her knees.

   What was her name? Trooper wondered. What difference did it make? All the same, every last one of them.
Pigs stuffed together in a filthy hot concrete coffin.

   "What's your hurry?" the redhead asked.

   "Why don't you read your book?" Trooper said rudely.

"Pretty damned stuck-up, ain't you?" the girl said.

"Look . . ." Trooper began. He considered the futility of arguing with her, added, "The hell with you."

He started into the building, a black uninviting maw. For an instant, he turned to look at the street again. Dull gray tenements reaching concrete fingers toward a gray sky.

Doesn't the sun ever shine here? He wondered. Stinking city. Stinking dirty city pressing against a guy. All day and all night, reaching for him, ready to snatch him up and turn him into a machine like all the rest.

He took a last disgusted look at the street and walked into the gloomy hallway. The redhead stared at him curiously. He stopped before the row of mailboxes, peered into the one marked *Joseph Trupa*. The lock had been broken long ago. He lifted the flap of the box and reached inside for a blue official-looking envelope.

His name was visible in the cellophane window on the front of the envelope. In the upper left hand corner, in bold black letters, were the words OFFICE OF THE MILITARY. Below that was the crest of Earth Seven.

He stuffed the envelope into the back pocket of his breeches and started up the steps in the dim hallway. She'd be waiting, probably drunk again, fat and sloppy. *Mother!*

He passed another tenant in the hallway, quickly looked away. *Everyone with a gimmick*, he thought. *Everyone trying to slit everyone else's throat. A nice big cheerful rat race in a concrete-and-steel maze. I don't trust any of them. And I'll never trust them.*

He stopped before the door of his apartment and listened. Inside a woman was singing in an offkey voice, loud and raucous. Drunk, as usual, no doubt.

He opened the door and stepped into the ancient living room. Mrs Trupa came from the kitchen. She was a short squat woman with black hair clinging wetly to the back of her neck. Her sloppy house tunic bore the filth of kitchen drippings. She walked flatfooted, like a big duck in oversized slippers.

"About time you're home," she complained in her usual whine.

"Lay off," Trooper replied. "Lay off, will you?"

"Ingrate, that's all you are. An ingrate. Ain't done a stitch of work since you served your Compulsory. Think all I got to do is slave all day for—"

"Oh, cut it out, for God's sake."

"Sure, sure. Your father can break his back for you, though, can't he? Out every morning early just to—"

"I said cut it out! A guy comes home and gets a lecture. Always lectures. Why don't you get yourself a soap-box?"

"Don't talk to *me* like that, you little . . ."

Trooper whipped the blue envelope out of his pocket and walked over to the window, where it was lighter. He tore open the flap and read the brief message. His eyes narrowed and then a strange smile spread over his face.

"What is it?" Mrs Trupa asked.

"I'm leaving," Trooper said. "I have to report to the Military in two hours."

Maybe they'll call me again, he thought. *Maybe it's goodbye again, you lousy fat slob!*

2

They stood before the desk of Commander Altz – Tod Bellew and Fred Trupa. Tod wore an expensive tunic, carefully molded to fit his body. Trooper wore dark ill-fitting breeches and a shirt with a tear in the left sleeve.

They stood and waited for the commander to speak, two men with two things in common – their youth and a deep aversion toward all of mankind.

The commander wore the bright yellow uniform of the Military with the Earth Seven insignia on his collar. His hair was snow-white, clipped short. His eyes were brown. He was tapping a pencil on the desk, looking at the two young men standing before him.

Tod shifted uneasily. Trooper clenched and unclenched his hands in anticipation. Commander Altz cleared his throat.

"You're both wondering why you're here, I imagine," he said.

"Yes," Tod replied with a trace of arrogance.

The commander lifted black eyebrows. "There's a seed on Venus," he said abruptly. "Earth Seven wants it, must have it."

He looked at the two men, appraising their reactions to his blunt statement.

"And?" Tod asked.

"You two are going after it," Altz went on.

Tod and Trooper looked at each other, then back to the commander. "Why us?" Tod asked. "Why not somebody else?"

Altz lifted his eyebrows again. "Oh, various reasons – progress reports during both your Compulsories – physical condition – Height, stature, general bone structure, facial proportions – things like that."

"What's that got to do with it?" Trooper wanted to know. He was anxious to leave New York but the idea of Venus didn't exactly appeal.

Altz smiled. "A great deal – a great deal."

"I wish you'd get to the point," Tod said, forgetting for a moment that Altz, in this particular situation, commanded more authority than he did himself.

"All right, I'll get to the point. Earth Seven is strong. We've got more weapons and machinery than practically all the other Earth Sectors put together. There's only one thing we lack – people. Men to man the weapons and the machines – fighting men. The entire population of Earth Seven is hardly equal to one third that of the other Sectors combined."

Tod sighed. "And for this we have to go to Venus?"

"Earth Seven is ready for a merger," Altz continued. "I don't have to tell you, of course, that this is top-secret stuff. The balance here is a stagnant one. We're ready to expand – west to Earth Eight and Nine, east to Earth Six, Five, and Four."

"Expand?" Trooper asked.

"A consolidated Earth," Altz explained, "with a central command here in Earth Seven."

Trooper nodded.

"We're ready to go, as soon as we get what we need. I'll describe the seed you're to bring back from Venus."

"I still don't understand why we were chosen for this particular job." Tod frowned. "What's our physical appearance got to do with this job? Why *us?*"

"We've tried to get the seed before. We've failed each time. This time we can't afford to fail. We either get it now or drop our plan entirely. The men we've already sent to Venus never returned."

"Why?" This was Trooper.

"The Venerians are somewhat reluctant about giving up this seed. It's fairly important to their culture."

"And how will we succeed where the others have failed?" Tod asked.

"That's where your physical appearance comes in. You'll go to Venus as Venerians. Tall, blue and big-boned."

"There must be a million men in Earth Seven who are tall and big-boned," Trooper protested.

"Yes, but a certain mental attitude is necessary for the job too. Your records seemed to indicate you were the right men."

"What kind of mental attitude?" Tod asked.

"That's not important. We've made the choice and you're the men we want."

"This is fantastic," Tod said. "Of what possible use can a Venerian seed be? I'm afraid I don't approve of this at—"

"I feel I should tell you both that from here on in it's no longer a matter of choice. You are both under martial law."

"We've already served our Compulsory," Tod reminded the commander.

"I'm well aware of that, Bellew." Altz' voice hardened.

A deep silence shouldered its way into the room. Altz began tapping the pencil on the desk again.

"You'll leave in a week. The necessary adjustments in appearance will be made before then. You'll be instructed in language, culture, topography – everything you'll need to know to pass as Venerians."

"And the seed?"

"It's small, no more than a quarter of an inch in diameter. It's a pale blue in color, with a thin network of fibre under the translucent covering. You'll see pictures of it and you'll study models before you leave. Everything will be taken care of."

"How many of these seeds will you want?" Trooper asked.

"Two will be sufficient. You'll be given specific orders before you leave."

"And this seed is so very important?" Tod asked.

"Very important."

"How?"

"I've already told you. It can mean the difference between a stagnant *status quo* – or a vibrant new change."

"How?" Tod asked again.

"You'll report to surgery first," Altz said, completely ignoring Tod's question.

Bellew and Trupa turned to go. Altz rapped on the desk with the end of his pencil.

"You're forgetting something, aren't you?"

Trooper was the first to turn. Tod moved more slowly.

"I told you that you're both under military orders now, didn't I?"

Instantly Trooper brought up his hand in salute. Tod eyed the commander for a hostile instant. Slowly he brought his hand in salute.

"Dismissed," Altz snapped.

The room was long and white and antiseptic. The doctor hovered over Trooper's body, carefully making measurements.

"Wrist to elbow, thirteen," he called.

An assistant in a white gown wrote the figures down.

"Elbow to shoulder, thirteen and one quarter."

Again the pencil moved over the pad.

"Ankle to knee, eighteen and one half."

On and on, measurements, measurements, measurements. Trooper lay stretched out on the long table, waiting for it to end.

"Hair, brown," the doctor said. "Eyes . . ." he looked at Trooper's face, ". . . brown."

"Will I live?" Trooper cracked.

"I think so." The doctor smiled. "We'll have to add a few inches to your elbows but that'll be fairly simple. And your legs are a little short but they can be fixed too, of course."

Trooper frowned as the doctor went on.

"Your eyes, of course, are all wrong. Blue lenses should take care of that nicely. Your hair will have to be dyed blue. And your skin, of course . . ."

"Is all this permanent?" Trooper asked.

"Worried about your good looks, eh?" The doctor chuckled. "No, it's not permanent. We can undo anything we do and the skin coloring will wear off in a year or so of its own accord."

Trooper sighed loudly and deeply.

"We'll start whenever you're ready," the doctor said.

"I'm ready right now," Trooper answered, somewhat resigned to his fate. If it wasn't one damned rat race it was another. Always being pushed, always being pushed, always . . .

The anesthetic cup covered his nose and mouth and he drifted off into a peaceful blackness in which tiny rodents scurried back and forth noiselessly.

*　　　*　　　*

What Price Venus?

They sat together in the Hypnobooth, earphones clapped tightly to their ears. Before them the Tridim flashed brilliant scenes of Venus as the words droned on and on and on in their ears.

They saw its position in the galaxy, were told its diameter, its density, its atmospheric conditions, its allotment of heat and light.

Now a picture of a large plant flashed onto the screen. It was a pale pink, with enormous petals that flapped like the ears of a cocker spaniel.

"Among the varied plants found on Venus is the Pink Eucador, startling for its enormous size and sensitivity to sunlight. The Eucador family includes the Striped Eucador, the Violet Eucador, and the Pink Eucador."

In rapid succession, pictures of these plants were flashed onto the three-dimensional screen.

"The Striped Eucador" – here the striped flower, pink, and pale violet, flashed onto the screen – "is smallest of the group. There are five petals on each bloom. The stem is short and the plant grows close to the ground. Its smell may be compared, to a mixture between Earth's muskmelon and magnolia."

At this point there was a slight hissing in the Hypnobooth. The odor slithered from holes in the walls and into the nostrils of Trooper and Tod.

There were more plants, so many plants that the mind reeled. Slowly the voice went through each variety, from the simplest to the infinitely complex.

"Most startling in the development of plant life on Venus, however," the voice said, "is the . . ."

Came a scratching sound and a garbled medley of noises. Undoubtedly a defective tape, Trooper thought. The screen flashed through a series of blinding colors, then focused on the tall blue figure of a Venerian native.

" . . . closely resembling the human being," the voice began abruptly. "Notice the long limbs, tapering toward the wrists and ankles. The skull covering is much like human hair, deep blue in color, as are the eyes. The skin, if we may call it such, is blue."

The screen presented a closeup of the hands, showing long sensitive-looking blue fingers.

"The hands are probably the most important part of the entire structure. It is with these that nourishment . . ."

Again, the annoying scratching garbled the tape as the screen continued to display the picture of the hand. Scraps of meaning penetrated the uproar in disjointed phrases.

". . . after the free-moving stage has been achieved . . . pedal extremities no longer . . . Venerian soil is . . . and blossoming . . ."

The scratching stopped abruptly and the screen went blank. A man in white snapped on the lights. He removed the headphones from Tod's head and snapped his fingers. Tod blinked and stared around him. The attendant repeated the process with Trooper.

"That's all for today, boys," he said cheerfully.

"Better get a new tape," Trooper said. "That one's pretty muddled."

"Nothing really important," the attendant said. "You're getting enough to keep you going up there, never fear."

"I hope so," Tod said. He looked at Trupa who was now almost a carbon copy of himself. They were both tall and blue – their bones lengthened, their skins dyed, their hair blue.

It was remarkable how much they resembled the natives they'd seen on the screen, Tod thought. For an instant, his mind flashed back to Miami and the whole foolish mission washed over him despairingly. Venus! Of all the idiotic places to . . .

"You coming along?" Trooper asked.

Tod turned appraising eyes on Trooper. *A gutter rat*, he thought. *Straight from the slums. Give him a new skin and a few lengthened bones and he thinks he's my equal.*

"No, thanks," Tod answered. "I've got a few things to do."

Trooper nodded curtly. *Just like all the rest*, he thought.

What Price Venus?

A rich bastard with his own particular gimmick. This was going to be some picnic. Some damned picnic!

The language lessons had already begun. At night it droned into their ears via Somnophone. During the day, they spoke it to instructors, catching the inflection, the subtle undertones of the speech.

And in the meantime they were constantly exposed to the Hynobooth, with its three-dimensional screen and its tape recordings. There were pictures of the seed and it was almost as Altz had described it.

Actually it appeared to be a tiny celluloid pellet, pale blue and translucent. Beneath the outside covering a network of blue lines could be seen criss-crossing wildly. These terminated, it appeared, just below the surface of the seed, probably ready to burst forth as roots, once the seed was nourished.

There were models too. Trooper held one in his fingers, turning it over slowly. "All the way to Venus for this," he said to Tod.

Tod didn't answer.

Trooper turned and held up the seed. "All the way to——" he repeated.

"I heard you," Tod snapped angrily.

Trooper's eyes narrowed behind their blue contact lenses. "I don't like this any better than you do, friend," he said.

"Don't 'friend' me," said Tod.

"That would suit me just fine," Trooper said.

"It had better, because that's the way it's going to be."

"Let's get one thing straight," Trooper said. "I'm here because the job was assigned to me. I don't like blue skin, blue hair *or* blue eyes. And while I hadn't given much thought to it before, I don't think I like you a hell of a lot either."

"The feelings are mutual, I assure you," Tod said.

"Just so we understand each other. This isn't a fraternity

45

reunion. We're going after that goddamned seed. Once we get it and bring it back, that's that."

"Precisely," Tod said. "And now, if you'll excuse me."

He turned on his heel, a tall blue figure striding regally down the wide corridor.

Trooper stared after him. He had the feeling, as he'd had many times before, that he was standing on a fast-moving treadmill.

3

The long silver ship streaked through space. The stars blinked around it in mute disapproval. Commander Altz stood before the two men in space-suits. They were tall men with blue skins and the suits had been constructed especially for them. Altz wore his yellow uniform with a maroon cape slung over his shoulder. A smart officer's cap perched on his white hair. He seemed to be in a cheerful mood.

"A few minutes," he said. "Just a few minutes and you'll be on Venus – on your own."

Tod nodded. It had been a grueling business but he felt he knew as much about Venus as there was to know. Now, if everything went well, they'd get the seed, make the necessary radar contact with Earth and be picked up as soon as a rocket could be dispatched. That, of course, was still in the future. Once they left the security of the ship they would indeed be on their own.

"You understand, of course, that you're to contact us as soon as you've found the seed," said Altz.

"We understand," Trooper said.

"Then, you'll stay in the exact spot from which you sent the signal. A ship will pick you up in five days."

"We've gone over this at least a dozen times," Tod snapped. "Do we look like first-grade morons?"

What Price Venus?

"What was that, Bellew?" Altz asked, anger in his voice.

"Do we look like first grade morons, *sir?*" Tod asked, emphasizing the last word in mock respect for Altz' rank.

"That's better," Altz said, appearently satisfied. "I just wanted to make sure everything was understood. We can't afford to bungle this again."

A uniformed cadet poked his head into the cabin. "Three minutes to peak, sir," he said.

"Ah, good," Altz said. He turned to the two blue men. "We're almost at the peak of our orbit. You understand, of course, that we're not landing. Our orbit is plotted to overshoot the planet. When we reach the turning point we'll decellerate slightly. You'll leave us then."

"We've gone over this before too," Tod said.

"I'm not sure I like your attitude, Bellew," Altz warned.

"Why, Commander," Tod said in surprise, "you said it was my attitude that was partly responsible for this lovely assignment."

A warning buzzer sounded in the cabin, a red light flashed on the bulkhead. "Get your helmets on," Altz said.

Trooper and Tod slipped plasteel bubbles over their heads. Rapidly they tightened the bolts on each other's helmets, as they had practiced so many times on Earth.

Tod cut in his oxygen, hearing a slight hiss in his helmet as he adjusted the flow. He pressed the button set in the chest of his suit and tested his radio. "Can you hear me?" he asked Trooper.

Trooper's hand went to his chest and a moment later his voice sounded in Tod's helmet. "I can hear you."

A cadet opened the airlock as a green light flashed on the bulkhead. Ponderously the two men stepped into the lock. Altz saluted. He was the last being they saw before the door clanged shut at their backs.

Tod turned the big wheel on the outer hatch, held

47

it for a moment as he waited for the light in the bulkhead to blink.

"There it is," Trooper's voice said.

The blue light over their heads blinked rapidly, on and off, on and off. Tod threw his shoulder against the hatch as the big ship seemed to hang in space for a moment, preparing to reverse its course. He pushed outward into the blackness, fell free for a few seconds to give Trooper time to clear the wash of his jets, then turned them on full.

A yellow-red trail of dust seared backward from the shoulder jets and he streaked through the blackness, feeling terribly alone for the first time in his life, alone in a pinpointed blackness that seemed to stretch away forever.

He glanced backward, saw Trooper clear the ship and turn on his jets. Trooper pulled alongside as the big ship dipped around, shuddered with a new burst of power and vanished into the blackness.

"That's that," Tod said.

"That's that," Trooper said.

Below them, covered with pale shifting clouds, was Venus. They hung in space, two bloated grotesque figures against a glistening backdrop of stars, watching the wash of the big ship smoulder and die.

Like a startled rabbit then Tod whirled, jets flashing, and dived for the shrouded planet.

They dropped silently into the jungle, lay flat on their stomachs for several moments, waiting, waiting. When they were sure they had landed unseen Tod Bellew pressed the speaker button on his chest.

"You think we should take off our helmets?"

"They *said* the atmosphere was breathable," Trooper answered.

Tod peered through the bubble and looked at Trooper suspiciously. "Come on," Trooper said, "I'll unhitch you."

"No," Tod said sharply. "I'll help you with *your* helmet first."

Trooper shrugged and stood before Tod as he unscrewed the bolts that held the helmet to the breast-plate. Trooper reached for Tod's helmet and Tod backed away.

"We've got to get that seed," he told Trooper. "One of us has to get back with it. No sense in both of us taking off our helmets until we're sure about the atmosphere."

Trooper smiled grimly and said, "What makes you think I'm volunteering? What makes you think I trust Altz any more than you do?"

"This is ridiculous," Tod said, pressing the button on his chest. "We can't just stand here all day, waiting to take off our helmets."

"Then why don't you take *yours* off," Trooper asked.

Tod's eyes suddenly widened in fear. "Look out," he called, "behind you!"

Trooper whirled, reaching for the blaster that hung on the trouser leg of the space-suit. At the same instant, Tod lurched forward, putting the strength of his shoulders and back against Trooper's turning body. Caught off balance, Trooper toppled to the ground.

Tod leaped onto his body, straddling Trooper's chest with his knees. With a deft movement he snapped the helmet from Trooper's head and tossed it into the tall grass. He held Trooper pinned to the ground as he waited, his eyes glued to Trooper's angry face.

After a long while, Trooper smiled and said something. Tod watched his lips, unable to hear inside the plastic bubble. Trooper nodded and formed the letters O and K with his lips.

It was then that Tod let him up and unscrewed the bolts he could reach on his helmet. Trooper unloosened the rest of the bolts and Tod lifted the plastic bubble from his head.

He took a deep breath and turned to Trooper. "Looks as if Altz was telling the truth after all," he said.

S.A. Lombino

Trooper's eyes narrowed. "Lucky, aren't we?"

Tod glanced sharply at Trooper, startled by the tone of his voice. "We'd better get out of these suits," he said softly.

They shrugged out of the suits, standing blue and tall in the Venerian jungle. They wore loin cloths, nothing else. Quickly, they extracted folding shovels from the pockets of the suits and began to spade the soft earth.

Trooper stopped digging once to examine the portable radar unit encased in the breastplate of the suit.

"Come on," Tod said. "Come on."

Trooper joined in the digging again, beginning to sweat freely. "I wonder if this stuff runs," he said, dead-panned.

"Very funny," Tod said drily. He began stuffing his suit into the hole he had dug. "We'd better speak Venerian from here on in," he suggested.

Trooper considered this as he began burying his suit. "You go for this cloak-and-dagger stuff, don't you?" he asked.

Tod glanced up. "Sure, I adore it. Nothing I like better than sweating in a stinking jungle with a—"

He cut himself short and finished covering his suit. "Can't you hurry?" he asked.

"I'm doing my best," Trooper replied. "What's the rush anyway? Have you got any idea where we're going to find this damn seed? It might be in any one of these plants."

"The sooner we get started the sooner we get back. That's all I'm interested in."

Trooper dumped his shovel on top of the space-suit and covered the rest with his hands. He tore up some weeds and scattered them over the fresh mound of earth.

"Okay," he said, "let's go."

4

They struck out through the jungle, speaking only Venerian now, stopping at each plant to examine the

50

petals, to prod deep within the flower, searching for a translucent blue-veined seed.

"A botanist," Trooper said, frowning. "A goddamn botanist."

They pushed on, the sun searing down through the magnifying layers of clouds that covered the planet. Trooper was hot – he was hotter than he ever remembered being. Somehow, he was sure that if his skin weren't blue he'd be cooler. He began to curse the color of his skin, began to curse the plants that stretched in endless monotony around them, began to curse the planet itself.

A seed – a lousy seed! All the way to Venus for a seed. Like looking for a needle in a haystack. Why hadn't they told them just what plant the seed belonged to? Why all the hush-hush?

He trudged along behind Tod, stopping at a tall flowering plant, tearing open an elongated pod near the top. Six brown seeds tumbled to the ground and Trooper scrambled after them, cutting his hand on the jagged weeds in the undergrowth. He picked up the seeds and stared at them.

"Brown," he muttered. *"Brown!"*

"Any luck?" Tod asked.

"No," Trooper said sullenly. "No luck."

"Let's get moving."

They began to move again, pushing their way through the jungle, scrutinizing each plant, each shrub, each bush, each weed, with inquisitive eyes and probing fingers. Trooper was sweating more freely now, the moisture oozing from every pore in his body.

"Let's go," Tod said.

Let's go, Trooper thought. *Let's go. Let's go. Let's go.*

And all at once, quite unreasonably, all the heat, all the plants, all the treacherous undergrowth, the reaching thorns, the pulling weeds, all of these seemed to center themselves in the plodding figure of Tod Bellew. A surging hatred boiled up in Trooper's being. For a blind moment he thought of killing the blue figure that trudged along before him, of killing him, of sending the radar signal back, of sitting down to wait for the pickup ship.

It would be nice to sit somewhere in the shade – somewhere out of this heat that . . .

"Wake up, damn you." It was Tod's voice. "There's something up ahead."

"What?" Trooper said wearily.

"I think it's a village. You remember the pictures they showed us."

"Glory be," Trooper said, "a village! Goody goody gum drop."

"The next time you speak Terran . . ." Tod warned.

"Shove it," Trooper said. Then, in Venerian, "Do you see any natives?"

"No. Let me do the talking until we're on safe ground."

"Who nominated you for leader of this little party?" Trooper asked, sarcasm thick in his voice.

"I just nominated myself."

"And who seconded the nomination, may I ask?"

They were close to the village now. A cluster of huts, conical in shape, thatched, laid out in a neat circle, the center of which seemed to be a high mound of soft earth.

Quite suddenly a tall Venerian crossed the clearing in the center of the huts. He saw Tod and Trooper and waved his arm in a gesture of friendly greeting.

"I'll handle this," Tod whispered.

Trooper was about to answer, thought better of it.

The Venerian grinned and approached the two Terrans. It was amazing what a job the surgeons and magic men on Earth had done, Trooper mused. If he hadn't known better he would have sworn he was watching himself cross the clearing.

The Venerian stopped before the two men and raised his arm, folding the other across his chest.

Trooper automatically made the greeting sign they'd practiced on Earth.

"Welcome," the Venerian said. "Our village is honored twice."

"And we," Tod repeated the customary acknowledgement of welcome, "are honored to be welcome – doubly honored because we are two."

"I am called Ragoo," the Venerian said, "son of Tandor."

"Toda do they call me," Tod answered, "son of Palla, and here with my brother Troo."

"Welcome, Toda and Troo."

"We have traveled far," Tod said, "and would know the name of your village that we may honor it when we return home again."

"Crescent Eight," the Venerian replied, "and to which village do we owe the honor of your presence?"

Trooper watched Tod carefully. He knew he was probably making a few fast mental calculations, picturing Crescent Eight on the projected diagram they'd seen back on Earth.

Crescent Eight – that would be pretty close to Crescent Eleven, Nine and Ten being far distant to the South. A good safe bet would . . .

"Crescent Five," Tod said, just as Trooper completed the same mental calculation.

"Welcome," the Venerian Ragoo said again. Trooper wondered how many times he was going to repeat *welcome* before he invited them in and gave them something to eat or a place to sleep.

They started into the village and natives appeared magically, swarming over the clearing, shouting their welcomes loudly. The men were dressed exactly like Tod and Trooper, naked except for loin-cloths.

They looked amazingly human, except for their peculiar proportions. Long and thin they were, with a subtle hint of strength rippling beneath their bright blue skins.

Trooper stared in interest as he noticed some women

come into the clearing for the first time. The women too were naked, except for a waist cloth that reached almost to their knees. Their breasts were bare, full, blooming like the flowers of a rare tropical plant.

And where the peculiar length gave the men an elongated somewhat-stretched appearance, it added a willowy sensuous beauty to the women of the village.

Their skin too seemed to shimmer and glow in the intense glare of the filtered sunlight. Their hair, long and blue, hung like vibrant seaweed about their shoulders. Their eyes tilted slightly, giving them an Oriental slant. But Trooper saw nothing exotic in the eyes themselves. They were open and frank and honest.

About the necks of each of the women, glistening brightly in the sunlight, were strands of jewels – delicate beautifully-rounded spheres that glowed in incandescent beauty.

As the women came closer Trooper noticed that the older ones among them wore no jewelry at all. And the youngest of the group wore tiny spheres, lacking in lustre – dull rounded pebbles. It was the middle group, those who were neither girls nor matrons, those who were women in the full bloom of maturity, that wore the brightest largest spheres.

Trooper stared at these until he felt his close scrutiny was becoming too obvious. He realized they were being led to one of the thatched huts. Ragoo chattered incessantly to Tod as they walked slowly across the clearing.

"You will stay," Ragoo was saying, "for at least a little while. The Planting is not far off, you know."

Trooper watched Tod as the cloud of confusion spread over his face. "The Planting?" Tod asked.

Trooper searched in his mind for some record, some mention of the Planting. He could remember nothing about a planting.

Ragoo smiled and put an arm around each of the men. His arm felt cool to the touch, almost like the arm of a dead man.

"Then you have not sown," Ragoo said, still smiling. "It is an even greater honor that you visit our village at this time."

Trooper smiled wearily as Tod went through the *mutual honor* business once more.

"You must be weary," Ragoo said. "You will rest here and feed whenever you are ready."

"Thank you," Tod said.

"Thank you," Trooper said.

Ragoo left them alone in the cool interior of the hut.

"*Well!*" Trooper said in English.

"If I have to tell you again!" Tod warned. "Venerian! Speak Venerian, do you understand?"

"Keep your shirt on," Trooper said. "I'm as anxious to get out of here with my blue skin on as you are."

Tod glanced out at the clearing, then lowered the flap of the opening. The hut grew darker instantly. "What did you think of them?" he asked Trooper.

Trooper shrugged. "No different from anyone else. They're all the same – Earth, Venus." He shrugged again.

"They seem like a simple lot," Tod said.

"Yeah," Trooper said. He wiped a hand across his sweating brow. "You know, I can't figure out how Ragmop, or whatever his name is, stays so cool."

"Did you notice that too?"

For the length of a heartbeat the two men's eyes met. They had noticed something together, had shared an instant of mutual recognition, however small.

And then, like a fist smothering a dim candle, distrust closed tightly about them, bringing with it the old wariness.

"Sure, I noticed it," Trooper snapped. "I wouldn't have mentioned it if I hadn't."

Tod's brow wrinkled in a frown. He turned to the flap and threw it backward. "Simple dolts," he said vehemently.

"I'm getting hungry," Trooper said.

He lifted his loin-cloth. Strapped about his waist was a

S.A. Lombino

leather belt inset with a series of pockets. He unsnapped two, removed blue tablets from one, white tablets from the other.

These he threw into his mouth, swallowing quickly. "Some meal," he said.

"They warned us against trying any Venerian food," Tod said. "They're not sure whether it's edible or not."

"I'm not sure whether these pills are edible or not, either."

"They're not supposed to be tasty," Tod said. "They're supposed to supply all of our daily calory requirements."

"I wonder what I should have for dessert," Trooper said. He reached into one of the pockets and extracted a pink pill which he popped into his mouth. "Lemon meringue pie," he said sarcastically.

"I hope we find that seed soon."

Trooper burped. "I should have tried the chocolate pudding," he said morosely.

5

The next day they started out into the jungle long before the natives were up. It was hot – just as hot as it had been the day before.

Tod thought of Miami Beach, thought of the luxurious hotel and the swimming pool. And then his mind reverted to the present situation. He rubbed a hand across his forehead, breathing deeply. There was a rank smell to the jungle, a smell of ancient crowded growth, a smell of plants growing in wild profusion.

He pushed a vine aside, ducked under it, stared around him. There were so many plants, too many plants. Altz had been crazy to send two men on this ridiculous hunt. What he needed was an army of botanists, equipped to stay on Venus for thirty years, searching for a seed as elusive as truth.

What Price Venus?

The simile pleased him somehow. *As elusive as truth.* As elusive as truth in a world of thieves and liars, he should have added. Again he thought of Earth and he compared it to Venus.

There wasn't very much difference, he realized. Venus was a jungle of plants, Earth a jungle of animals. Here in this primitive sprawling jungle the plants fought for supremacy, putting tendril against tendril, vine against vine, root against root. Arguing for the right to a stretch of soil or a ray of sunshine. The weaker plant succumbed, smothered by the stronger, and was left to rot on the fetid floor of the jungle.

On Earth it was the same. He was lucky. He was one of the stronger plants. He was capable of buying and selling a hundred stinking crawling Earth humans – the animal counterparts of the weaker Venerian plants.

He had no sympathy for the sniveling creatures of Earth, no more sympathy than he had for a strangled bush here in the vicious jungle. But he was a paradox in that he had no sympathy for the stronger plants either, the men who controlled the Earth, the men like Altz who were ready to grab more and more, smothering, strangling like the powerful denizens of this jungle.

With an honesty he had previously fancied himself incapable of, he realized that he too was one of these men, that he too would as soon squelch a trembling beggar as look at him.

A product of my society, he mused. *A product of the society I hate.*

He sighed deeply and stopped, turning to face Trooper behind him. "Let's take a break," he said. "I'm tired."

Trooper nodded and dropped to the jungle floor, stretching out languorously. Tod dropped down beside him, mopping his brow again.

After awhile, Trooper sat up and stood staring into the jungle. "There's a new one," he said.

"A new *what?*"

"Plant. Haven't seen that one before."

57

"Mmm," Tod murmured lazily.

"Might as well take a look," Trooper said. He struggled to his feet. "Might be the one we're after."

Tod closed his eyes as Trooper made his way toward the bright yellow plant ahead. The plant had a long thick stem. Branches, stout and green, jutted out from the stem and tendrils dropped from these to trail limply on the ground. An enormous yellow bloom topped the stem, exuding a peculiarly sweet smell.

Trooper stepped up to the plant, close to the stem, and started to part the closed petals of the yellow bloom.

"Holy . . . !"

The cry tore through the jungle like the abortive scream of a wounded animal. Tod leaped to his feet, his eyes widening in terror. He stood glued to the spot, incapable of moving. Sweat broke out on his brow, streamed down his neck, cascaded off his chest in little rivulets. He shivered, tried to summon up the muscle-power he no longer possessed.

Not more than seven feet away Trooper clawed at his throat, trying to loosen the tendril that was wrapped tightly about it. The plant had suddenly come to life, limp tendrils snapping like bull-whips, lashing about his body, curling tightly about his arms and legs, pulling him closer to the yellow bloom.

"Tod!" Trooper screamed. "For *God's* sake . . . !"

He kicked out at the stem and a tendril dropped from his arm. He coughed, pried at the steely vine that was tightening about his throat. Another tendril lashed out, wrapped itself around his wrist, pulled it away from Trooper's throat.

"Tod!"

Silence – a silence as heavy as the clouds that smothered the planet, as intense as the sun that beat down firecely through the treetops. Silence – except for the thrashing of plant and a human.

Tod stood motionless, watching the struggle like a spectator in a box seat. Trooper loosened the tendril from his throat, tried to step back. Another tendril slapped out across his face and he blinked his eyes in pain. The tendril curled about his throat again, slowly, like a boa-constrictor tightening its death grip. Trooper thrashed about wildly as the plant seemed to exert itself in a supreme effort to lift him off his feet.

He kicked again as he was raised from the ground. And at the same instant, the yellow blossom parted, petals opening wide to reveal a fuzzy opening.

Tod sprang forward and wrapped his arms about Trooper's legs. A probing tendril reached out for him and he slapped it aside. He held onto Trooper, fighting the tremendous lifting power of the plant. A tendril loosened from Trooper's waist and curled around Tod's arm. Tod sank his teeth into it and a bitter taste flooded over his tongue. He spit and bit again as the tendril loosened.

Trooper hung limply in the grip of the plant while Tod tore at it, ripping, scratching, biting. He kicked at the stem, dodged the swinging vines, pulled at the petals of the yellow bloom. Trooper dropped to the ground, one tendril wrapped tightly about his ankle.

Tod descended on this with a fanatic fury, stamping it with his feet, kicking. He fell to the ground and pounded it with his fists, sinking his teeth into it at last. The tendril withdrew slowly, slithering across the jungle floor.

Tod seized Trooper's wrists and pulled him away from the plant – far away.

When at last he stopped, he looked back at a peaceful-looking yellow flower blooming in the distance. He sat down, panting his lungs out. Trooper lay at his feet, his eyes closed.

When Tod had caught his breath he reached over and slapped Trooper across the face. Trooper's eyes blinked. Tod slapped him again.

This time the eyes fluttered open. Trooper stared blankly at Tod Bellew for several minutes, then his face cracked into a weak smile. "Thanks," he said.

Every instinct in Tod's body shouted for him to snap

at Trooper. Every facet of his training, every ounce of experience, every previous human relationship, urged him to say, "I'd do the same for any dog."

But he didn't say it. He was sweating with the struggle and his hands trembled a little but he didn't say it. Instead he looked off to the side, avoiding Trooper's eyes and murmured, "You had a close call, Trupa."

Trooper nodded, still smiling weakly. "Goddamn seed," he said. This time Tod smiled with him in spite of himself.

When they told Ragoo about the encounter with the plant he nodded sagely and said, "There are good and bad in everything."

They didn't understand what he meant at the time but they learned a little more fully later.

Every since they'd come to the village they had been living on the calory pills from their belts. They hadn't had a real chance to observe the eating habits of the Venerians and it hadn't really interested them anyway. But after the experience with the plant, they spent more and more time in the village and were puzzled to note that the Venerians seemed to have no regular eating habits. In fact they never saw one of them eating.

"It's impossible," Tod said. "Everyone has to eat."

"Have *you* ever seen them eat?"

"No, but . . ." Tod stopped, shrugging his shoulders. "We'll just have to watch more closely."

They began to watch more closely.

The Venerians were a simple race. They rose early, escaping the rays of the sun in the conical huts for long rest periods. They seemed to do little work during the day. Their time was spent in playing games, singing, dancing. The only work they really did was of a seemingly religious nature. Or so Trooper and Tod thought.

In the center of the village was the large mound of earth. The huts were clustered about it, the mound was easily accessible to all of them. Parties of men would go off into the jungle and return with fresh soil daily. This they would pile onto the mound.

Tod and Trooper were confused until they hit on their hosts' religious theory. The theory seemed to be substantiated by the peculiar rites the Venerians performed.

At irregular intervals one or another of them would go to the mound and thrust his hands deep into the soft soil. He would leave them there for several minutes and then withdraw them.

"It's a ritual," Tod said. "It can't be anything else."

But they continued watching.

They were surprised that they saw no Venerians they could classify as children. There were the old, the middle-aged, the mature and the adolescent. But no children.

"I can't understand a society without children," Tod said, still confused.

"Maybe they eat their young," Trooper suggested.

Tod frowned. "I doubt it. I've never seen an easier-going people."

"They *do* kind of grow on you," Trooper admitted. "They're just what you said they were in the beginning – a simple people."

It was about then that a new activity began in the village. The mound in the center was replenished daily but in addition to that a new area of soil was being laid down. The area was a large rectangle, also within the ring of huts. But in contrast to the mount it was flat.

Trooper stopped Ragoo and asked him what it was all about.

Ragoo smiled. "You are joking."

"No – no, really," Trooper said.

Ragoo chuckled out loud this time. "Be patient, my friend. We are preparing for the Planting."

"Oh," Trooper said.

"You will sow," Ragoo promised.

When the rectangle had reached a size approximately sixty by a hundred feet the Venerians stopped carrying soil from the jungle.

After this a new sort of game began to be played. The young girls of the village, their translucent jewelry gleaming at their throats, began to circulate among the young men. They danced for them and sang for them, displayed their breasts and their hair, followed them about the village.

Trooper was surprised to find a doe-eyed Venerian parked outside his hut after his sleep one morning. He blinked at her, his eyes still not accustomed to the glare of the sun.

"Hello," she said. "You are the one they call Troo."

"I am he," Trooper said, "son of Palla, here with my brother Toda."

The girl smiled, her teeth glistening like the baubles around her throat. Trooper noticed that they were set in a single line, curving gracefully about her neck, gleaming brilliantly in the sunlight.

"Are you not sorry to be away from your village at the time of the Planting?" she asked.

Trooper hesitated.

"Or do you find our village a worthy one in which to sow?"

Trooper nodded. "Indeed," he faltered, "it is a worthy one."

The girl smiled again and looked shyly at the ground. "I am happy," she said. "I am called Donya and this is my first Season of the Planting."

"It is my first too," Trooper said.

The girl looked up with wonder in her eyes. "Really?" she asked. "Is it really?"

"Why, yes."

"And have you already made arrangements?"

"No. No, I – er – haven't."

The girl lowered her eyes again. "You will consider me bold."

"Why, no, not at all. I think you're very sweet."

She smiled up at him. "I will come to you," she said, then she fled in my embarrassment.

When Trooper told Tod what had happened Tod nodded knowingly. "Me, too," he said. "Perhaps there's a sort of festival at the Planting. Perhaps the girls are asking us to escort them or something."

"Sure," Trooper said, snapping his fingers. "I should have realized."

"After all," Tod said, "we are eligible Venerian males, you know."

"Oh, you kid," Trooper said.

6

The time of the Planting came the following week. Trooper and Tod stood in the opening of their hut as the men watched the young women dance before them in the circle formed by the huts.

Donya came to Trooper, a secret smile on her face. She knelt before him and lowered her head.

"I come, as I promised."

Trooper nodded.

She rose then and took Trooper's hand in hers. Her hand was cool to the touch. She led him into the darkness of the hut and lowered the flap. She turned then and huddled into his arms. Trooper caressed her cautiously, unfamiliarly.

"You hesitate," she said shyly. "We will learn together."

The afternoon was one of whispered words and fond caresses. Slowly, tenderly, Donya guided Trooper's hands to the glowing spheres at her throat. He didn't know what to do. She closed his fingers on the first sphere, then gently pulled his hand away. The sphere clung to her skin for an instant and then shook loose. Donya gripped him tightly.

They waited and again she guided his fingers to the spheres. One by one they fell loose into his hands.

And then, when all the spheres had been plucked, Donya whispered, "I will wait while you sow."

He lifted the flap and stepped out into the sunshine. Tod met him there and they stared in bewilderment at each other.

They followed the other young men to the new rectangular plot of earth. They watched silently.

The young men gripped the translucent spheres in the palms of their hands, closed their eyes and thrust their fists deeply into the soft soil. When they withdrew their hands the spheres were gone.

Tod turned a glistening, translucent sphere in his fingers. "Trooper," he whispered, "I think we have finally found the seed!"

"What?" His mouth fell open.

"The seed, Trooper. This is *it!*"

Trooper stared at the glistening ball for a long time. "No," he said. "You're wrong. The other seed had blue veins beneath the surface."

Tod nodded his head. "The other seeds were fertilized, Trooper."

"Fertilized? What are you saying, Tod? You're talking as if these people were . . ." The word caught in his throat as they approached the rectangular plot. "*Plants.*"

They went through the motions, thrusting their hands into the soil, releasing the seeds. Over and over again they repeated the process until all the seeds were in the ground.

Trooper went back to the hut then and Donya was waiting. "And have you sown?" she asked. She touched him with cold fingers.

"Yes," he said, "I have sown."

"Thank you," she murmured, "thank you, thank you!"

Tod and Trooper watched the development of the seeds. After a week, they plucked one from the earth and studied it. A blue network of lines had begun to form beneath the surface of the sphere. .

"That bastard," Trooper said. "He wants us to bring back people. *Seeds!* Seeds that grow people!"

"We're not sure," Tod cautioned. "We'll wait and see."

They waited. The weeks dragged into months and the seeds began to sprout. A tall stem at first, then four secondary branches. A large bulb formed slowly at the top of the stem and by the fourth month this bulb had assumed the half-shaped contours of a face. The branches had grown longer, bright blue in color.

Trooper thought back to the sessions in the Hypnobooth, to the garbled sentences the tape had tried to reveal through the scratches.

. . . after the free-moving stage has been achieved . . .

This was after the eighth month. The plants seemed to shake themselves free of the soil, emerged as perfect figures.

. . . pedal extremities no longer . . .

No longer *what*, Trooper wondered. Why, no longer provide nourishment to the plant, he realized in amazement. The hands became a substitute. And he knew then that the mound in the village was the Venerian method of feeding.

. . . Venerian soil is . . .

Venerian soil was the staff of Venerian life – because all Venerian life was plant life.

. . . and blossoming . . .

And blossoming around the throat of the female of the species, he filled in, *is the precious seed that guarantees preservation of the species.*

And Altz would have them bring these seeds back. So that he could plant them, and use them as robots in his expansion plans.

People – men to man the weapons and the machines . . .

And Altz would have them bring back the seed of a slave race, a race to fight the wars. What was it he had said? . . . *a certain mental attitude is necessary for the job.*

And he and Tod had that mental attitude. Their records showed it.

Bellew and Trupa pondered this together for long hours, the rich boy and the poor boy – the two Altz had thought specially fitted for the job of securing a slave race.

It was difficult at first to break down the walls each had built through the years – difficult to override the pull of inbred instinct – difficult to pour out their emotions to each other, to break the wall of hate and loneliness.

But they turned the problem over, comparing the simple, happy existence these people now led to the one awaiting them on Earth.

They made the only decision possible.

They said their goodbyes the next morning. The young girls, the new crop that was now free-moving, were already beginning to develop tiny translucent spheres around their necks.

The space-suits were where they'd left them. Bellew and Turba dug them up, two men who knew exactly what they were ready to do. The radar units were intact and they sent the signal back to Earth.

The ship came promptly five days later, hovering over the planet like a silver needle in the sky. They adjusted their bubbles, took blasters in hand and turned on the power in their shoulder jets.

The men on the ship were jubilant. "The Commander will blow his top," they shouted. "You'll get medals, both of you."

The two were strangely silent throughout the entire trip. Their skins were beginning to fade back to normal colors. They talked little, answered questions tersely.

When the ship landed on Earth five days later they had subdued the small crew. They dropped them off on the outskirts of New York, bound and gagged, then headed for the Office of the Military.

Commander Altz greeted Bellew and Turba with a broad grin. They wore the clothes the crew had provided for them and their holstered blasters hung at their sides.

"Well," Altz cried. "You made it!"

"We made it," Tod repeated.

"And the seeds – did you get the seeds?"

Trooper's blaster flicked into his hand.

"Wha –?" Altz began.

"Here's the only seed you'll ever know," Trooper said. His finger tightened on the trigger and a searing yellow beam knifed across the room. Tod's blaster echoed Trooper's as Altz dropped to the floor.

They ran to the ship, slammed the hatches, pointed the nose toward the sky.

It streaked out into space, a slim promise, trailing the sparks of a dead civilization. The stars in infinite numbers blinked curiously.

"There must be other worlds," Tod said.

"Better worlds," Trooper said.

They aimed the nose of the ship at one of the curious stars and smiled in the darkness of the cabin.

THE QUATERMASS EXPERIMENT

(BBC TV 1953–1979)
Starring: Reginald Tate, Isabel Dean &
Duncan Lamont
Directed by Rudolph Cartier
Story 'Enderby and the Sleeping Beauty' by
Nigel Kneale

Saturday nights on British television were never to be the same after 8.15 p.m. on 18 July, 1953 when the first 30-minute episode of *The Quatermass Experiment* entitled 'Contact Has Been Established' was transmitted live after an afternoon of sport, children's TV and news. Those who might have been in any doubt about what they were about to see were warned by an unseen announcer, "This programme may be unsuitable for children or persons of a nervous disposition." At a stroke Science Fiction was introduced to the nation's viewers and a legend was born that has endured to this day. The bold decision to feature an SF story on TV was taken by the BBC's new Head of Drama, Michael Barry, who gave the go-ahead to staff writer Nigel Kneale to dramatize his idea about a space mission which inadvertently brings back an alien virus to Earth. What made the series so remarkable was that it anticipated the Apollo moonshot by 16 years as well as many of the fears about manned space-flight which were later to be proved uncannily accurate. To those like myself who can remember the series with its rudimentary special effects – still no mean achievement by Richard R. Greenhough and Stewart Marshall on a total budget of just £3,500

– and the show's frequent tendency to overrun its alloted time span, it was nevertheless a landmark production that Rudolph Cartier's direction made believable and somehow far beyond the confines of the studios in which it was acted. Unknown to us at the time, the spectacular finale in which the apparently 100-foot high vegetable-like 'monster' wrecked havoc in Westminster Abbey was actually the author Nigel Kneale using his gloved hands covered with vegetation inside a blown-up photograph of the famous cathedral!

Nigel Kneale (1922-) had trained to be a lawyer before becoming a playwright and even undertook a little acting prior to joining the BBC. The success of Quatermass lead to three sequels: *Quatermass II* (1955), *Quatermass and the Pit* (1958) and *Quatermass* (1979) which was comissioned by the BBC but when the production was cancelled on cost grounds, Thames TV took up the option and transmitted it in four episodes with Sir John Mills as Professor Bernard Quatermass – a name, incidentally, that Kneale had plucked from the London telephone directory! Since then he has continued to enhance his reputation with a number of TV dramas, contributions to several series and the creation of two more of his own: *Beasts* (1976), a horror series about human attitudes towards animals, and the much underrated *Kinvig* (1987). This series had grown out of Nigel's fascination then with stories of contacts with aliens. Profoundly cynical at the claims of numbers of people to have seen flying saucers and by others to have actually flown in them, he devised the story of an everyday little repair man, Kinvig (Tony Haygarth) who unexpectedly encounters a beutiful alien from Mercury (Pruncella Gee) who takes him on board her spaceship. Overnight the statuesque Miss Gee in her revealing costumes – mostly variations on swimsuits and bikinis – became unmissable to a lot of the adult male population, while

Nigel Kneale

Nigel Kneale's brillaintly comic scripts put meetings with aliens into a whole new context. *Kinvig* remains a series that deserves a reshowing – and here as a reminder is an earlier story by Kneale written in 1949 which explores the same theme of an ordinary man suddenly coming face to face with an otherworld beauty . . .

A double-size chin. With a wide, pleasant mouth to say the thoughts from the long, tipped-back cranium above. These thoughts were just so many, docile and wholesome, like a well-ordered flock. Most concerned the laws and functions of machines, for Fred Enderby had been a mechanic since he began to screw strips of painted tin together in his mother's back-yard in Warrington.

L.A.C. Enderby, Frederick, is the only man, I believe, to know the factual core of a legend that every child can tell when it has reached half a dozen years. How a princess pricked her finger on a magic needle and slept for a hundred years, with the whole palace, courtiers, scullions, dogs, in a trance where they fell. Round the palace grew a hedge of thorns so that no one could get in, or, once in, out. Until at the end of the appointed time, a handsome prince broke through and kissed the princess back to life, while every creature in the court stirred and moved again. That is the legend. Here are the facts:

In 1942, Enderby was in North Africa on maintenance duty with an R.A.F. survey truck. They were far to the south of the battle area when the great retreat to El Alamein reached its height. Helpless in the radio silence, knowing only from the rumbling, and the glow by night, that the enemy was closing on Egypt.

Several times the party spotted planes, slow, sightless specks. To avoid the chance of capture they turned to the south-east, deeper into the desert. Flat barrenness gave place gradually to the wallowing Sahara.

They were deep in that wilderness when the kamsin storm came upon them.

The wind was of unnatural violence, Enderby said. Sand shifted in whole dunes. The party were totally unprepared. To go on was impossible. To leave the truck seemed suicidal. The sides of the thing trembled and drummed. Cans of petrol and a spare wheel tumbled away into the whirling dust.

The truck itself became unstable. Twice they felt the three offside wheels lift and settle again. Then, even while they shifted gear to balance it, the vehicle went over.

The officer in charge had his head crushed by falling equipment. Another man was trapped. A third smelt petrol, forced his way out, and was choked to death a few yards from the truck he could no longer see.

Enderby was in the cab, unconscious.

He woke at last from his own coughing. There was sand in his mouth. He lay upside down across the body of the driver.

Enderby levered himself up and examined his mate. The man was dead, his face buried in a soft, suffocating layer that covered the inside of the splintered window.

Enderby forced up the other door. Sand poured from it. The simoon had become a gritty breeze across the reshaped land. He slid out, coughing.

The truck was half-buried. The rear door, once opened, had been held wide by the blast that poured inside. Nothing lived in there now. The man from Warrington rested a while, still half-stunned, among the smothered shapes.

When Enderby set off alone the sun was still fierce. He had water in a full bottle: some fresh, some from the truck's tank: and sufficient emergency rations to reach safety, if he could trust the sun and himself. He felt weakly bitter that the radio had smashed itself.

At the top of each rise he stopped and turned about, shading his eyes: blinked and went on. He walked slowly, to conserve his strength. The glare beat up against his body.

It was perhaps an hour after starting, Enderby says, that he first saw the thing.

As he came to the sliding, coarse top of a shallow dune, its brighter colour struck his eye. A few hundred yards away. There was something man-made about that pale stone that he could just barely see.

Enderby shouted once and began to run, slithering among the brown ripples.

It was a building. Sand was heaped about it on every side. Only a part jutted from the desert, like a half-buried box. The roof and corners were formless, the pale walls deeply corroded.

Enderby's heart sank. He walked haltingly along the bare side of the place, turned a corner into the black, cool shadow. Just where the desert rose up under his feet and hid the building, he found a door.

It was recessed between two of the flat, shallow buttresses that ran up the walls at intervals. Surprisingly, the lock was on the outside of the thin stone. (As Enderby said later, "An ordinary lock mechanism with no cover. It was all made of stone bars and big – it must 'ave spread over 'alf the door.")

He was able to open it. His dread of the desert forced and fought the lock until it submitted. The door ground and scraped until there was a gap wide enough for a man to enter. On the other side was complete blackness. "'Allo, in there!" Enderby shouted. "Ey!"

The answer was a long, clapping echo.

He found matches, stepped into the cool darkness and struck one. He was in a small, bricked antechamber. As the second match flared up he saw a heap of faggots. ("Sort of compressed fibre, they were made of," Enderby said. "They lit easily. Queer. Made you feel you were kind of expected.")

With the slow-burning, smoky torch held high, and two cold spares stuffed inside his shirt, he entered a passage. The air was dry and dead and sweet.

Then he dived to the wall, crouching, quivering.

Nothing stirred.

"Who's that?" said Enderby. "If it's anybody, come 'ere!" Then, remembering, he threw the torch.

("I saw a statue," he said afterwards. "I felt – well, a sort of daft relief. Like a false alarm in a U certificate thriller.")

The figure stood man-high against the wall. Stone drapes exposed one polished shoulder and its arms were crossed. Round the head was a wide beaded band of blue stones. And the face—

("That's what'd given me the start," said Enderby. "The eyes, long, bulging black ovals – no pupils – they were the worst. And the mouth and that – as if 'e'd sucked every dirty thing in the world into 'is mind, and was damn 'appy about it.")

When he picked up the torch he began to see others. They stood in two facing rows, lining the walls of the high tunnel.

He walked in the middle. The black eyes flickered in the light. His feet were like a cat's in the deep, black dust.

The figures were of both men and women. Some were painted, in dull colours: blue and green stones sparkled in their dress: more than once Enderby saw gold in the carved folds of a woman's hair. And every face repelled him.

They were amazingly expressive, he said. Each seemed to have a double meaning. A twisting of the brows and a wrinkling round the empty eyes, and madness showed through the face's laugh. Were they heavy and stupid, there was vicious cunning also. In eagerness was slavering depravity: in innocence treachery. Gentleness meant cruelty. ("It was like people in a bad dream. They wanted to make y' see through them. Indecent.") He was puzzled by small holes drilled in the centre of each forehead and throat, and in the robes below.

On the walls between them, depressed in the brick, were tablets of writing. Symbols were nicked out like tiny tooth-prints, row upon row. ("Like something a tike's chewed.")

The tunnel curved gradually. Enderby reckoned himself fifty yards along when he could no longer see the entrance. He began to whistle without a tune because hope had dropped to vague curiosity. The walls echoed against him. He walked in silence.

Then he saw that the figures ended just ahead. He passed the last leering face into an open darkness that must have been far under the desert. The air was thick.

Enderby crept like a glow-worm in his circle of light. His eyes went left and right.

He watched the guiding walls so intently that his knee struck what he did not see. It was a high-mounted slab. The top was carved to such a likeness of soft cushioning. ("Like petrified silk. It'd 'ave made y' sleepy to look at it. Like the mattress adverts.")

Enderby strongly disclaims any knowledge of art. Sculpture bores him and his only visit to a gallery was to the engineering section.

But what he saw on the stone couch, he says, was not sculpture.

He forgot the darkness, the unnatural figures, the choking air. He forgot the truck disaster and that he was lost in the desert.

("She wasn't just wonderful in the ordinary way. I can't tell you 'ow. Look 'ere, if y' take the most smashing film stars – Betty 'Utton, Garson – as many as y' like – and all they've got between 'em, and multiply it by ten, and then . . . oh, I dunno! She was different to them anyway – Eastern, of course – but so different in other ways. What I said, I just can't begin to describe her . . .")

But she was made of stone.

Enderby stood worshipping until the torch hand sank and the figure was shadowed.

He went to the magnificent head. The stone, he says, was tinted to life, but no paint showed itself.

Light from one raised hand smoked down across the

Lancashire man's wide eyes and long chin and tunic: and over the pale-sallow nestling stone creature with the sleeping eyes. At last Enderby leaned forward.

Very gently he kissed the sculpture on the mouth.

("She was – I've told you. Oh, I suppose it was, well – perverted. A statue, I mean. Her lips were cold.")

Then fear replaced all he felt.

For the figure moved.

Enderby started back. The delicate face had turned away. Now it came back again, very slowly. Coy. Away, back. Away, back. Rhythmically, swivelling on the carved throat, the beautiful lady shook her head.

"'Inge," said Enderby's whisper, because he was very much afraid. "'Inge, that."

The movement grew stronger, pendulum-regular. And now the eyes opened, black, horribly void. His throat seemed to wither.

Points of light moved. In the tunnel. From side to side they went, slowly. Jet eyes in metronome faces. ("Like the Chinese ornaments that keep rocking their 'eads when y've started them. Only slowly. Terribly slowly. And these shook them.")

Enderby sweated. He pulled the other faggots from his shirt. A moment later the whole chamber flared into light.

From it led not one passage, he saw, but five. And in each were figures that leered in perfect time. Somewhere there was a heavy murmuring rumble.

Enderby collected himself. He touched the icy stone body of the beauty. From a pocket of his shirt he fumbled a stump of blue copying pencil.

Across the perfect waist he printed, thick and almost steadily: 'F. ENDERBY, WARRINGTON, R.A.F. 1942.'

He stuffed the defiling pencil away. "And now," he said, much too loudly, "I will go and get started again."

It was when he turned towards the tunnels that he saw the spikes.

They were coming out very slowly. About the pace of

a common slug in a Warrington allotment, and with no more noise.

One from the forehead, one from the throat and one from the folded hands; others from the studded robes. From each figure, and above to the ceiling, the points shone and grew, sprouting across the passages. Closing them.

"Christ!" Enderby said.

He sprang into the centre tunnel, opposite the slab, ran with the waving treble torch. It cast stubby points in a forest of pikes upon the ceiling. Nightmarishly, the dust muffled his boots.

Twice he kicked up yellow-white human fragments. He tripped on a carpeted cage of ribs and slashed his hand on a lengthening spike.

He saw no daylight.

Instead, a wall of arrow-lettered brick faced him at the end. He tore and kicked, trying to open it, before he realised he could be in the wrong passage.

Then he was flying back between the sprouting pikes. They covered half the space with a mass of jagged bars. Even the spaces between them would be death cages. Back across the bones.

The chamber itself, when he reached it, sprouted iron from each wall. A deep throb shook everything. The whole building was thrusting at him.

Enderby panted by the slab without a glance. Down the left-hand tunnel.

At each nod from the jet-eyed lines, the points sprang a little farther across.

If he had not seen the light of the entrance, Enderby swears he would have been insane before the points took him.

As it was, he dragged himself through the last twenty feet when they were little more than a foot apart. Another second and the spike which ripped open his water-bottle would have held him by the rib bones.

But he was outside. He stood in the shadowed sand with

blood and water trickling together down his body ("In the nick of time. Like a film 'ero.") One of the last things he remembers is heaving the door shut and stumbling away from the ponderous booming that hung in the still heat.

Four days later Enderby was spotted by a reconnaissance car. He was walking in small circles.

When they brought him in, three of the deep lacerations in his side and arms were infected. He was totally collapsed. During his travels he had written two half-legible letters in his pay-book. One to his fiancée, a feverishly confused apology for something unspecified. The second was addressed to the Warrington Town Council, complaining of floods. He had almost died of thirst.

As he recovered, Enderby was eager at first to tell his story. Coupled with his letters, it made them prescribe further sleep.

"Do y' think it could 'ave been only that?" he asked me later. "Sometimes it makes y' wonder." Then he indicated the parallel scars. "Truck accident I don't think!"

He told me the story while he carved a piece of perspex into a Spitfire badge to send his fiancée. "Y' know," said Enderby, as I had not laughed, "if I 'ad a lot more leave and that, I wouldn't mind 'aving a look back there some time. Bet it's covered up again, though.

"Y' see, I 'ardly touched 'er face more than a feather, like. And it started all that. Stone weights and pendulums, I suppose.

"Now, listen! Where did the acceleration come from? Tell me that!" He put down the transparent Spitfire and prodded me and paused to impress.

"There's a machine in that place, boy! Damn near perpetual motion, that's what. They'd be worth something, I tell y', them plans—"

First and last a mechanic, Enderby.

But also a prince. Who left his claim in writing.

THE TWILIGHT ZONE

(CBS TV, 1959–64)
Starring: Claude Atkins, Jack Weston &
Mary Gregory
Directed by Ron Winston
Story 'The Monsters Are Due on Maple Street'
by Rod Serling

Like *The Quatermass Experiment, The Twilight Zone*
now enjoys a celebrity that has transcended the passage of time and changes in TV fashions. Such was
the programme's sheer originality and bredth of
imagination that it has been frequently rerun since the
Sixties as well as inspiring a sequel in the Eighties and
a big-budget film, *Twilight Zone – The Movie*, made by
Steven Speilberg, a fan who used all the special effects
wizardry of Hollywood to pay his own tribute to the
landmark programme. The series had originally been
the brainchild of Rod Serling (1924–1975), a highly
respected television scritpwriter whose plays *Patterns*
(1955), *Requiem for a Heavyweight* (1956) and *The
Comedian* (1957) all won Emmy awards. He turned his
back on television drama after growing increasingly
frustrated at the way his more outspoken scripts were
censored by network executives anxious not to offend
sponsors. The format of *The Twilight Zone* enabled
him to mix fantasy and science fiction and give free
reign to his boundless imagination. The result was a
programme that was memorable from the opening
lines of each half hour episode which Serling himself
spoke in a measured and matter-of-fact voice: "There
is a fifth dimension beyond that which is known to

man. It is a dimension as vast as space and as timeless as infinity. It is the middle ground between science and superstition; between the pit of man's fears and the summit of his knowledge. It is an area we call . . . *The Twilight Zone*."

During its critically acclaimed run on American TV, a total of 156 episodes of the *Zone* were screened, many written by Serling and the rest by two popular SF writers, Charles Beaumont and Richard Matheson. The series also featured a number of actors who would later become famous including Robert Redford, Charles Bronson, Lee Marvin and Burt Reynolds; as well as a duo destined to be the mainstays of another legendary TV series, *Star Trek*: William Shatner and Leonard Nimoy. Apart from occasionally poking fun at the mentality of the TV executives who had so enraged him – in stories like 'The Bard' in which Jack Weston played a hack writer who summoned up William Shakespeare to help him finish a script – Serling also tackled a number of controversial themes including Fascism (in 'He Lives') and mass hysteria in 'The Monsters Are Due on Maple Street', the episode included here. It is a salutory tale of how hysteria can turn neighbour against neighbour when confronted with inexplicable events that are actually the work of aliens. Serling introduced a typical wry joke for those able to spot the fact by filming the scenes of hysteria on a set normally used by M.G.M. for their comic Andy Hardy series. He also clothed the two visitors from space in outfits that had been used in the movie *Forbidden Planet*, and cleverly utilized a clip from the same picture for his own UFO. What he did was to take some footage of the alien craft flying through space and run it upside down and going backwards! Jack West from 'The Bard' returned to the series as one of the people accused of being an alien. Curiously, just before the episode was transmitted Serling once more found himself at the centre of controversy

when several newspapers accused him of writing a story *about* prejudice – the complete opposite of his intention!

It was Saturday afternoon on Maple Street and the late sun retained some of the warmth of a persistent Indian summer. People along the street marveled at winter's delay and took advantage of it. Lawns were being mowed, cars polished, kids played hopscotch on the sidewalks. Old Mr. Van Horn, the patriarch of the street, who lived alone, had moved his power saw out on his lawn and was fashioning new pickets for his fence. A Good Humor man bicycled in around the corner and was inundated by children and by shouts of "Wait a minute!" from small boys hurrying to con nickels from their parents. It was 4:40 P.M. A football game blared from a portable radio on a front porch, blending with the other sounds of a Saturday afternoon in October. Maple Street. 4:40 P.M. Maple Street in its last calm and reflective moments – before the monsters came.

Steve Brand, fortyish, a big man in an old ex-Marine set of dungarees, was washing his car when the lights flashed across the sky. Everyone on the street looked up at the sound of the whoosh and the brilliant flash that dwarfed the sun.

"What was that?" Steve called across at his neighbor, Don Martin, who was fixing a bent spoke on his son's bicycle.

Martin, like everyone else, was cupping his hands over his eyes, to stare up at the sky. He called back to Steve, "Looked like a meteor, didn't it? I didn't hear any crash though, did you?"

Steve shook his head. "Nope. Nothing except that roar."

Steve's wife came out on the front porch. "Steve?" she called. "What was that?"

Steve shut off the water hose. "Guess it was a meteor, honey. Came awful close, didn't it?"

"Much too close for my money," his wife answered. "Much too close."

She went back into the house, and became suddenly conscious of something. All along Maple Street people paused and looked at one another as a gradual awareness took hold. All the sounds had stopped. All of them. There was a silence now. No portable radio. No lawn mowers. No clickety-click of sprinklers that went round and round on front lawns. There was a silence.

Mrs Sharp, fifty-five years of age, was talking on the telephone, giving a cake recipe to her cousin at the other end of town. Her cousin was asking Mrs Sharp to repeat the number of eggs when her voice clicked off in the middle of the sentence. Mrs Sharp, who was not the most patient of women, banged furiously on the telephone hook, screaming for an operator.

Pete Van Horn was right in the middle of sawing a 1×4 piece of pine when the power saw went off. He checked the plug, the outlet on the side of the house and then the fuse box in his basement. There was just no power coming in.

Steve Brand's wife, Agnes, came back out on the porch to announce that the oven had stopped working. There was no current or something. Would Steve look at it? Steve couldn't look at it at that moment because he was preoccupied with a hose that suddenly refused to give any more water.

Across the street Charlie Farnsworth, fat and dumpy, in a loud Hawaiian sport shirt that featured hula girls with pineapple baskets on their heads, barged angrily out toward the road, damning any radio outfit that manufactured a portable with the discourtesy to shut off in the middle of a third-quarter forward pass.

Voices built on top of voices until suddenly there was no more silence. There was a conglomeration of questions

and protests; of plaintive references to half-cooked din-
ners, half-watered lawns, half-washed cars, half-finished
phone conversations. Did it have anything to do with the
meteor? That was the main question – the one most asked.
Pete Van Horn disgustedly threw aside the electric cord of
his power mower and announced to the group of people
who were collected around Steve Brand's station wagon
that he was going on over to Bennett Avenue to check and
see if the power had gone off there, too. He disappeared
into his back yard and was last seen heading into the back
yard of the house behind his.

Steve Brand, his face wrinkled with perplexity, leaned
against his car door and looked around at the neighbors
who had collected. "It just doesn't make sense," he said.
"Why should the power go off all of a sudden *and* the
phone line?"

Don Martin wiped bicycle grease off his fingers.
"Maybe some kind of an electrical storm or something."

Dumpy Charlie's voice was always unpleasantly high.
"That just don't seem likely," he squealed. "Sky's just as
blue as anything. Not a cloud. No lightning. No thunder.
No nothin'. How could it be a storm?"

Mrs Sharp's face was lined with years, but more deeply
by the frustrations of early widowhood. "Well, it's a
terrible thing when a phone company can't keep its line
open," she complained. "Just a terrible thing."

"What about my portable radio," Charlie demanded.
"Ohio State's got the ball on Southern Methodist's
eighteen-yard line. They throw a pass and the damn
thing goes off just then."

There was a murmur in the group as people looked at
one another and heads were shaken.

Charlie picked his teeth with a dirty thumbnail. "Steve,"
he said in his high, little voice, "why don't you go
downtown and check with the police?"

"They'll probably think we're crazy or something,"
Don Martin said. "A little power failure and right away
we get all flustered and everything."

"It isn't just the power failure," Steve answered. "If if was, we'd still be able to get a broadcast on the portable."

There was a murmur of reaction to this and heads nodded.

Steve opened the door to his station wagon. "I'll run downtown. We'll get this all straightened out."

He inched his big frame onto the front seat behind the wheel, turned on the ignition and pushed the starter button. There was no sound. The engine didn't even turn over. He tried it a couple of times more, and still there was no response. The others stared silently at him. He scratched his jaw.

"Doesn't that beat all? It was working fine before."

"Out of gas?" Don offered.

Steve shook his head. "I just had it filled up."

"What's it mean?" Mrs Sharp asked.

Charlie Farnsworth's piggish little eyes flapped open and shut. "It's just as if – just as if everything had stopped. You better *walk* downtown, Steve."

"I'll go with you," Don said.

Steve got out of the car, shut the door and turned to Don. "Couldn't be a meteor," he said. "A meteor couldn't do *this*." He looked off in thought for a moment, then nodded. "Come on, let's go."

They started to walk away from the group, when they heard the boy's voice. Tommy Bishop, aged twelve, had stepped out in front of the others and was calling out to them.

"Mr Brand! Mr Martin. You better not leave!"

Steve took a step back toward him.

"Why not?" he asked.

"They don't want you to," Tommy said.

Steve and Don exchanged a look.

"*Who* doesn't want us to?" Steve asked him.

Tommy looked up toward the sky. "Them," he said.

"Them?" Steve asked.

"Who are 'them'?" Charlie squealed.

"Whoever was in that thing that came by overhead," Tommy said intently.

Steve walked slowly back toward the boy and stopped close to him. "What, Tommy?" he asked.

"Whoever was in that thing that came over," Tommy repeated. "I don't think they want us to leave here."

Steve knelt down in front of the boy "What do you mean, Tommy? What are you talking about?"

"They don't want us to leave, that's why they shut everything off."

"What makes you say that?" Irritation crept into Steve's voice. "Whatever gave you *that* idea?"

Mrs Sharp pushed her way through to the front of the crowd. "That's the craziest thing I ever heard," she announced in a public-address-system voice. "Just about the craziest thing I ever did hear!"

Tommy could feel the unwillingness to believe him. "It's always that way," he said defensively, "in every story I've ever read about a space ship landing from outer space!"

Charlie Farnsworth whinnied out his derision.

Mrs Sharp waggled a bony finger in front of Tommy's mother. "If you ask me, Sally Bishop," she said, "you'd better get that boy of yours up to bed. He's been reading too many comic books or seeing too many movies or something."

Sally Bishop's face reddened. She gripped Tommy's shoulders tightly. "Tommy," she said softly. "Stop that kind of talk, honey."

Steve's eyes never left the boy's face. "That's all right, Tom. We'll be right back. You'll see. That wasn't a ship or anything like it. That was just a – a meteor or something, likely as not—" He turned to the group, trying to weight his words with an optimism he didn't quite feel. "No doubt it did have something to do with all this power failure and the rest of it. Meteors can do crazy things. Like sun spots."

"That's right," Don said, as if picking up a cue. "Like

sun spots. That kind of thing. They can raise cain with radio reception all over the world. And this thing being so close – why there's no telling what sort of stuff it can do." He wet his lips nervously. "Come on, Steve. We'll go into town and see if that isn't what's causing it all."

Once again the two men started away.

"Mr Brand!" Tommy's voice was defiant and frightened at the same time. He pulled away from his mother and ran after them. "Please, Mr Brand, please don't leave here."

There was a stir, a rustle, a movement among the people. There was something about the boy. Something about the intense little face. Something about the words that carried such emphasis, such belief, such fear. They listened to these words and rejected them because intellect and logic had no room for spaceships and green-headed things. But the irritation that showed in the eyes, the murmuring and the compressed lips had nothing to do with intellect. A little boy was bringing up fears that shouldn't be brought up; and the people on Maple Street this Saturday afternoon were no different from any other set of human beings. Order, reason, logic were slipping, pushed by the wild conjectures of a twelve-year-old boy.

"Somebody ought to spank that kid," an angry voice muttered.

Tommy Bishop's voice continued defiant. It pierced the murmurings and rose above them. "You might not even be able to get to town," he said. "It was that way in the story. *Nobody* could leave. Nobody except—"

"Except who?" Steve asked.

"Except the people they'd sent down ahead of them. They looked just like humans. It wasn't until the ship landed that—"

His mother grabbed him by the arm and pulled him back. "Tommy," she said in a low voice. "Please, honey . . . don't talk that way."

"Damn right he shouldn't talk that way," came the

voice of the man in the rear again. "And we shouldn't stand here listening to him. Why this is the craziest thing I ever heard. The kid tells us a comic-book plot and here we stand listening—"

His voice died away as Steve stood up and faced the crowd. Fear can throw people into a panic, but it can also make them receptive to a leader and Steve Brand at this moment was such a leader. The big man in the ex-Marine dungarees had an authority about him.

"Go ahead, Tommy," he said to the boy. "What kind of story was this? What about the people that they sent out ahead?"

"That was the way they prepared things for the landing, Mr Brand," Tommy said. "They sent four people. A mother and a father and two kids who looked just like humans. But they weren't."

There was a murmur – a stir of uneasy laughter. People looked at one another again and a couple of them smiled.

"Well," Steve said, lightly but carefully, "I guess we'd better run a check on the neighborhood, and see which ones of us are really human."

His words were a release. Laughter broke out openly. But soon it died away. Only Charlie Farnsworth's horse whinny persisted over the growing silence and then he too lapsed into a grim quietness, until all fifteen people were looking at one another through changed eyes. A twelve-year-old boy had planted a seed. And something was growing out of the street with invisible branches that began to wrap themselves around the men and women and pull them apart. Distrust lay heavy in the air.

Suddenly there was the sound of a car engine and all heads turned as one. Across the street Ned Rosen was sitting in his convertible trying to start it, and nothing was happening beyond the labored sound of a sick engine getting deeper and hoarser, and finally giving up altogether. Ned Rosen, a thin, serious-faced man in his thirties, got out of his car and closed the door. He stood there staring at it for a moment, shook his head, looked across the street at his neighbors and started toward them.

"Can't get her started, Ned?" Don Martin called out to him.

"No dice," Ned answered. "Funny, she was working fine this morning."

Without warning, all by itself, the car started up and idled smoothly, smoke briefly coming out of the exhaust. Ned Rosen whirled around to stare at it, his eyes wide. Then, just as suddenly as it started, the engine sputtered and stopped.

"Started all by itself!" Charlie Farnsworth squealed excitedly.

"How did it do that?" Mrs Sharp asked. "How could it just start all by itself?"

Sally Bishop let loose her son's arm and just stood there, shaking her head. "How in the world—" she began.

Then there were no more questions. They stood silently staring at Ned Rosen who looked from them to his car and then back again. He went to the car and looked at it. Then he scratched his head again.

"Somebody explain it to me," he said. "I sure never saw anything like that happen before!"

"He never did come out to look at that thing that flew overhead. He wasn't even interested," Don Martin said heavily.

"What do you say we ask him some questions," Charlie Farnsworth proposed importantly. "I'd like to know what's going on here!"

There was a chorus of assent and the fifteen people started across the street toward Ned Rosen's driveway. Unity was restored, they had a purpose, a feeling of activity and direction. They were *doing* something. They weren't sure what, but Ned Rosen was flesh and blood – askable, reachable and seeable. He watched with growing apprehension as his neighbors marched toward him. They stopped on the sidewalk close to the driveway and surveyed him.

Ned Rosen pointed to his car. "I just don't understand it, any more than you do! I tried to start it and it *wouldn't* start. You saw me. All of you saw me."

His neighbors seemed massed against him, solidly, alarmingly.

"I don't understand it!" he cried. "I swear – I don't understand. What's happening?"

Charlie Farnsworth stood out in front of the others. "Maybe you better tell us," he demanded. "Nothing's working on this street. Nothing. No lights, no power, no radio. Nothing except one car – *yours!*"

There were mutterings from the crowd. Steve Brand stood back by himself and said nothing. He didn't like what was going on. Something was building up that threatened to grow beyond control.

"Come on, Rosen," Charlie Farnsworth commanded shrilly, "let's hear what goes on! Let's hear how you explain your car startin' like that!"

Ned Rosen wasn't a coward. He was a quiet man who didn't like violence and had never been a physical fighter. But he didn't like being bullied. Ned Rosen got mad.

"Hold it!" he shouted. "Just hold it. You keep your distance. All of you. All right, I've got a car that starts by itself. Well, that's a freak thing – I admit it! But does that make me some sort of a criminal or something? I don't know why the car works – it just does!"

The crowd were neither sobered nor reassured by Rosen's words, but they were not too frightened to listen. They huddled together, mumbling, and Ned Rosen's eyes went from face to face till they stopped on Steve Brand's. Ned knew Steve Brand. Of all the men on the street, this seemed the guy with the most substance. The most intelligent. The most essentially decent.

"What's it all about, Steve?" he asked.

"We're all on a monster kick, Ned," he answered quietly. "Seems that the general impression holds that maybe one family isn't what we think they are. Monsters from outer space or something. Different from us. Fifth columnists from the vast beyond." He couldn't keep the sarcasm out of his voice. "Do you know anybody around here who might fit that description?"

Rosen's eyes narrowed. "What is this, a gag?" He looked around the group again. "This a practical joke or something?" And without apparent reason, without logic, without explanation, his car started again, idled for a moment, sending smoke out of the exhaust, and stopped.

A woman began to cry, and the bank of eyes facing Ned Rosen looked cold and accusing. he walked to his porch steps and stood on them, facing his neighbors.

"Is that supposed to incriminate me?" he asked. "The car engine goes on and off and that really does it, huh?" He looked down into their faces. "I don't understand it. Not any more than you do."

He could tell that they were unmoved. This couldn't really be happening, Ned thought to himself.

"Look," he said in a different tone. "You all know me. We've lived here four years. Right in this house. We're no different from any of the rest of you!" He held out his hands toward them. The people he was looking at hardly resembled the people he'd lived alongside of for the past four years. They looked as if someone had taken a brush and altered every character with a few strokes. "Really," he continued, "this whole thing is just . . . just weird—"

"Well, if that's the case, Ned Rosen," Mrs Sharp's voice suddenly erupted from the crowd – "maybe you'd better explain why—" She stopped abruptly and clamped her mouth shut, but looked wise and pleased with herself.

"Explain what?" Rosen asked her softly.

Steve Brand sensed a special danger now. "Look," he said, "let's forget this right now—"

Charlie Farnsworth cut him off. "Go ahead. Let her talk. What about it? Explain what?"

Mrs Sharp, with an air of great reluctance, said, "Well, sometimes I go to bed late at night. A couple of times – a couple of times I've come out on the porch, and I've seen Ned Rosen here, in the wee hours of the morning, standing out in front of his house looking up at the sky." She looked around the circle of faces. "That's right, looking up at the sky as if – as if he was waiting for something." She paused for emphasis, for dramatic effect. "As if he was looking for something!" she repeated.

The nail on the coffin, Steve Brand thought. One, dumb, ordinary, simple idiosyncrasy of a human being – and that probably was all it would take. He heard the murmuring of the crowd rise and saw Ned Rosen's face turn white. Rosen's wife, Ann, came out on the porch. She took a look at the crowd and then at her husband's face.

"What's going on, Ned?" she asked.

"I don't know what's going on," Ned answered. "I just don't know, Ann. But I'll tell you this. I don't like these people. I don't like what they're doing. I don't like them standing in my yard like this. And if any one of them takes another step and gets close to my porch – I'll break his jaw. I swear to God, that's just what I'll do. I'll break his jaw. Now go on, get out of here, all of you!" he shouted at them. "Get the hell out of here."

"Ned," Ann's voice was shocked.

"You heard me," Ned repeated. "All of you get out of here."

None of them eager to start an action, the people began to back away. But they had an obscure sense of gratification. At least there was an opponent now. Someone who wasn't one of them. And this gave them a kind of secure feeling. The enemy was no longer formless and vague. The enemy had a front porch and a front yard and a car. And he had shouted threats at them.

They started slowly back across the street forgetting for the moment what had started it all. Forgetting that there was no power, and no telephones. Forgetting even that there had been a meteor overhead not twenty minutes earlier. It wasn't until much later, as a matter of fact, that anyone posed a certain question.

Old man Van Horn had walked through his back yard over to Bennett Avenue. He'd never come back. Where was he? It was not one of the questions that passed through the minds of any of the thirty or forty people on Maple Street who sat on their front porches and watched the night come and felt the now menacing darkness close in on them.

There were lanterns lit all along Maple Street by ten o'clock. Candles shone through living-room windows and cast flickering, unsteady shadows all along the street. Groups of people huddled on front lawns around their lanterns and a soft murmur of voices was carried over the Indian-summer night air. All eyes eventually were drawn to Ned Rosen's front porch.

He sat there on the railing, observing the little points of light spotted around in the darkness. He knew he was surrounded. He was the animal at bay.

His wife came out on the porch and brought him a glass of lemonade. Her face was white and strained. Like her husband, Ann Rosen was a gentle person, unarmored by temper or any proclivity for outrage. She stood close to her husband now on the darkened porch feeling the suspicion that flowed from the people around lanterns, thinking to herself that these were people she had entertained in her house. These were women she talked to over clotheslines in the back yard; people who had been friends and neighbors only that morning. Oh dear God, could all this have happened in those few hours? It must be a nightmare, she thought. It had to be a nightmare that she could wake up from. It couldn't be anything else.

Across the street Mabel Farnsworth, Charlie's wife, shook her head and clucked at her husband who was drinking a can of beer. "It just doesn't seem right though, Charlie, keeping watch on them. Why he was right when he said he was one of our neighbors. I've known Ann Rosen ever since they moved in. We've been good friends."

Charlie Farnsworth turned to her disgustedly. "That don't prove a thing," he said. "Any guy who'd spend his time lookin' up at the sky early in the morning – well there's something wrong with that kind of person. There's something that ain't legitimate. Maybe under normal circumstances we could let it go by. But these aren't normal circumstances." He turned and pointed toward the street. "Look at that," he said. "Nothin' but candles and lanterns. Why it's like goin' back into the Dark Ages or something!"

He was right. Maple Street had changed with the night. The flickering lights had done something to its character. It looked odd and menacing and very different. Up and down the street, people noticed it. The change in Maple Street. It was the feeling one got after being away from home for many, many years and then returning. There was a vague familiarity about it, but it wasn't the same. It was different.

Ned Rosen and his wife heard footsteps coming toward their house. Ned got up from the railing and shouted out into the darkness.

"Whoever it is, just stay right where you are. I don't want any trouble, but if anybody sets foot on my porch, that's what they're going to get – trouble!" He saw that it was Steve Brand and his features relaxed.

"Ned—" Steve began.

Ned Rosen cut him off. "I've already explained to you people, I don't sleep very well at night sometimes. I get up and I take a walk and I look up at the sky. I look at the stars."

Ann Rosen's voice shook as she stood alongside of him. "That's exactly what he does. Why this whole thing, it's – it's some kind of a madness or something."

Steve Brand stood on the sidewalk and nodded grimly. "That's exactly what it is – some kind of madness."

Charlie Farnsworth's voice from the adjoining yard was

spiteful. "You'd best watch who you're seen with, Steve. Until we get this all straightened out, you ain't exactly above suspicion yourself."

Steve whirled around to the outline of the fat figure that stood behind the lantern in the other yard. "Or you either, Charlie," he shouted. "Or any of the rest of us!"

Mrs Sharp's voice came from the darkness across the street. "What I'd like to know is – what are we going to do? Just stand around here all night?"

"There's nothin' else we can do," Charlie Farnsworth said. He looked wisely over toward Ned Rosen's house. "One of 'em'll tip their hand. They *got* to."

It was Charlie's voice that did it for Steve Brand at this moment. The shrieking, pig squeal that came from the layers of fat and the idiotic sport shirt and the dull, dumb, blind prejudice of the man. "There's something *you* can do, Charlie," Steve called out to him. "You can go inside your house and keep your mouth shut!"

"You sound real anxious to have that happen, Steve," Charlie's voice answered him back from the little spot of light in the next yard. "I think we'd better keep our eye on you, too!"

Don Martin came up to Steve Brand, carrying a lantern. There was something hesitant in his manner, as if he were about to take a bit in his teeth, but wondered whether it would hurt. "I think everything might as well come out now," Don said. "I really do. I think everything should come out."

People came off porches, from front yards, to stand around in a group near Don who now turned directly toward Steve.

"Your wife's done plenty of talking, Steve, about how odd you are," he said.

Charlie Farnsworth trotted over. "Go ahead. Tell us what she said," he demanded excitedly.

Steve Brand knew this was the way it would happen. He was not really surprised but he still felt a hot anger rise up inside of him. "Go ahead," he said. "What's my wife said? Let's get it *all* out." He peered around at the shadowy figures of the neighbors. "Let's pick out every Goddamned peculiarity of every single man, woman and child on this street! Don't stop with me and Ned. How about a firing squad at dawn, so we can get rid of all the suspects! Make it easier for you!"

Don Martin's voice retreated fretfully. "There's no need getting so upset, Steve—"

"Go to hell, Don," Steve said to him in a cold and dispassionate fury.

Needled, Don went on the offensive again but his tone held something plaintive and petulant. "It just so happens that, well, Agnes has talked about how there's plenty of nights you've spent hours in your basement working on some kind of a radio or something. Well none of us have ever *seen* that radio—"

"Go ahead, Steve," Charlie Farnsworth yelled at him. "What kind of a 'radio set' you workin' on? I never seen it. Neither has anyone else. Who do you talk to on that radio set? And who talks to you?"

Steve's eyes slowly traveled in an arc over the hidden faces and the shrouded forms of neighbors who were now accusers. "I'm surprised at you, Charlie," he said quietly. "I really am. How come you're so God-damned dense all of a sudden? Who do I talk to? I talk to monsters from outer space. I talk to three-headed green men who fly over here in what look like meteors!"

Agnes Brand walked across the street to stand at her husband's elbow. She pulled at his arm with frightened intensity. "Steve! Steve, please," she said. "It's just a ham radio set," she tried to explain. "That's all. I bought him a book on it myself. It's just a ham radio set. A lot of people have them. I can show it to you. It's right down in the basement."

Steve pulled her hand off his arm. "You show them nothing," he said to her. "If they want to look inside our house, let them get a search warrant!"

Charlie's voice whined at him. "Look, buddy, you can't afford to—"

"Charlie," Steve shouted at him. "Don't tell me what I can afford. And stop telling me who's dangerous and who isn't. And who's safe and who's a menace!" He walked over to the edge of the road and saw that people backed away from him. "And you're with him – all of you," Steve bellowed at them. "You're standing there all set to crucify – to find a scapegoat – desperate to point some kind of a finger at a neighbor!" There was intensity in his tone and on his face, accentuated by the flickering light of the lanterns and the candles. "Well look, friends, the only thing that's going to happen is that we'll eat each other up alive. Understand? *We are going to eat each other up alive!*"

Charlie Farnsworth suddenly ran over to him and grabbed his arm. "That's not the *only* thing that can happen to us," he said in a frightened, hushed voice. "Look!"

"Oh, my God," Don Martin said.

Mrs Sharp screamed. All eyes turned to look down the street where a figure had suddenly materialized in the darkness and the sound of measured footsteps on concrete grew louder and louder as it walked toward them. Sally Bishop let out a stifled cry and grabbed Tommy's shoulder.

The child's voice screamed out, "It's the monster! It's the monster!"

There was a frightened wail from another woman, and the residents of Maple Street stood transfixed with terror as something unknown came slowly down the street. Don Martin disappeared and came back out of his house a moment later carrying a shotgun. He pointed it toward the approaching form. Steve pulled it out of his hands.

"For God's sake, will somebody think a thought around here? Will you people wise up? What good would a shotgun do against—"

A quaking, frightened Charlie Farnsworth grabbed the

gun from Steve's hand. "No more talk, Steve," he said. "You're going to talk us into a grave! You'd let whoever's out there walk right over us, wouldn't yuh? Well, some of us won't!"

He swung the gun up and pulled the trigger. The noise was a shocking, shattering intrusion and it echoed and reechoed through the night. A hundred yards away the figure collapsed like a piece of clothing blown off a line by the wind. From front porches and lawns people raced toward it.

Steve was the first to reach him. He knelt down, turned him over and looked at his face. Then he looked up toward the semi-circle of silent faces surveying him.

"All right, friends," he said quietly. "It happened. We got our first victim – Pete Van Horn!"

"Oh, my God," Don Martin said in a hushed voice. "He was just going over to the next block to see if the power was on—"

Mrs Sharp's voice was that of injured justice. "You killed him, Charlie! You shot him dead!"

Charlie Farnsworth's face looked like a piece of uncooked dough, quivering and shaking in the light of the lantern he held.

"I didn't know who he was," he said. "I certainly didn't know who he was." Tears rolled down his fat cheeks. "He comes walking out of the dark – how am I supposed to know who he was?" He looked wildly around and then grabbed Steve's arm. Steve could explain things to people. "Steve," he screamed, "you know why I shot. How was I supposed to know he wasn't a monster or something?"

Steve looked at him and didn't say anything. Charlie grabbed Don.

"We're all scared of the same thing," he blubbered. "The very same thing. I was just tryin' to protect my home, that's all. Look, all of you, that's all I was tryin' to do!" He tried to shut out the sight of Pete Van Horn who stared up at him with dead eyes and a shattered chest. "Please, please, please," Charlie Farnsworth sobbed, "I didn't know it was somebody we knew. I swear to God I didn't know—"

The lights went on in Charlie Farnsworth's house and shone brightly on the people of Maple Street. They looked suddenly naked. They blinked foolishly at the lights and their mouths gaped like fishes'.

"Charlie," Mrs Sharp said, like a judge pronouncing sentence, "how come you're the only one with lights on now?"

Ned Rosen nodded in agreement. "That's what I'd like to know," he said. Something inside tried to check him, but his anger made him go on. "How come, Charlie? You're quiet all of a sudden. You've got nothing to say out of that big, fat mouth of yours. Well, let's hear it, Charlie? Let's hear why you've got lights!"

Again the chorus of voices that punctuated the request and gave it legitimacy and a vote of support. "Why, Charlie?" the voices asked him. "How come you're the only one with lights?" The questions came out of the night to land against his fat wet cheeks. "You were so quick to kill," Ned Rosen continued, "and you were so quick to tell us who we had to be careful of. Well maybe you *had* to kill, Charlie. Maybe Pete Van Horn, God rest his soul, was trying to tell us something. Maybe he'd found out something and had come back to tell us who there was among us we should watch out for."

Charlie's eyes were little pits of growing fear as he backed away from the people and found himself up against a bush in front of his house. "No," he said. "No, please." His chubby hands tried to speak for him. They waved around, pleading. The palms outstretched, begging for forgiveness and understanding. "Please – please, I swear to you – it isn't me! It really isn't me."

A stone hit him on the side of the face and drew blood. He screamed and clutched at his face as the people began to converge on him.

"No," he screamed. "No."

Like a hippopotamus in a circus, he scrambled over the

bush, tearing his clothes and scratching his face and arms.
His wife tried to run toward him, somebody stuck a foot
out and she tripped, sprawling head first on the sidewalk.
Another stone whistled through the air and hit Charlie on
the back of the head as he raced across his front yard
toward his porch. A rock smashed at the porch light and
sent glass cascading down on his head.

"It isn't me," he screamed back at them as they came
toward him across the front lawn. "It isn't me, but I know
who it is," he said suddenly, without thought. Even as he
said it, he realized it was the only possible thing to say.

People stopped, motionless as statues, and a voice
called out from the darkness. "All right, Charlie, who
is it?"

He was a grotesque, fat figure of a man who smiled
now through the tears and the blood that cascaded down
his face. "Well, I'm going to tell you," he said. "I am now
going to tell you, because I know who it is. I really know
who it is. It's . . ."

"Go ahead, Charlie," a voice commanded him. "Who's
the monster?"

Don Martin pushed his way to the front of the crowd.
"All right, Charlie, now! Let's hear it!"

Charlie tried to think. He tried to come up with a name.
A nightmare engulfed him. Fear whipped at the back of
his brain. "It's the kid," he screamed. "That's who it is.
It's the kid!"

Sally Bishop screamed and grabbed at Tommy, burying
his face against her. "That's crazy," she said to the people
who now stared at her. "That's crazy. He's a little boy."

"But he knew," said Mrs Sharp. "He was the only one
who knew. He told us all about it. Well how did he know?
How *could* he have known?"

Voices supported her. "How could he know?" "Who
told him?" "Make the kid answer." A fever had taken hold
now, a hot, burning virus that twisted faces and forced
out words and solidified the terror inside of each person
on Maple Street.

Tommy broke away from his mother and started to run. A man dove at him in a flying tackle and missed. Another man threw a stone wildly toward the darkness. They began to run after him down the street. Voices shouted through the night, women screamed. A small child's voice protested – a playmate of Tommy's one tiny voice of sanity in the middle of a madness as men and women ran down the street, the sidewalks, the curbs, looking blindly for a twelve-year-old boy.

And then suddenly the lights went on in another house – a two-story, gray stucco house that belonged to Bob Weaver. A man screamed, "It isn't the kid. It's Bob Weaver's house!"

A porch light went on at Mrs Sharp's house and Sally Bishop screamed, "It isn't Bob Weaver's house. It's Mrs Sharp's place."

"I tell you it's the kid," Charlie screamed.

The lights went on and off, on and off down the street. A power mower suddenly began to move all by itself lurching crazily across a front yard, cutting an irregular path of grass until it smashed against the side of the house.

"It's Charlie," Don Martin screamed. "He's the one." And then he saw his own lights go on and off.

They ran this way and that way, over to one house and then back across the street to another. A rock flew through the air and then another. A pane of glass smashed and there was the cry of a woman in pain. Lights on and off, on and off. Charlie Farnsworth went down on his knees as a piece of brick plowed a two-inch hole in the back of his skull. Mrs Sharp lay on her back screaming, and felt the tearing jab of a woman's high heel in her mouth as someone stepped on her, racing across the street.

From a quarter of a mile away, on a hilltop, Maple Street looked like this, a long tree-lined avenue full of lights going on and off and screaming people racing back and forth. Maple Street was a bedlam. It was an outdoor asylum for the insane. Windows were broken, street lights sent clusters of broken glass down on the heads of women and children. Power mowers started up and car engines and radios. Blaring music mixed with the screams and shouts and the anger.

Up on top of the hill two men, screened by the darkness, stood near the entrance to a space ship and looked down on Maple Street.

"Understand the procedure now?" the first figure said. "Just stop a few of their machines and radios and telephones and lawn mowers. Throw them into darkness for a few hours and then watch the pattern unfold."

"And this pattern is always the same?" the second figure asked.

"With few variations," came the answer. "They pick the most dangerous enemy they can find and it's themselves. All we need do is sit back – and watch."

"Then I take it," figure two said, "this place, this Maple Street, is not unique?"

Figure one shook his head and laughed. "By no means. Their world is full of Maple Streets and we'll go from one to the other and let them destroy themselves." He started up the incline toward the entrance of the space ship. "One to the other," he said as the other figure followed him. "One to the other." There was just the echo of his voice as the two figures disappeared and a panel slid softly across the entrance. "One to the other," the echo said.

When the sun came up on the following morning Maple Street was silent. Most of the houses had been burned. There were a few bodies lying on sidewalks and draped over porch railings. But the silence was total. There simply was no more life. At four o'clock that afternoon there was no more world, or at least not the kind of world that had greeted the morning. And by Wednesday afternoon of the following week, a new set of residents had moved into Maple Street. They were a handsome race of people. Their faces showed great character. Great character indeed. Great character and excellently shaped heads. Excellently shaped heads – two to each new resident!

From Rod Serling's closing narration, 'The Monsters Are Due on Maple Street,' The Twilight Zone, January 1, 1960, CBS Television Network.

Now the CAMERA PANS UP for a shot of the starry sky and over this we hear the Narrator's Voice.

NARRATOR'S VOICE
The tools of conquest do not necessarily come
with bombs and explosions and fall-out. There
are weapons that are simply thoughts, attitudes,
prejudices – to be found only in the minds of men.
For the record, prejudices can kill and suspicion
can destroy and a thoughtless, frightened search
for a scapegoat has a fall-out all of its own for the
children . . . and the children yet unborn.
    (a pause)
And the pity of it is, that these things cannot be
confined to . . . The Twilight Zone!
FADE TO BLACK

OUT OF THIS WORLD

(ABC TV, 1962)
Starring: William Lucas, Hilda Schroder &
Ray Barrett
Directed by Charles Jarrott
Story: 'Dumb Martian' by John Wyndham

In 1962, Boris Karloff who had starred in the first American Science Fiction TV series, *Tales of Tomorrow*, returned to his native England to host Britain's first SF anthology show, *Out Of This World*. This pioneer show which ran to 13, one hour long episodes through the summer of 1962 saw SF finally come of age on the small screen in the UK through a combination of excellent stories by leading genre writers and fine acting by accomplished players obviously enjoying working in a completely different entertainment medium. The success of the ambitious, black and white series was also very much due to the dedicated work of its producer Leonard White and story editor Irene Shubik, who had earlier launched the very popular *Armchair Theatre*. The Science Fiction stories adapted for the screen varied from tense dramas to black comedies and included the work of such distinguished names as Isaac Asimov, Clifford Simak, Philip K. Dick and Britain's own John Wyndham. Among the scriptwriters who worked on the series were Leon Griffiths, Clive Exton and Terry Nation whose place in the pantheon of SF TV writers was assured the day he created the infamous Daleks for *Dr Who*. The cast lists of many of the episodes also looked like a Who's Who of the best contemporary television actors and actress including – among others – Dinsdale Landen, Peter Wyngarde, Maurice Denham, Charles Gray, Geraldine McEwan and Jane Asher.

'Dumb Martian' by John Wyndham (1903–1969), one of Britain's leading Twentieth Century SF writers and forever remembered for *The Day of the Triffids* (1951) which has also been filmed and adapted for TV, was chosen as the story to launch the series and was transmitted on June 24, 1962. Following the closing credits, Karloff materialized onto the nation's screens to urge viewers to watch the impending series. In Wyndham's tale an uncouth space pilot, Duncan Weaver (Lucas) buys a Martian girl Lellie (Schroder) to act as his wife and housekeeper, but when he begins treating her badly soon finds he has underestimated her intelligence as well as provoking an unexpected rival to his domestic harmony. The episode offered a form of entertainment that few viewers had seen before, but *Out Of This World* quickly caught on in the following weeks. It would not be long, in fact, before the BBC would latch onto the popularity of the anthology format and put out their own rival show.

When Duncan Weaver bought Lellie for – no, there could be trouble putting it that way – when Duncan Weaver paid Lellie's parents one thousand pounds in compensation for the loss of her services, he had a figure of six, or, if absolutely necessary, seven hundred in mind.

Everybody in Port Clarke that he had asked about it assured him that that would be a fair price. But when he got up country it hadn't turned out quite as simple as the Port Clarkers seemed to think. The first three Martian families he had tackled hadn't shown any disposition to sell their daughters at all; the next wanted £1,500, and wouldn't budge; Lellie's parents had started at £1,500, too, but they came down to £1,000 when he'd made it plain that he wasn't going to stand for extortion. And

when, on the way back to Port Clarke with her, he came
to work it out, he found himself not so badly pleased
with the deal after all. Over the five-year term of his
appointment it could only cost him £200 a year at the
worst – that is to say if he were not able to sell her for
£400, maybe £500 when he got back. Looked at that way,
it wasn't really at all unreasonable.

In town once more, he went to explain the situation
and get things all set with the Company's Agent.

"Look," he said, "you know the way I'm fixed with this
five-year contract as Way-load Station Superintendent on
Jupiter IV/II? Well, the ship that takes me there will be
travelling light to pick up cargo. So how about a second
passage on her?" He had already taken the precautionary
step of finding out that the Company was accustomed
to grant an extra passage in such circumstances, though
not of right.

The Company's Agent was not surprised. After con-
sulting some lists, he said that he saw no objection to an
extra passenger. He explained that the Company was also
prepared in such cases to supply the extra ration of food
for one person at the nominal charge of £200 per annum,
payable by deduction from salary.

"What! A thousand pounds!" Duncan exclaimed.

"Well worth it," said the Agent. "It *is* nominal for the
rations, because it's worth the Company's while to lay
out the rest for something that helps to keep an employee
from going nuts. That's pretty easy to do when you're
fixed alone on a way-load station, they tell me – and I
believe them. A thousand's not high if it helps you to
avoid a crack-up."

Duncan argued it a bit, on principle, but the Agent had
the thing cut and dried. It meant that Lellie's price went
up to £2,000 – £400 a year. Still, with his own salary at
£5,000 a year, tax free, unspendable during his term on
Jupiter IV/II, and piling up nicely, it wouldn't come to
such a big slice. So he agreed.

"Fine," said the Agent. "I'll fix it, then. All you'll

need is an embarkation permit for her, and they'll grant that automatically on production of your marriage certificate."

Duncan stared.

"Marriage certificate! What, me! Me marry a Mart!"

The Agent shook his head reprovingly.

"No embarkation permit without it. Anti-slavery regulation. They'd likely think you meant to sell her – might even think you'd bought her."

"What, me!" Duncan said again, indignantly.

"Even you," said the Agent. "A marriage licence will only cost you another ten pounds – unless you've got a wife back home, in which case it'll likely cost you a bit more later on."

Duncan shook his head.

"I've no wife," he assured him.

"Uh-huh," said the Agent, neither believing, nor disbelieving. "Then what's the difference?"

Duncan came back a couple of days later, with the certificate and the permit. The Agent looked them over.

"That's okay," he agreed. "I'll confirm the booking. My fee will be one hundred pounds."

"Your fee! What the— ?"

"Call it safeguarding your investment," said the Agent.

The man who had issued the embarkation permit had required one hundred pounds, too. Duncan did not mention that now, but he said, with bitterness:

"One dumb Mart's costing me plenty."

"Dumb?" said the Agent, looking at him.

"Speechless plus. These hick Marts don't know they're born."

"H'm," said the Agent. "Never lived here, have you?"

"No," Duncan admitted. "But I've laid-over here a few times."

The Agent nodded.

"They act dumb, and the way their faces are makes them look dumb," he said, "but they were a mighty clever people, once."

"Once, could be a long time ago."

"Long before we got here they'd given up bothering to think a lot. Their planet was dying, and they were kind of content to die with it."

"Well, I call that dumb. Aren't all planets dying, anyway?"

"Ever seen an old man just sitting in the sun, taking it easy? It doesn't have to mean he's senile. It may do, but very likely he can snap out of it and put his mind to work again if it gets really necessary. But mostly he finds it not worth the bother. Less trouble just to let things happen."

"Well, this one's only about twenty – say ten and a half of your Martian years – and she certainly lets 'em happen. And I'd say it's a kind of acid test for dumbness when a girl doesn't know what goes on at her own wedding ceremony."

And then, on top of that, it turned out to be necessary to lay out yet another hundred pounds on clothing and other things for her, bringing the whole investment up to £2,310. It was a sum which might possibly have been justified on a really *smart* girl, but Lellie . . . But there it was. Once you made the first payment, you either lost on it, or were stuck for the rest. And, anyway, on a lonely way-load station even she would be company – of a sort . . .

The First Officer called Duncan into the navigating room to take a look at his future home.

"There it is," he said, waving his hand at a watch-screen.

Duncan looked at the jagged-surfaced crescent. There was no scale to it: it could have been the size of Luna, or of a basket-ball. Either size, it was still just a lump of rock, turning slowly over.

"How big?" he asked.

"Around forty miles mean diameter."

"What'd that be in gravity?"

"Haven't worked it out. Call it slight, and reckon there isn't any, and you'll be near enough."

"Uh-huh," said Duncan.

On the way back to the mess-room he paused to put his head into the cabin. Lellie was lying on her bunk, with the spring-cover fastened over her to give some illusion of weight. At the sight of him she raised herself on one elbow.

She was small – not much over five feet. Her face and hands were delicate; they had a fragility which was not simply a matter of poor bone-structure. To an Earthman her eyes looked unnaturally round, seeming to give her permanently an expression of innocence surprised. The lobes of her ears hung unusually low out of a mass of brown hair that glinted with red among its waves. The paleness of her skin was emphasized by the colour on her cheeks and the vivid red on her lips.

"Hey," said Duncan. "You can start to get busy packing up the stuff now."

"Packing up?" she repeated doubtfully, in a curiously resonant voice.

"Sure. Pack," Duncan told her. He demonstrated by opening a box, cramming some clothes into it, and waving a hand to include the rest. Her expression did not change, but the idea got across.

"We are come?" she asked.

"We are nearly come. So get busy on this lot," he informed her.

"Yith – okay," she said, and began to unhook the cover.

Duncan shut the door, and gave a shove which sent him floating down the passage leading to the general mess and living-room.

Inside the cabin, Lellie pushed away the cover. She reached down cautiously for a pair of metallic soles, and attached them to her slippers by their clips. Still cautiously holding on to the bunk, she swung her feet over the side and lowered them until the magnetic soles clicked into contact with the floor. She stood up, more confidently. The brown overall suit she wore revealed

107

proportions that might be admired among Martians, but by Earth standards they were not classic – it is said to be the consequence of the thinner air of Mars that has in the course of time produced a greater lung capacity, with consequent modification. Still ill at ease with her condition of weightlessness, she slid her feet to keep contact as she crossed the room. For some moments she paused in front of a wall mirror, contemplating her reflection. Then she turned away and set about the packing.

"– one hell of a place to take a woman to," Wishart, the ship's cook, was saying as Duncan came in.

Duncan did not care a lot for Wishart – chiefly on account of the fact that when it had occurred to him that it was highly desirable for Lellie to have some lessons in weightless cooking, Wishart had refused to give the tuition for less than £50, and thus increased the investment cost to £2,360. Nevertheless, it was not his way to pretend to have misheard.

"One hell of a place to be given a job," he said, grimly.

No one replied to that. They knew how men came to be offered way-load jobs.

It was not necessary, as the Company frequently pointed out, for superannuation at the age of forty to come as a hardship to anyone: salaries were good, and they could cite plenty of cases where men had founded brilliant subsequent careers on the savings of their space-service days. That was all right for the men who had saved, and had not been obsessively interested in the fact that one four-legged animal can run faster than another. But this was not even an enterprising way to have lost one's money, so when it came to Duncan's time to leave crew work they made him no more than the routine offer.

He had never been to Jupiter IV/II, but he knew just what it would be like – something that was second moon to Callisto; itself fourth moon, in order of discovery, to Jupiter; would inevitably be one of the grimmer kinds of cosmic pebble. They offered no alternative, so he signed up at the usual terms: £5,000 a year for five years, all found, plus five months waiting time on half-pay before he could get there, plus six months afterwards, also on half-pay, during 'readjustment to gravity'.

Well – it meant the next six years taken care of; five of them without expenses, and a nice little sum at the end.

The splinter in the mouthful was: could you get through five years of isolation without cracking up? Even when the psychologist had okayed you, you couldn't be sure. Some could: others went to pieces in a few months, and had to be taken off, gibbering. If you got through two years, they said, you'd be okay for five. But the only way to find out about the two was to try . . .

"What about my putting in the waiting time on Mars? I could live cheaper there," Duncan suggested.

They had consulted planetary tables and sailing schedules, and discovered that it would come cheaper for them, too. They had declined to split the difference on the saving thus made, but they had booked him a passage for the following week, and arranged for him to draw, on credit, from the Company's agent there.

The Martian colony in and around Port Clarke is rich in ex-spacemen who find it more comfortable to spend their rearguard years in the lesser gravity, broader morality, and greater economy obtaining there. They are great advisers. Duncan listened, but discarded most of it. Such methods of occupying oneself to preserve sanity as learning the Bible or the works of Shakespeare by heart, or copying out three pages of the Encyclopaedia every day, or building model spaceships in bottles, struck him not only as tedious, but probably of doubtful efficacy, as well. The only one which he had felt to show sound practical advantages was that which had led him to picking Lellie to share his exile, and he still fancied it was a sound one, in spite of its letting him in for £2,360.

He was well enough aware of the general opinion about it to refrain from adding a sharp retort to Wishart. Instead, he conceded:

"Maybe it'd not do to take a *real* woman to a place like that. But a Mart's kind of different . . ."

"Even a Mart—" Wishart began, but he was cut short by finding himself drift slowly across the room as the arrester tubes began to fire.

Conversation ceased as everybody turned-to on the job of securing all loose objects.

Jupiter IV/II was, by definition, a sub-moon, and probably a captured asteroid. The surface was not cratered, like Luna's: it was simply a waste of jagged, riven rocks. The satellite as a whole had the form of an irregular ovoid; it was a bleak, cheerless lump of stone splintered off some vanished planet, with nothing whatever to commend it but its situation.

There have to be way-load stations. It would be hopelessly uneconomic to build big ships capable of landing on the major planets. A few of the older and smaller ships were indeed built on Earth, and so had to be launched from there, but the very first large, moon-assembled ships. established a new practice. Ships became truly *space*ships and were no longer built to stand the strains of high gravitational pull. They began to make their voyages, carrying fuel, stores, freight, and changes of personnel, exclusively between satellites. Newer types do not put in even at Luna, but use the artificial satellite, Pseudos, exclusively as their Earth terminus.

Freight between the way-loads and their primaries is customarily consigned in powered cylinders known as crates; passengers are ferried back and forth in small rocket-ships. Stations such as Pseudos, or Deimos, the main way-load for Mars, handle enough work to keep a crew busy, but in the outlying, little-developed posts one man who is part-handler, part-watchman is enough. Ships visited them infrequently. On Jupiter IV/II one might, according to Duncan's information, expect an average of one every eight or nine months (Earth).

The ship continued to slow, coming in on a spiral, adjusting her speed to that of the satellite. The gyros started up to give stability. The small, jagged world grew until it overflowed the watch-screens. The ship was manoeuvred into a close orbit. Miles of featureless, formidable rocks slid monotonously beneath her.

The station site came sliding on to the screen from the left; a roughly levelled area of a few acres; the first and only sign of order in the stony chaos. At the far end was a pair of hemispherical huts, one much larger than the other. At the near end, a few cylindrical crates were lined up beside a launching ramp hewn from the rock. Down each side of the area stood rows of canvas bins, some stuffed full of a conical shape; others slack, empty or half-empty. A huge parabolic mirror was perched on a crag behind the station, looking like a monstrous, formalized flower. In the whole scene there was only one sign of movement – a small, space-suited figure prancing madly about on a metal apron in front of the larger dome, waving its arms in a wild welcome.

Duncan left the screen, and went to the cabin. He found Lellie fighting off a large case which, under the influence of deceleration, seemed determined to pin her against the wall. He shoved the case aside, and pulled her out.

"We're there," he told her. "Put on your space-suit."

Her round eyes ceased to pay attention to the case, and turned towards him. There was no telling from them how she felt, what she thought. She said, simply:

"Thpace-thuit. Yith – okay."

Standing in the airlock of the dome, the outgoing Superintendent paid more attention to Lellie than to the pressure-dial. He knew from experience exactly how long equalizing took, and opened his face-plate without even a glance at the pointer.

"Wish I'd had the sense to bring one," he observed. "Could have been mighty useful on the chores, too."

He opened the inner door, and led through.

"Here it is – and welcome to it," he said.

The main living-room was oddly shaped by reason of the dome's architecture, but it was spacious. It was also exceedingly, sordidly untidy.

"Meant to clean it up – never got around to it, some way," he added. He looked at Lellie. There was no visible sign of what she thought of the place. "Never can tell with Marts," he said uneasily. "They kind of non-register."

Duncan agreed: "I've figured this one looked astonished at being born, and never got over it."

The other man went on looking at Lellie. His eyes strayed from her to a gallery of pinned-up terrestrial beauties, and back again.

"Sort of funny shape Marts are," he said, musingly.

"This one's reckoned a good enough looker where she comes from," Duncan told him, a trifle shortly.

"Sure. No offence, Bud. I guess they'll all seem a funny shape to me after this spell." He changed the subject. "I'd better show you the ropes around here."

Duncan signed to Lellie to open her face-plate so that she could hear him, and then told her to get out of her suit.

The dome was the usual type: double-floored, double-walled, with an insulated and evacuated space between the two; constructed as a unit, and held down by metal bars let into the rock. In the living-quarters there were three more sizable rooms, able to cope with increased personnel if trade should expand.

"The rest," the outgoing man explained, "is the regular station stores, mostly food, air cylinders, spares of one kind and another, and water – you'll need to watch her on water; most women seem to think it grows naturally in pipes."

Duncan shook his head.

"Not Marts. Living in deserts gives 'em a natural respect for water."

The other picked up a clip of store-sheets.

"We'll check and sign these later. It's a nice soft job here. Only freight now is rare metalliferous earth. Callisto's not been opened up a lot yet. Handling's easy. They tell you when a crate's on the way: you switch on the radio beacon to bring it in. On dispatch you can't go wrong if you follow the tables." He looked around the room. "All home comforts. You read? Plenty of books." He waved a hand at the packed rows which covered half the inner partition wall. Duncan said he'd never been much of a reader. "Well, it helps," said the other. "Find pretty well anything that's known in that lot. Records there. Fond of music?"

Duncan said he liked a good tune.

"H'm. Better try the other stuff. Tunes get to squirrelling inside your head. Play chess?" He pointed to a board, with men pegged into it.

Duncan shook his head.

"Pity. There's a fellow over on Callisto plays a pretty hot game. He'll be disappointed not to finish this one. Still, if I was fixed up the way you are, maybe I'd not have been interested in chess." His eyes strayed to Lellie again. "What do you reckon she's going to do here, over and above cooking and amusing you?" he asked.

It was not a question that had occurred to Duncan, but he shrugged.

"Oh, she'll be okay, I guess. There's a natural dumbness about Marts – they'll sit for hours on end, doing damn all. It's a gift they got."

"Well, it should come in handy here," said the other.

The regular ship's-call work went on. Cases were unloaded, the metalliferous earths hosed from the bins into the holds. A small ferry-rocket came up from Callisto carrying a couple of time-expired prospectors, and left again with their two replacements. The ship's engineers checked over the station's machinery, made renewals, topped up the water tanks, charged the spent air cylinders, tested, tinkered, and tested again before giving their final okay.

John Wyndham

Duncan stood outside on the metal apron where not long ago his predecessor had performed his fantastic dance of welcome, to watch the ship take off. She rose straight up, with her jets pushing her gently. The curve of her hull became an elongated crescent shining against the black sky. The main driving jets started to gush white flame edged with pink. Quickly she picked up speed. Before long she had dwindled to a speck which sank behind the ragged skyline.

Quite suddenly Duncan felt as if he, too, had dwindled. He had become a speck upon a barren mass of rock which was itself a speck in the immensity. The indifferent sky about him had no scale. It was an utterly black void wherein his mother-sun and a myriad more suns flared perpetually, without reason or purpose.

The rocks of the satellite itself, rising up in their harsh crests and ridges, were without scale, too. He could not tell which were near or far away; he could not, in the jumble of hard-lit planes and inky shadows, even make out their true form. There was nothing like them to be seen on Earth, or on Mars. Their unweathered edges were sharp as blades: they had been just as sharp as that for millions upon millions of years, and would be for as long as the satellite should last.

The unchanging millions of years seemed to stretch out before and behind him. It was not only himself, it was all life that was a speck, a briefly transitory accident, utterly unimportant to the universe. It was a queer little mote dancing for its chance moment in the light of the eternal suns. Reality was just globes of fire and balls of stone rolling on, senselessly rolling along through emptiness, through time unimaginable, for ever, and ever, and ever . . .

Within his heated suit, Duncan shivered a little. Never before had he been so alone; never so much aware of the vast, callous, futile loneliness of space. Looking out into the blackness, with light that had left a star a million years ago shining into his eyes, he wondered.

114

"*Why?*" he asked himself. "What the heck's it all about, anyway?"

The sound of his own unanswerable question broke up the mood. He shook his head to clear it of speculative nonsense. He turned his back on the universe, reducing it again to its proper status as a background for life in general and human life in particular, and stepped into the airlock.

The job was, as his predecessor had told him, soft. Duncan made his radio contacts with Callisto at pre-arranged times. Usually it was little more than a formal check on one another's continued existence, with perhaps an exchange of comment on the radio news. Only occasionally did they announce a dispatch and tell him when to switch on his beacon. Then, in due course, the cylinder-crate would make its appearance, and float slowly down. It was quite a simple matter to couple it up to a bin to transfer the load.

The satellite's day was too short for convenience, and its night, lit by Callisto, and sometimes by Jupiter as well, almost as bright; so they disregarded it, and lived by the calender-clock which kept Earth time on the Greenwich Meridian setting. At first much of the time had been occupied in disposing of the freight that the ship had left. Some of it into the main dome – necessities for themselves, and other items that would store better where there was warmth and air. Some into the small, airless, unheated dome. The greater part to be stowed and padded carefully into cylinders and launched off to the Callisto base. But once that work had been cleared, the job was certainly soft, too soft . . .

Duncan drew up a programme. At regular intervals he would inspect this and that, he would waft himself up to the crag and check on the sun-motor there, et cetera. But keeping to an unnecessary programme requires resolution. Sun-motors, for instance, are very necessarily built to run for long spells without attention. The only action one could take if it should stop would be to call on

Callisto for a ferry-rocket to come and take them off until a ship should call to repair it. A breakdown there, the Company had explained very clearly, was the only thing that would justify him in leaving his station, with the stores of precious earth, unmanned (and it was also conveyed that to contrive a breakdown for the sake of a change was unlikely to prove worth while). One way and another, the programme did not last long.

There were times when Duncan found himself wondering whether the bringing of Lellie had been such a good idea after all. On the purely practical side, he'd not have cooked as well as she did, and probably have pigged it quite as badly as his precessor had, but if she had not been there, the necessity of looking after himself would have given him some occupation. And even from the angle of company – well, she was that, of a sort, but she was alien, queer; kind of like a half-robot, and dumb at that; certainly no fun. There were, indeed, times – increasingly frequent times, when the very look of her irritated him intensely; so did the way she moved, *and* her gestures, *and* her silly pidgin-talk when she talked, *and* her self-contained silence when she didn't, *and* her withdrawness, *and* all her differentness, *and* the fact that he would have been £2,360 better off without her . . . Nor did she make a serious attempt to remedy her shortcomings, even where she had the means. Her face, for instance. You'd think any girl would try to make her best of that – but did she, hell! There was that left eyebrow again: made her look like a sozzled clown, but a lot she cared . . .

"For heaven's sake," he told her once more, "put the cockeyed thing straight. Don't you know how to fix 'em *yet?* And you've got your colour on wrong, too. Look at that picture – now look at yourself in the mirror: a great daub of red all in the wrong place. And your hair, too: getting all like seaweed again. You've got the things to wave it, then for crysake wave it again, and stop looking like a bloody mermaid. I know you can't help being a damn Mart, but you can at least *try* to look like a real woman."

Lellie looked at the coloured picture, and then compared her reflection with it, critically.

"Yith – okay," she said, with an equable detachment.
Duncan snorted.

"And that's another thing. Bloody baby-talk! It's not
'yith', it's 'yes'. Y-E-S, yes. So say 'yes'."

"Yith," said Lellie, obligingly.

"Oh, for – Can't you *hear* the difference? S-s-s, not
th-th-th. Ye-sss."

"Yith," she said.

"No. Put your tongue further back like this—"

The lesson went on for some time. Finally he grew
angry.

"Just making a monkey out of me, huh! You'd better
be careful, my girl. Now, say 'yes'."

She hesitated, looking at his wrathful face.

"Go on, say it."

"Y-yeth," she said, nervously.

His hand slapped across her face harder than he had
intended. The jolt broke her magnetic contact with the
floor, and sent her sailing across the room in a spin of arms
and legs. She struck the opposite wall, and rebounded to
float helplessly, out of reach of any hold. He strode after
her, turned her right way up, and set her on her feet. His
left hand clutched her overall in a bunch, just below her
throat, his right was raised.

"Again!" he told her.

Her eyes looked helplessly this way and that. He
shook her. She tried. At the sixth attempt she managed: "Yeths."

He accepted that for the time being.

"You *can* do it, you see – when you try. What you
need, my girl, is a bit of firm handling."

He let her go. She tottered across the room, holding
her hands to her bruised face.

A number of times while the weeks drew out so slowly
into months Duncan found himself wondering whether he
was going to get through. He spun out what work there

was as much as he could, but it left still too much time hanging heavy on his hands.

A middle-aged man who has read nothing longer than an occasional magazine article does not take to books. He tired very quickly, as his predecessor had prophesied, of the popular records, and could make nothing of the others. He taught himself the moves in chess from a book, and instructed Lellie in them, intending after a little practice with her to challenge the man on Callisto. Lellie, however, managed to win with such consistency that he had to decide that he had not the right kind of mind for the game. Instead, he taught her a kind of double solitaire, but that didn't last long, either; the cards seemed always to run for Lellie.

Occasionally there was some news and entertainment to be had from the radio, but with Earth somewhere round the other side of the sun just then, Mars screened off half the time by Callisto, and the rotation of the satellite itself, reception was either impossible, or badly broken up.

So mostly he sat and fretted, hating the satellite, angry with himself, and irritated by Lellie.

Just the phlegmatic way she went on with her tasks irritated him. It seemed an injustice that she could take it all better than he could simply *because* she was a dumb Mart. When his ill-temper became vocal, the look of her as she listened exasperated him still more.

"For crysake," he told her one time, "can't you make that silly face of yours *mean* something? Can't you laugh, or cry, or get mad, or something? It's enough to drive a guy nuts going on looking at a face that's fixed permanent like it was a doll just heard its first dirty story. I know you can't help being dumb, but for heaven's sake crack it up a bit, get some expression into it."

She went on looking at him without a shadow of a change.

"Go on, you heard me! Smile, damn you – Smile!"

Her mouth twitched very slightly.

"Call that a smile! Now, there's a smile!" He pointed

118

to a pin-up with her head split pretty much in half by a smile like a piano keyboard. "Like that! Like this!" He grinned widely.

"No," she said. "My face can't wriggle like Earth faces."

"Wriggle!" he said, incensed. "Wriggle, you call it!" He freed himself from the chair's spring-cover, and came towards her. She backed away until she fetched up against the wall. "I'll make yours wriggle, my girl. Go on, now – smile!" He lifted his hand.

Lellie put her hands up to her face.

"No!" she protested. "No-no-no!"

It was on the very day that Duncan marked off the eighth completed month that Callisto relayed news of a ship on the way. A couple of days later he was able to make contact with her himself, and confirm her arrival in about a week. He felt as if he had been given several stiff drinks. There were the preparations to make, stores to check, deficiencies to note, a string of nil-nil-nil entries to be made in the log to bring it up to date. He bustled around as he got on with it. He even hummed to himself as he worked, and ceased to be annoyed with Lellie. The effect upon her of the news was imperceptible – but then, what would you expect . . . ?

Sharp on her estimated time the ship hung above them, growing slowly larger as her upper jets pressed her down. The moment she was berthed Duncan went aboard, with the feeling that everything in sight was an old friend. The Captain received him warmly, and brought out the drinks. It was all routine – even Duncan's babbling and slightly inebriated manner was the regular thing in the circumstances. The only departure from pattern came when the Captain introduced a man beside him, and explained him.

"We've brought a surprise for you, Superintendent. This is Doctor Whint. He'll be sharing your exile for a bit."

Duncan shook hands. "Doctor . . . ?" he said, surprisedly.

"Not medicine – science," Alan Whint told him. "The Company's pushed me out here to do a geological survey – if geo isn't the wrong word to use. About a year. Hope you don't mind."

Duncan said conventionally that he'd be glad of the company, and left it at that for the moment. Later, he took him over to the dome. Alan Whint was surprised to find Lellie there; clearly nobody had told him about her. He interrupted Duncan's explanations to say:

"Won't you introduce me to your wife?"

Duncan did so, without grace. He resented the reproving tone in the man's voice; nor did he care for the way he greeted Lellie just as if she were an Earth woman. He was also aware that he had noticed the bruise on her cheek that the colour did not altogether cover. In his mind he classified Alan Whint as one of the smooth, snooty type, and hoped that there was not going to be trouble with him.

It could be, indeed, it was, a matter of opinion who made the trouble when it boiled up some three months later. There had already been several occasions when it had lurked uneasily near. Very likely it would have come into the open long before had Whint's work not taken him out of the dome so much. The moment of touch-off came when Lellie lifted her eyes from the book she was reading to ask: "What does 'female emancipation' mean?"

Alan started to explain. He was only half-way through the first sentence when Duncan broke in:

"Listen – who told you to go putting ideas into her head?"

Alan shrugged his shoulders slightly, and looked at him.

"That's a damn silly question," he said. "And, anyway, why shouldn't she have ideas? Why shouldn't anyone?"

"You know what I mean."

"I never understand you guys who apparently can't *say* what you mean. Try again."

"All right then. What I mean is this: you come here with your ritzy ways and your snazzy talk, and right from the start you start shoving your nose into things that aren't your business. You begin right off by treating her as if she was some toney dame back home."

"I hoped so. I'm glad you noticed it."

"And do you think I didn't see why?"

"I'm quite sure you didn't. You've such a well-grooved mind. You think, in your simple way, that I'm out to get your girl, and you resent that with all the weight of two thousand, three hundred and sixty pounds. But you're wrong: I'm not."

Duncan was momentarily thrown off his line, then:

"My *wife*," he corrected. "She may be only a dumb Mart, but she's legally my wife: and what I say goes."

"Yes, Lellie is a Mart, as you call it; she may even be your wife, for all I know to the contrary; but dumb, she certainly is not. For one example, look at the speed with which she's learned to read – once someone took the trouble to show her how. I don't think you'd show up any too bright yourself in a language where you only knew a few words, and which you couldn't read."

"It was none of your business to teach her. She didn't need to read. She was all right the way she was."

"The voice of the slaver down the ages. Well, if I've done nothing else, I've cracked up your ignorance racket there."

"And why? – So she'll think you're a great guy. The same reason you talk all toney and smarmy to her. So you'll get her thinking you're a better man than I am."

"I talk to her the way I'd talk to any woman anywhere – only more simply since she's not had the chance of an education. If she does think I'm a better man, then I agree with her. I'd be sorry if I couldn't."

"I'll show you who's the better man—" Duncan began.

121

"You don't need to. I knew when I came here that you'd be a waster, or you'd not be on this job – and it didn't take long for me to find out that you were a goddam bully, too. Do you suppose I've not noticed the bruises? Do you think I've enjoyed having to listen to you bawling out a girl whom you've deliberately kept ignorant and defenceless when she's potentially ten times the sense you have? Having to watch a *clodkopf* like you lording it over your 'dumb Mart'? You emetic!"

In the heat of the moment, Duncan could not quite remember what an emetic was, but anywhere else the man would not have got that far before he had waded in to break him up. Yet, even through his anger, twenty years of space experience held – as little more than a boy he had learnt the ludicrous futility of weightless scrapping, and that it was the angry man who always made the bigger fool of himself.

Both of them simmered, but held in. Somehow the occasion was patched up and smoothed over, and for a time things went on much as before.

Alan continued to make his expeditions in the small craft which he had brought with him. He examined and explored other parts of the satellite, returning with specimen pieces of rock which he tested, and arranged, carefully labelled, in cases. In his off times he occupied himself, as before, in teaching Lellie.

That he did it largely for his own occupation as well as from a feeling that it should be done, Duncan did not altogether deny; but he was equally sure that in continued close association one thing leads to another, sooner or later. So far, there had been nothing between them that he could put his finger on – but Alan's term had still some nine months to go, even if he were relieved to time. Lellie was already hero-worshipping. And he was spoiling her more every day by this fool business of treating her as if she were an Earth woman. One day they'd come alive to it – and the next step would be that they would see him as an obstacle that would be better removed. Prevention being better than cure, the sensible course was to see that the situation should never develop. There need not be any fuss about it . . .

There was not.

One day Alan Whint took off on a routine flight to prospect somewhere on the other side of the satellite. He simply never came back. That was all.

There was no telling what Lellie thought about it; but something seemed to happen to her.

For several days she spent almost all her time standing by the main window of the living-room, looking out into the blackness at the flaring pinpoints of light. It was not that she was waiting or hoping for Alan's return – she knew as well as Duncan himself that when thirty-six hours had gone by there was no chance of that. She said nothing. Her expression maintained its exasperating look of slight surprise, unchanged. Only in her eyes was there any perceptible difference: they looked a little less live, as if she had withdrawn herself further behind them.

Duncan could not tell whether she knew or guessed anything. And there seemed to be no way of finding out without planting the idea in her mind – *if* it were not already there. He was, without admitting it too fully to himself, nervous of her – too nervous to turn on her roundly for the time she spent vacantly mooning out of the window. He had an uncomfortable awareness of how many ways there were for even a dimwit to contrive a fatal accident in such a place. As a precaution he took to fitting new air-bottles to his suit every time he went out, and checking that they were at full pressure. He also took to placing a piece of rock so that the outer door of the airlock could not close behind him. He made a point of noticing that his food and hers came straight out of the same pot, and watched her closely as she worked. He still could not decide whether she knew, or suspected . . . After they were sure that he was gone, she never once mentioned Alan's name . . .

The mood stayed on her for perhaps a week. Then

it changed abruptly. She paid no more attention to the blackness outside. Instead, she began to read, voraciously and indiscriminately.

Duncan found it hard to understand her absorption in the books, nor did he like it, but he decided for the moment not to interfere. It did, at least, have the advantage of keeping her mind off other things.

Gradually he began to feel easier. The crisis was over. Either she had not guessed, or, if she had, she had decided to do nothing about it. Her addiction to books, however, did not abate. In spite of several reminders by Duncan that it was for *company* that he had laid out the not inconsiderable sum of £2,360, she continued, as if determined to work her way through the station's library.

By degrees the affair retreated into the background. When the next ship came Duncan watched her anxiously in case she had been biding her time to hand on her suspicions to the crew. It turned out, however, to be unnecessary. She showed no tendency to refer to the matter, and when the ship pulled out, taking the opportunity with it, he was relievedly able to tell himself that he had really been right all along – she was just a dumb Mart: she had simply forgotten the Alan Whint incident, as a child might.

And yet, as the months of his term ticked steadily away, he found that he had, bit by bit, to revise that estimate of dumbness. She was learning from books things that he did not know himself. It even had some advantages, though it put him in a position he did not care for – when she asked, as she sometimes did now, for explanations, he found it unpleasant to be stumped by a Mart. Having the practical man's suspicion of book-acquired knowledge, he felt it necessary to explain to her how much of the stuff in the books was a lot of nonsense, how they never really came to grips with the problems of life as he had lived it. He cited instances from his own affairs, gave examples from his experience, in fact, he found himself teaching her.

She learnt quickly, too; the practical as well as the book stuff. Of necessity he had to revise his opinion of Marts slightly more – it wasn't that they were altogether dumb as he had thought, just that they were normally too dumb to start using the brains they had. Once started, Lellie was a regular vacuum-cleaner for knowledge of all sorts: it didn't seem long before she knew as much about the way-load station as he did himself. Teaching her was not at all what he had intended, but it did provide an occupation much to be preferred to the boredom of the early days. Besides, it had occurred to him that she was an appreciating asset . . .

Funny thing, that. He had never before thought of education as anything but a waste of time, but now it seriously began to look as if, when he got her back to Mars, he might recover quite a bit more of the £2,360 than he had expected. Maybe she'd make quite a useful secretary to someone . . . He started to instruct her in elementary book-keeping and finance – insofar as he knew anything about it . . .

The months of service kept on piling up; going a very great deal faster now. During the later stretch, when one had acquired confidence in his ability to get through without cracking up, there was a comfortable feeling about sitting quietly out there with the knowledge of the money gradually piling up at home.

A new find opened up on Callisto, bringing a slight increase in deliveries to the satellite. Otherwise, the routine continued unchanged. The infrequent ships called in, loaded up, and went again. And then, surprisingly soon, it was possible for Duncan to say to himself: "Next ship but one, and I'll be through!" Even more surprisingly soon there came the day when he stood on the metal apron outside the dome, watching a ship lifting herself off on her under-jets and dwindling upwards into the black sky, and was able to tell himself: "That's the last time I'll see that! When the next ship lifts off this dump, I'll be aboard her, and then – boy, oh boy . . . !"

He stood watching her, one bright spark among the others, until the turn of the satellite carried her below his horizon. Then he turned back to the airlock – and found the door shut . . .

Once he had decided that there was going to be no repercussion from the Alan Whint affair he had let his habit of wedging it open with a piece of rock lapse. Whenever he emerged to do a job he left it ajar, and it stayed that way until he came back. There was no wind, or anything else on the satellite to move it. He laid hold of the latch-lever irritably, and pushed. It did not move.

Duncan swore at it for sticking. He walked to the edge of the metal apron, and then jetted himself a little round the side of the dome so that he could see in at the window. Lellie was sitting in a chair with the spring-cover fixed across it, apparently lost in thought. The inner door of the airlock was standing open, so of course the outer could not be moved. As well as the safety-locking device, there was all the dome's air pressure to hold it shut.

Forgetful for the moment, Duncan rapped on the thick glass of the double window to attract her attention; she could not have heard a sound through there, it must have been the movement that caught her eye and caused her to look up. She turned her head, and gazed at him, without moving. Duncan stared back at her. Her hair was still waved, but the eyebrows, the colour, all the other touches that he had insisted upon to make her look as much like an Earth woman as possible, were gone. Her eyes looked back at him, set hard as stones in that fixed expression of mild astonishment.

Sudden comprehension struck Duncan like a physical shock. For some seconds everything seemed to stop.

He tried to pretend to both of them that he had not understood. He made gestures to her to close the inner door of the airlock. She went on staring back at him, without moving. Then he noticed the book she was holding in her hand, and recognized it. It was not one of the books which the Company had supplied for the station's library. It was a book of verse, bound in blue. It had once belonged to Alan Whint . . .

Panic suddenly jumped out at Duncan. He looked down at the row of small dials across his chest, and then sighed with relief. She had not tampered with his air-supply: there was pressure there enough for thirty hours or so. The sweat that had started out on his brow grew cooler as he regained control of himself. A touch on the jet sent him floating back to the metal apron where he could anchor his magnetic boots, and think it over.

What a bitch! Letting him think all this time that she had forgotten all about it. Nursing it up for him. Letting him work out his time while she planned. Waiting until he was on the very last stretch before she tried her game on. Some minutes passed before his mixed anger and panic settled down and allowed him to think.

Thirty hours! Time to do quite a lot. And even if he did not succeed in getting back into the dome in twenty or so of them, there would still be the last, desperate resort of shooting himself off to Callisto in one of the cylinder-crates.

Even if Lellie were to spill over later about the Whint business, what of it? He was sure enough that she did not know *how* it had been done. It would only be the word of a Mart against his own. Very likely they'd put her down as space-crazed.

. . . All the same, some of the mud might stick; it would be better to settle with her here and now – besides, the cylinder idea was risky; only to be considered in the last extremity. There were other ways to be tried first.

Duncan reflected a few minutes longer, then he jetted himself over to the smaller dome. In there, he threw out the switches on the lines which brought power down from the main batteries charged by the sun-motor. He sat down to wait for a bit. The insulated dome would take some time to lose all its heat, but not very long for a drop in the temperature to become perceptible, and visible on the thermometers, once the heat was off. The small capacity, low voltage batteries that were in the place wouldn't be much good to her, even if she did think of lining them up.

He waited an hour, while the faraway sun set, and the arc of Callisto began to show over the horizon. Then he went back to the dome's window to observe results. He arrived just in time to see Lellie fastening herself into her space-suit by the light of a couple of emergency lamps.

He swore. A simple freezing out process wasn't going to work, then. Not only would the heated suit protect her, but her air supply would last longer than his – and there were plenty of spare bottles in there even if the free air in the dome should freeze solid.

He waited until she had put on the helmet, and then switched on the radio in his own. He saw her pause at the sound of his voice, but she did not reply. Presently she deliberately switched off her receiver. He did not; he kept his open to be ready for the moment when she should come to her senses.

Duncan returned to the apron, and reconsidered. It had been his intention to force his way into the dome without damaging it, if he could. But if she wasn't to be frozen out, that looked difficult. She had the advantage of him in air – and though it was true that in her space-suit she could neither eat nor drink, the same, unfortunately, was true for him. The only way seemed to be to tackle the dome itself.

Reluctantly, he went back to the small dome again, and connected up the electrical cutter. Its cable looped behind him as he jetted across to the main dome once more. Beside the curving metal wall, he paused to think out the job – and the consequences. Once he was through the outer shell there would be a space; then the insulating material – that was okay, it would melt away like butter, and without oxygen it could not catch fire. The more awkward part was going to come with the inner metal skin. It would be wisest to start with a few small cuts to let the air-pressure down – and stand clear of it: if it were all to come out with a whoosh he would stand a good chance in his weightless state of being blown a considerable distance by it. And what would she do? Well, she'd very likely try covering up the holes as he made them – a bit awkward if she had the sense to use asbestos packing: it'd have to be the whoosh then . . . Both shells could be welded up again before he re-aerated the place from cylinders . . . The small loss of insulating material wouldn't matter . . . Okay, better get down to it, then . . .

He made his connexions, and contrived to anchor himself enough to give some purchase. He brought the cutter up, and pressed the trigger-switch. He pressed again, and then swore, remembering that he had shut off the power.

He pulled himself back along the cable, and pushed the switches in again. Light from the dome's windows suddenly illuminated the rocks. He wondered if the restoration of power would let Lellie know what he was doing. What if it did? She'd know soon enough, anyway.

He settled himself down beside the dome once more. This time the cutter worked. It took only a few minutes to slice out a rough, two-foot circle. He pulled the piece out of the way, and inspected the opening. Then, as he levelled the cutter again, there came a click in his receiver: Lellie's voice spoke in his ear:

"Better not try to break in. I'm ready for that."

He hesitated, checking himself with his finger on the switch, wondering what counter-move she could have thought up. The threat in her voice made him uneasy. He decided to go round to the window, and see what her game was, if she had one.

She was standing by the table, still dressed in her space-suit, fiddling with some apparatus she had set up there. For a moment or two he did not grasp the purpose of it.

There was a plastic food-bag, half-inflated, and attached in some way to the table top. She was adjusting
a metal plate over it to a small clearance. There was a
wire, scotch-taped to the upper side of the bag. Duncan's
eye ran back along the wire to a battery, a coil, and on
to a detonator attached to a bundle of half a dozen
blasting-sticks . . .

He was uncomfortably enlightened. It was very simple
– ought to be perfectly effective. If the air-pressure in the
room should fall, the bag would expand: the wire would
make contact with the plate: up would go the dome . . .

Lellie finished her adjustment, and connected the second wire to the battery. She turned to look at him through
the window. It was infuriatingly difficult to believe that
behind that silly surprise frozen on her face she could be
properly aware what she was doing.

Duncan tried to speak to her, but she had switched
off, and made no attempt to switch on again. She simply
stood looking steadily back at him as he blustered and
raged. After some minutes she moved across to a
chair, fastened the spring-cover across herself, and
sat waiting.

"All right then," Duncan shouted inside his helmet.
"But you'll go up with it, damn you!" Which was, of
course, nonsense since he had no intention whatever of
destroying either the dome or himself.

He had never learnt to tell what went on behind that
silly face – she might be coldly determined, or she might
not. If it had been a matter of a switch which she must
press to destroy the place he might have risked her nerve
failing her. But this way, it would be he who operated
the switch, just as soon as he should make a hole to let
the air out.

Once more he retreated to anchor himself on the apron.
There must be *some* way round, some way of getting
into the dome without letting the pressure down . . .
He thought hard for some minutes, but if there was
such a way, he could not find it – besides, there was

no guarantee that she'd not set the explosive off herself if she got scared . . .

No – there was no way that he could think of. It would have to be the cylinder-crate to Callisto.

He looked up at Callisto, hanging huge in the sky now, with Jupiter smaller, but brighter, beyond. It wasn't so much the flight, it was the landing there. Perhaps if he were to cram it with all the padding he could find . . . Later on, he could get the Callisto fellows to ferry him back, and they'd find some way to get into the dome, and Lellie would be a mighty sorry girl – *mighty* sorry . . .

Across the levelling there were three cylinders lined up, charged and ready for use. He didn't mind admitting he was scared of that landing: but, scared or not, if she wouldn't even turn on her radio to listen to him, that would be his only chance. And delay would do nothing for him but narrow the margin of his air-supply.

He made up his mind, and stepped off the metal apron. A touch on the jets sent him floating across the levelling towards the cylinders. Practice made it an easy thing for him to manoeuvre the nearest one on to the ramp. Another glance at Callisto's inclination helped to reassure him; at least he would reach it all right. If their beacon there was not switched on to bring him in, he ought to be able to call them on the communication radio in his suit when he got closer.

There was not a lot of padding in the cylinder. He fetched more from the others, and packed the stuff in. It was while he paused to figure out a way of triggering the thing off with himself inside, that he realized he was beginning to feel cold. As he turned the knob up a notch, he glanced down at the meter on his chest – in an instant he knew . . . She had known that he would fit fresh air-bottles and test them; so it had been the battery, or more likely, the circuit, she had tampered with. The voltage was down to a point where the needle barely kicked. The suit must have been losing heat for some time already.

He knew that he would not be able to last long – perhaps not more than a few minutes. After its first stab, the fear abruptly left him, giving way to an impotent fury. She'd tricked him out of his last chance, but, by God, he could make sure she didn't get away with it. He'd be going, but just one small hole in the dome, and he'd not be going alone . . .

The cold was creeping into him, it seemed to come lapping at him icily through the suit. He pressed the jet control, and sent himself scudding back towards the dome. The cold was gnawing in at him. His feet and fingers were going first. Only by an immense effort was he able to operate the jet which stopped him by the side of the dome. But it needed one more effort, for he hung there, a yard or so above the ground. The cutter lay where he had left it, a few feet beyond his reach. He struggled desperately to press the control that would let him down to it, but his fingers would no longer move. He wept and gasped at the attempt to make them work, and with the anguish of the cold creeping up his arms. Of a sudden, there was an agonizing, searing pain in his chest. It made him cry out. He gasped – and the unheated air rushed into his lungs, and froze them . . .

In the dome's living-room Lellie stood waiting. She had seen the space-suited figure come sweeping across the levelling at an abnormal speed. She understood what it meant. Her explosive device was already disconnected; now she stood alert, with a thick rubber mat in her hand, ready to clap it over any hole that might appear. She waited one minute, two minutes . . . When five minutes had passed she went to the window. By putting her face close to the pane and looking sideways she was able to see the whole of one space-suited leg and part of another. They hung there horizontally, a few feet off the ground. She watched them for several minutes. Their gradual downward drift was barely perceptible.

She left the window, and pushed the mat out of her

hand so that it floated away across the room. For a moment or two she stood thinking. Then she went to the bookshelves and pulled out the last volume of the encyclopaedia. She turned the pages, and satisfied herself on the exact status and claims which are connoted by the word 'widow'.

She found a pad of paper and a pencil. For a minute she hesitated, trying to remember the method she had been taught, then she started to write down figures, and became absorbed in them. At last she lifted her head, and contemplated the result: £5,000 per annum for five years, at 6 per cent compound interest, worked out at a nice little sum – quite a small fortune for a Martian.

But then she hesitated again. Very likely a face that was not set for ever in a mould of slightly surprised innocence would have frowned a little at that point, because, of course, there was a deduction that had to be made – a matter of £2,360.

DOCTOR WHO

(BBC TV, 1963–?)
Starring: William Hartnell, Roslyn de Winter
& Martin Jarvis
Directed by Richard Martin
Story 'The Lair of the Zarbi' by Bill Strutton

The phenomenon of *Doctor Who* is almost without precedent in television history. Although off the screen at the time of writing – only temporarily, its countless millions of fans around the world hope – this SF series which was devised in 1963 by the BBC's new Head of Drama, Sydney Newman (recently recruited from ABC where he had also been instrumental in the success of *Armchair Theatre*), embodies a concept that literally gives it an indefinite life. The idea of a Time Lord who can travel wherever he pleases and 'regenerate' at will, allows any producer to recast his leading actor without destroying the audience's identification with the central character. Hence there have been seven actors so far playing the man known only as the Doctor from the planet Gallifrey who journeys in his space vehicle, the TARDIS – which resembles an old-fashioned London police call box – confronting the enemies of interplanetary law and order: crotchety William Hartnell; the cosmic hobo Patrick Troughton; flamboyant Jon Pertwee; exhuberant Tom Baker; youthful Peter Davison; the brash Colin Baker; and comical Sylvester McCoy. All, of course, have had their companions ranging from leggy beauties given to screaming at any oportunity to streetwise, independently-minded young women.

The fame of the series was, of course, established very early on with the advent of the Daleks who frightened a whole generation of children behind their armchairs. Other favourite monsters have included the Cybermen, the Ice Warriors, the Sea Devils and many more: several of whom have generated the kind of public outcry and newspaper headlines which have given *Doctor Who* its special place in TV legend. The series has not only been well served by its scriptwriters such as the now famous Terry Nation, Kit Pedlar, Gerry Davis, Robert Holmes and Douglas Adams, but has attracted a host of guest stars, too – too numerous, in fact, to list. And to date, there have been almost 700 episodes of the Doctor's adventures . . .

'The Lair of the Zarbi' is based on the characters created by Bill Strutton (1931–) in his memorable adventure in the second season of the programme, 'The Web Planet' (1965), about a world inhabited by the hostile, ant-like Zarbi who are forever persecuting the gentle, moth-shaped Menoptra. The production was a landmark in the history of the series because of the huge cost of costuming every actor and actress from head to foot in layers of make-up plus building a set to resemble a planet with a surface like that of the Moon, all within the confines of the BBC studios. Although the first episode attracted the largest viewing figures for any of William Hartnell's apearances as the Doctor – over ten million – the overheads were so high that the experiment was never repeated. Here, though, as a reminder of that story which helped to establish one of the most famous of all TV Science Fiction series is another of the Doctor's adventure on the planet Vortis . . .

The shock of hearing the voice was so great that Dr Who had barely time to complete the materialisation processes. But old habit was strong, and smoothly and efficiently the *Tardis* slid in through the transdimensional flux and fitted its rearranged atoms into the new sphere. By all the doctor's co-ordinates and calculations this world should be the planet Vortis but just *where* on the planet, or *when* in the time-scale of that world, he could not as yet know. He drove home the last lever and, with hands on the edges of the control panel, panted with excitement. The voice through his radio had been talking in modern English!

He strapped the walkie-talkie apparatus on his shoulders, already clad in the Atmospheric Density Jacket he remembered having needed on his previous visit to this ill-omened world. Then, activating the great door, he stood waiting for it to open, fidgeting with impatience.

This was not at all like the Vortis he remembered, was his first thought as he peered out through the open portals. True, there were several moons in the sky, two of them so close to the planet that they could be seen in daylight. The sparkles he remembered were in the sky also, but the mists were not there, nor the white basaltic needle-like spires. Quite evidently, his *Tardis* had landed him in an entirely different part of the planet. He walked steadily through the doorway, the voice from the radio still murmuring in his ears.

He had first heard it during the materialisation of his ship from intra-dimensional non-space into the real space in which Vortis swam. The voice sounded low and weary and consisted of but few words. It was as though the effort to dredge the words out was almost too much for the throat uttering them. "Help, Help," the voice was muttering. "Beware Zarbi Supremo. Warn Earth. Warn Earth." That was all. It was so tantalisingly obscure that Dr Who was almost dancing with impatience as he set foot outside his ship. But what he saw when he looked round the landscape momentarily drove all else from his mind.

He was on a low plateau, overlooking a broad plain. At least it should have been a plain, for the ground itself seemed flat enough. It was the structures that reared themselves up from that plain that made the eyes almost start from his head. On every side and outwards as far as the horizon, there reared up from the ground a multitude of cone-like structures like dunces' caps, like sugar-loaves, like – and now he knew for certain that he was back on Vortis – just like ant hills. He darted back inside his ship and re-emerged with binoculars.

He trained the glasses on the cones nearest to him and his gaze roamed over the surface, confirming that his first deduction was only too true. These monstrous hills of maybe a hundred feet high were the counterparts of the ant hills or termitaries to be seen in the Southern Hemisphere of Earth and . . . crawling all over them, in and out of their holes, were hordes of the hideous inhabitants of Vortis, the huge ants or termites known as the Zarbi.

Fascinated, he allowed the glasses to lead his gaze over first one immense hill and then another. There they crawled, hundreds, thousands, perhaps millions of them. Those noxious mindless creatures, controlled from a distance by some unknown intelligence, who preyed upon the likeable innocent Butterfly people, the Menoptera, the other species native to Vortis, whom he had encountered on his last visit. He had seen but little of the Zarbi themselves then, but he had heard enough to know that they were to be dreaded.

"Help. Help. Beware Zarbi Supremo!" the voice in his earphone droned on. "Warn Earth. Warn Earth." He started as the voice again penetrated into his consciousness. Somewhere, not too far away from him, was a man of Earth. He seemed to be weak and was perhaps wounded or a prisoner – somewhere in that veritable maze of termitaries. The doctor stared sombrely at the forest of cones and lowered the glasses. On his walkie-talkie there was, of course, a directional aerial and he began to twist the knob, listening as the sound of the voice sank or grew louder.

At last he determined roughly the quarter where the

sound originated. He turned his face in that direction. It looked no different from any other part of the plain of ant hills; but somewhere out there must be the owner of that tired voice, that voice that cried out hopelessly on an alien planet for a rescue of which it had lost all hope. But Dr Who had made up his mind that rescue he would attempt, no matter where it led him or through what perils. That his first greeting on Vortis should be the sound of a human voice, speaking in his own native tongue, was so extraordinary a thing that the doctor knew that fate had directed his hands as they had locked home the controls which had precipitated the *Tardis* into the sphere of Vortis at this precise place and at this precise time.

As he approached the termitaries he was almost deafened by the shrill chirping of the millions of Zarbi as they crawled about their mysterious business. On Earth ants and termites have no real voices, they communicate by rubbing their back legs together. Dr Who reflected that he could very well be mightily in error if he was to assume that these Zarbi were just very large ants or termites. These loathsome creatures could very well be some entirely different type of creature from the ants and termites which had evolved on Earth, even though they were insectile.

They seemed to take no notice of him as he passed, trembling, close to their hills. Of course he avoided getting too close to any of them, for he could see that most of these Zarbi were of the soldier class. This was evident from their powerful huge mandibles, which in a creature of that size could tear the limbs from a man, just as a man might tear apart a roasted chicken.

The voice over the radio was stronger now so that the doctor felt that he was getting very close to its source. Walking as warily as he could and avoiding contact with any of the Zarbi, he trod softly on the sandy surface of the ground, his gaze moving constantly about. Now he switched on his sender and spoke urgently into the microphone. "Help is here," he said. "Direct me to where you are. Give me some landmark to go by. I am coming to you."

But the radio gave him back no reply, only the monotonous low repetition of the message he had first heard. Baffled he glowered round him at the jungle of termitaries and shuddered to think of his own position, one feeble, weaponless Earthman, alone amongst these hordes of malevolent giant insects, searching for the owner of a voice which could not hear him.

Looking for a needle in a haystack would be simplicity itself compared to his task, he told himself irritably. But, he reflected grimly, a needle would glitter, wouldn't it? That was just what he could see ahead of him now . . . a dull glitter that lay athwart two ant hills relatively close to each other. Excitedly now he pressed on until he came to the thing. It was circular and was half buried in the sandy soil. On every side rose the gigantic ant hills and here it lay, like a child's lost ball, unspied by the Zarbi, many of whom were even then crawling over the sand that had gathered on the top. Dr Who sensed that he had reached his objective. He was convinced that inside this sphere was the owner of the voice, now sounding much louder in his earphone. He squatted down on the sand and for five minutes he spoke urgently into his microphone.

But it was soon obvious that whoever was inside the sphere – if indeed there was anyone inside it – either had no receiver or else one that was out of order. He leaned forward and rapped sharply on the metal surface. There was no reaction. He felt in his pocket and producing a torch he began a tattoo on the same place as before. Then he moved on and around, speculating that the hull of a space-ship must be very thick and searching for a thinner place. Thus it was that he came upon the door, half buried in the sand. The hollowness of his knocking told him there was emptiness behind it. Getting to his knees he began to scoop away the sand and soon uncovered the door, a small circle just about large enough for a normal man to wriggle through. In his excitement he leaned against it and the next moment he had fallen in through the doorway and into an open space. The door closed behind him, evidently on powerful springs.

It was hot and close and dark and he reflected that it must be an airlock, now broken, and that there would be another door into the ship proper. His torch soon revealed it and he put his shoulder against the panel. It needed all his strength to force it open against extremely powerful springs, but finally, with a mighty heave, he was inside the ship. Breathing hard through the breathing apparatus necessary for the thin air of Vortis, he got to his feet and smoothed down his clothes. "My goodness," he murmured to himself. "Now here is a very fine thing. Not a soul to greet me. Upon my word—"

Then he stopped, for the voice he had been hearing in his radio was now coming directly to his ear, and it was coming from a cabinet on the opposite wall of the room. He went closer and saw the reels of the recorder going slowly round and round, while the voice seeped hopelessly and monotonously from the speaker, repeating over and over again the appeal for help and the warning. He stared round him bitterly. So this was the end of his search. A tape recorder, endlessly sending out its message while no one lived and breathed here. He was as much alone as he had been before. Exasperated, he stared round him at what was evidently the control cabin of a space-ship. Compared to his *Tardis* it was, of course, a very primitive space-ship but he could recognise many of the principles which in his own ship were so refined that only an expert could have seen the resemblance. A ship like this would require quite a crew. Where were they? Was this ship like the *Marie Celeste*, which was found drifting crewless on the sea of Earth? Just so this space-craft lay, marooned and crewless on this cruel planet of Vortis, so far from where men lived and laughed under the bright sun.

Then it was as though the heavens opened. He heard a voice. Something in him told him this was a human voice and no electronic reproduction. It was calling for help and the sound came from a round port. He struggled and fought with the unfamiliar mechanism and at last the door opened. He put his head through and his heart lightened. There were two people in there, a man and a boy. Both lay on mattresses and the man looked as though he was dead. His eyes were closed and his head had fallen sideways. But the boy was very much alive. He was sitting up on the mattress and crying out to the rescuer. Earth was the boy's original birthplace, the doctor decided. And the Twentieth Century was his period, that was obvious. His name was Gordon Hamilton and he was the son of the man who lay motionless on the mattress.

"All the others have gone," the boy told him. "Father was ill so they left us with food and water and went out to explore. You see we didn't know where we were. We crash-landed and father was injured. The others left us here and went off to get help. We could hear noises outside which told us the planet wasn't uninhabited and so—"

"The voice in the recorder?" asked the doctor. "What is that?"

"Father made that recording before he lost consciousness," Gordon said. "By that time we'd given up all hope that the others would ever return and also we'd seen through the other window those things out there. Dad said they must be for an invasion of Earth – there aren't any other planets inhabited in the Solar System. You should see them, hundreds and hundreds of them—"

"Now, sonny, wait a minute," Dr Who protested. "Not so fast. You talk of the Solar System. Why, this planet is nowhere near – tell me, how long had your ship been travelling? What is her motive-power?"

"Oh, we've been in space for two years," the boy said. "Father's ship moves by anti-gravity and can travel many times the speed of light."

The doctor reflected. This boy quite evidently had not the least notion that Vortis was not even in the Milky

Way. A space-ship travelling even at many times the speed of light would need millions of Earth-years to traverse the waste space between galaxies. There was a mystery here. But this was scarcely the time to argue, he must see what could be done for the poor fellow lying on the mattress.

In spite of all his ministrations, however, he could get no response at all from the unconscious man, although his breathing was even enough. He was bearded, but evidently not old. There seemed to be no injury to the body and, baffled, the doctor got up from his knees and looked round.

"How many were in the crew?" he asked, staring round the small cabin shaped like the segment of a circle, which he judged to be one of the living quarters.

"There were six," Gordon told him. "All scientists, like Father. They took weapons and food and they've been gone five days now. I looked through both ports and saw the space-ships on one side and the big hills on the other. There are things crawling about on the hills. You came from outside – what are they? And where did you come from? Have you a ship here?"

Which question should he answer first, the doctor wondered. The boy did not seem to be aware that the Zarbi he had seen outside were one of the dominant species on this planet. He was evidently thinking in terms of human beings living on this world and assuming that the six crewmen had been captured or killed outside. What a position to find himself in. He went to the other window and looked out. At first, all he could see was a continuation of the multitudes of termitaries.

Then a gleam caught his eye. The things were so superficially like the termitaries that he could see why he had not recognised them before. Now he found he could see scarcely anything else. The things were space-ships of the archair torpedo shape. They were almost as tall as the ant hills but, as he looked, he discerned that their outline was smooth and regular and that they gave out a deceptive gleam. He turned to the boy. "You said they were space-ships, my boy. How did you know that?"

"They couldn't very well be anything else, could they?" and the boy gave a youthful grin. "They're like the rockets they used on Earth in the first half of the century. They must travel by chemical explosions. They'll be slow enough and if we could get the *Solar Queen* repaired we could get back to Earth and warn them of the invasion."

"Bless my soul, boy," snapped Dr Who. "What nonsense are you talking? Warn Earth, indeed! Why, we are millions and millions of miles from Earth. We are in a different space and a different time. And what's this talk of invasion? Who is going to invade Earth?"

"I'm only telling you what Father told me," said the boy stubbornly. "Before he went unconscious he used to lie still as though he was listening. He said there were messages sort of drifting into his mind. He said it was almost like eavesdropping on someone else talking by radio or telephone. But it wasn't either of those because there wasn't any apparatus. He said there was a force on this world which was intent on invading Earth. Water was what they wanted, water and vegetation. There were millions of them but always the talk seemed to be about just one individual, Dad said. He didn't get many details, most of the images that came into his mind didn't have any meaning for him. But the parts about the space-ships were very clear – Father knows about things like that. He'll be very interested in your ship."

"I shouldn't be surprised at that," said the doctor dryly. "Well, all you tell me is very interesting, Gordon, but we are wasting time. I am a scientist. I came here by a-ahem – rather different route than you did. My ship is outside, in a safe place, I hope. What we must do now is to work out some plan of campaign."

"We've time enough," said the boy in a matter-of-fact tone. "Dad says Earth is at present on the other side of the system and it'll be months before this world is in a position, you see, for the space-ships to travel there."

Dr Who looked at him curiously. "Did your father tell you any more about his ideas as to where this planet is?" he asked.

"Oh, yes," said the boy brightly. "It's a rogue planet," he said. "Not one of the Sun's real family. Those moons we can see, he said, are the outer moons of Jupiter, some of them. All the other planets are in the plane of the ecliptic but this one isn't. He said it's been driven into the Solar System under power. He said that if we could get out into the open at night we'd see the Solar System from an angle no other people have ever seen it from."

Dr Who reflected within himself without answering. It sounded all very wild and unlikely and, he told himself, irritably, downright impossible. But then, many of his own voyages would sound impossible to other ordinary people. This boy sounded tough and strong. He had not seemed frightened when the doctor had come upon him, marooned on an alien world, his father motionless and speechless and all his friends vanished. The doctor realised that Gordon would be his only helper in what he had decided must be done.

"We've got to follow your friends," he said tersely. "No use cowering in here. I've got a feeling they won't come back without our help."

The boy caught in his breath. "You mean, they've been captured?" he muttered. "But they all had weapons, they were scientists . . . they . . ."

The doctor looked at him. The boy looked frightened enough now that the situation was put coldly to him. But this was no time for squeamishness.

"We've got to go and find them," he said as he got up. "Your father is as comfortable as we can make him. We'll take food and weapons and we'll secure your ship. And we've got to hurry. Five days, you say. We haven't a moment to lose."

After five days of confinement, the boy seemed glad

enough to go outside the marooned ship once the doctor had convinced him that his father would be in no greater danger alone and unconscious than with his son there, powerless to help him. They emerged from the broken airlock and the boy stood still, thunderstruck, staring round him.

"I saw it from the window," he stammered. "But I couldn't really believe. Why, they're insects – they're ants. They must be all as big as men. How can that be? Where are the *people* of this world?"

"These are the people of this world, which is called Vortis, Gordon," said Dr Who firmly. "They are named the Zarbi and they are one of two dominant races on this planet. I've met the others, a gentle, peaceful race, almost like Earth butterflies with great wings. They talk and they, too, are as big as men. But here I see none of the Menoptera, this is all Zarbi territory."

They stood looking in wonder round them. The crawling busy Zarbi seemed to be taking no more notice of them than they had of the doctor when he had passed them alone before finding the *Solar Queen*. Busily and furiously they crawled hither and thither about their mysterious business, each one seeming to be furiously intent on some unknown and urgent task. It was this furious haste that directed the doctor's attention to several of the creatures lying motionless on the sand between two of the hills. Maybe half a dozen in number they lay as still as stones. He cautiously led the way and they both stood looking down on them.

"Are they dead?" asked Gordon with a little shudder.

Dr Who gave the nearest Zarbi form a touch with the toe of his boot. It gave out a metallic ring and he started. "They're not dead, my boy," he said. "They've never even been alive. These are dummies, Gordon, dummies, or should I say robots? I wonder what is inside them."

Gordon looked round fearfully. It was evidently very strange to him that these hordes of loathsome huge insects appeared quite unaware of the existence amongst them of the humans. But Dr Who was not taking any notice at all of the creatures, he was too intent on this find.

"Upon my soul," he muttered. "It is only too true, these really are robots. Look, they are made of metal and they can be opened up and, do you know, a most ingenious idea occurs to me. Quick, lend a hand here. If we can use two of these things, we can follow the trail of your friends and see where it leads to and what has happened to them. Help me with this plate, it lifts off and inside . . . oh, my goodness gracious, what have we here?"

Inside the robot Zarbi there was indeed an inhabitant and Dr Who's memory went back to his previous visit to Vortis. It had then been in another galaxy but now it had crossed intergalactic space and was in the Milky Way. How many ages had passed since then? And yet these Earth people were of the modern era; time was indeed filled with paradoxes.

It was a dead Menoptera that lay inside the robot Zarbi and, with a certain amount of reverence, Dr Who removed the body from its case. "Quick, quick," he directed the boy. "That other one there, open it up, remove the body and get inside. We'll then lie still and talk and try to investigate the controls of these things. Without them we wouldn't get very far among those millions of brutes out there."

"But they aren't taking any notice of us," Gordon objected. "I don't like the idea of being cooped up in that dark thing. Can't we just leave them and go on and trust to luck? The Zarbi aren't interfering with us at all."

"That can't last," said the doctor testily. "Do as I say, boy. It's our best chance." He was mollified to see that Gordon at last gave way. As they lay inside the great metal replicas of the Zarbi, with the thorax plates half-open, Dr Who looked at anything that might be thought of as a control of these awkward creatures. In the dim light he could see levers which might move the legs and the feelers, the thorax and the abdomen.

The eyes, though seeming compound from outside, were clear enough vision-plates from inside. As he tried a few tentative experiments he heard a frightened squeal from Gordon. The great Zarbi robot, with the doctor inside, stood up on six legs and waved its feelers about. Inside the doctor chuckled.

"It looks so real," said the boy, "that I was scared. How did you do it? Oh, I can feel now, these levers and handles. It isn't too hard, is it? I say, this is a bit of fun, isn't it? We can go anywhere in these things."

"Yes, yes, anywhere," said the doctor. "The trouble will be to determine which way we *shall* go. There'll be no trails in this soft sand and these forests of ant hills are so confusing."

"I say," came Gordon's excited voice. "I've just thought of something. All the men had walkie-talkies, like that one of yours. If you send out a signal, at least some of them might hear it and reply."

"Now, why didn't I think of that?" mused Dr Who to himself as he switched on his radio. With the metal antenna protruding through the half-open thorax plate of his robot he sent out a powerful wave-band, designed to radiate to the outermost limit of the range of his set. The result of his action was astonishing in the extreme and was a total surprise to both of them. A sudden dead silence descended on the whole scene around them. Through the eye-plates the doctor saw that every one of the Zarbi in his view had stopped in its tracks as still as a stone. The sounds of their myriad cricket chirpings died away into utter silence, and on the surface of every termitary the hordes of Zarbi lay motionless, as though dead. The reason came to him like a thunderclap and feverishly he switched off his set and stayed trembling and sweating inside his metal prison.

"Can you hear me, Gordon?" he whispered after a while, and there came a muffled murmured reply. "I won't be able to use the radio, after all. You can see what has happened. There is something not too far away from us that is receiving our wave. Did you notice how all the Zarbi out there stopped moving and trilling as soon as I switched on? They're still motionless and silent. If I switch on again whatever it is will be able to get our location."

"The others have been captured then," came Gordon's hoarse reply. "Each of them had a walkie-talkie receiver but we've never heard any signal from any of them for four days. The last signal was cut off in the middle of a sentence."

"What did the message say?" asked Dr Who urgently.

Gordon considered a moment. "Something about being very dark and very hot – I didn't really pay much attention."

"Tut, tut," snapped the doctor angrily. "That might have told us quite a lot. Now, listen carefully, Gordon. Stay absolutely still where you are. Don't touch any of those controls at all. We'll have to wait and see. It's obvious that all the Zarbi out there are controlled at a distance in some weird way. These robot Zarbi were operated by Menoptera who were killed in some unknown way. I can't think when I've ever been in such hideous danger – there must be millions of those beasts out there."

"They're moving again, look," came an excited murmur from Gordon.

It was true. The Zarbi hordes had come to life and were moving. But now there was none of the haphazard zigzagging about they had seen before. Now their movement was like a surge of the sea, all in one direction. The sounds of their shrill trilling note rose in crescendo all around them and the thunder of those millions of feet and feelers made the ground tremble. The doctor operated his controls quickly and turned. A vast wave of the creatures was approaching them from the rear. On every side they were surrounded by approaching Zarbi. They would be swept along by a tidal wave of the hurrying Zarbi unless they could do something to avoid

148

it. But escape proved impossible. He called out sharply to Gordon.

"Close the plate and hang on, boy, we're going to be swept along wherever these monsters are going. It's like a landslide, an avalanche."

His words were swept away as the robot moved along with the multitude of Zarbi. Like corks on a turbulent sea they were carried along, over sandy ground, through and around the ant hills, past the great forest of torpedo ships.

Then Dr Who saw what was obviously their destination. It towered up over twice the height of all the other ant hills. It was squatter than the others too and there was only one entrance, not a number of holes like all the others, but a great black gaping hole at the base of the conical mountain. Within minutes the doctor and Gordon, inside their robot Zarbi, were swept along with the hordes into the darkness inside. By some miracle they were not separated and as soon as the doctor could manage it he manipulated his levers so that one of the robot feelers was round the cleft between the thorax and the abdomen of Gordon's steed. It locked there and he quickly locked the lever. Together they had a chance, but if they were separated their plight would be hopeless indeed.

The heat and the smells were almost overpowering and the doctor felt as though he would faint at any moment. But he knew he must hang on to consciousness as long as possible. Once let either of them lose control of their robot and they would be trampled to a sticky paste by the myriads of scurrying feet.

The Zarbi were being impelled in their head-long rush by some remote, but imperative call, he decided, for this was so obviously different from the previous random crawlings of the things. This great termitary must be the haunt of their ruler, or controller, great queen or whatever thing dominated these hordes of mindless creatures. Willy nilly, they were being swept along towards that thing. In reality this was just what he had wanted, the doctor thought wryly, and he shuddered. What sort of a mess had he landed himself in now? But the plight of this ill-fated expedition from Earth could not have been ignored. That he knew very well.

How did the Menoptera fit into all this? Was it an attempt by them to invade Zarbi territory by penetrating into it disguised as the native Zarbi? Or were the few they had seen merely spies? In that case why had they been killed, and how? There had been no time to examine the body he had hauled from the robot.

The air grew closer and hotter and now, through his vision-plates in the huge eyes of the thing, the doctor could see dim lights. What they were he could not discern: whether they were natural lights, such as fireflies or phosphorescence, or whether they were mechanical. By now he was a little lightheaded and he was ready to credit the mysterious something, towards which they were obviously being carried, with miraculous powers and unheard-of technology. But the Zarbi were after all, he told himself, merely huge insects, weren't they? But were they merely insects? What about that forest of torpedo space-craft outside? What about the radio? And what, to crown it all, about the mysterious control under which all these myriads of Zarbi were moving?

It was a nightmare journey. Afterwards, Dr Who scarcely knew whether he had dreamed it all; whether he had really seen and heard all he remembered or whether he had imagined it all. At the time it all seemed real enough but dreams sometimes have a quality of reality. There were caverns in which there was machinery, of that he was certain, *at the time*. He saw and heard great engines and vast furnaces with hordes of the Zarbi working round them. These would be the worker Zarbi, while the host in the midst of which they were being swept would be the soldiers.

He remembered the great mandibles of the robot in which he was imprisoned. Could it be possible that these monsters practised engineering? The idea was so fantastic that at first he scouted it. But then who or what had built those space-ships? And he was quite sure that the forms he saw working round the fires and at the machines were Zarbi.

They passed great galleries in which hung suspended, like sides of meat in a cold-store, thousands and thousands of grey shrouded forms. Of course, these would be the larvae of these creatures, the nurseries where the young ones were raised to make way for the dead Zarbi. Like grey unmoving spectres the rows and rows of larvae hung and the doctor shuddered violently.

A great opening to one side revealed, in a lightning glimpse, what he had suspected from the beginning. Perhaps two or three hundred feet in length she lay, a bloated queen with a host of workers feeding her and stroking her and attending to her wants. He saw and then it was gone and he felt very sick. There would be many of these queens in a termitary as large as this and from them had come the countless hordes of the Zarbi from outside.

Now the pace was slackening and Dr Who found a little more opportunity to see where they were being taken. Also the passages and the galleries were opening out. He felt certain that they were by now far underground, judging by the heat and the rising pressure. There came a time when the tide that bore them on stopped completely and they were at rest. Dazedly the doctor hung in his robot and then, moving gently, he knocked against the thing that held Gordon. An answering knock told him that the boy was at least alive. There had been no chance for them to communicate during that headlong flight.

It was like a vast amphitheatre, the doctor saw as he moved the great metal head from side to side, peering through the huge eye-plates. Rank upon rank of the Zarbi were there in great semi-circular rows, their number almost countless and all of them very still. Almost against his will his gaze was slowly, inexorably, drawn towards the middle of the great throng, where something sat upon a raised dais, with a glowing light shining down upon it from a roof that was almost out of sight. As the doctor's eyes reluctantly reached it, he recoiled in horror and downright disbelief.

That it was a Zarbi was obvious enough, for its form was the same as that of all the others crowding round him motionless on all sides.

But its size! It towered perhaps twenty feet tall standing on its dais, three times the height of a normal Zarbi and completely motionless on its pedestal.

The doctor tore away his eyes to gaze in startled astonishment at another scene. In a cleared space in front of the gigantic Zarbi were two parties of creatures, and one party was human. There were six of them and they were standing like marble statues in a tight group. Opposite them was another party and Dr Who knew that these were Menoptera, although they were wingless and as motionless as the human beings. He heard the hoarse voice of Gordon close by. "They're down there. They're still alive, all of them. How are we going to escape with them from here?"

"A very good question, my boy," muttered the doctor grimly. "If you have any ideas, now is the time to express them. I confess that at this very moment I must admit myself totally baffled. We got in easily enough, but I fancy it's going to be mightily harder to get out, hm?"

He could see now that all the members of each of the two parties, evidently all prisoners, were quite still as if made of stone. He tried to remember all he knew about the insect world of Earth, which was indeed remarkably little. Anyway, why try to relate these Zarbi to Earth ants or termites, or whatever? The conclusions would be quite mistaken. He went on examining the scene closely and saw that all the prisoners wore something that looked like a loose collar or ring round their necks. It shone a little and fitted very loosely. He watched as one of the Zarbi attendants on the Zarbi Supremo, for that is what the doctor had called the creature in his own mind, moved forward. The creature's mandibles hovered above the head of one of the motionless Menoptera prisoners and the ring was lifted from the Menoptera's neck. In the silence the doctor could just hear the voice of the Menoptera speaking to Zarbi Supremo up on its dais.

It was really most exasperating, the doctor thought irritably. He could hear the voice but not the words. From the giant Zarbi there came no sound at all. How it was replying he could get no idea unless perhaps it was through some electronic translator invisible to the doctor from where he stood.

They must somehow get closer to the centre of operations. His robot nudged Gordon's and pushed it forward through the massed ranks of motionless Zarbi. None of them took any notice and gradually inch by inch the two robots edged their way forward until at last they were on the rim of the cleared space. Now Dr Who found that he could hear what the Menoptera was saying.

"You will have to kill every one of the Menoptera on Vortis before we will agree to help you," the soft voice was saying. "We have watched you over the generations as your mighty engines have moved this planet into this alien system. You are transgressing the paths of Nature. Vortis can be made such a world as you want. A very little of the powers you have spent would have done this. But you cannot invade a peaceful world as you plan. First you would have to slaughter all of the creatures that live there. They are not insects, they are mammals and their world is suited to their needs. Vortis can be made suitable to beings of our own species. You say that you need us of the Menoptera as your ambassadors to the humans, because we speak as they do. You would have us speak to them as though we came in peace because you know they would kill you as soon as they saw what you were. Then, when their suspicions were lulled by us, you would turn on them all and exterminate them. We will not help you to do this."

There was a silence and the great Zarbi on the dais moved. A limb angled out and the doctor saw it manipulate a dial on an instrument board beside it. Almost dancing with rage the doctor knew that it was replying to the speaker. But not one sound could he hear. It was obvious, however, that the Menoptera was hearing something. That instrument must be some means by which the Zarbi brainwaves were translated into speech in the brain of the Menoptera.

"You must kill us all then," came the reply from the Menoptera. "It will be war between us as has never happened before. On our hemisphere we are building weapons which will give you pause. We who speak to you now are doomed, that we well know. These humans also will die, for we recognise that in you has arisen a new spirit among the Zarbi, the spirit of cruelty and destruction. We cannot halt you now, we are too few. But later you will not find your task easy, I promise you that."

A limb shot out from the great Zarbi body and hovered above the head of the Menoptera. Like a moth caught in a flame the creature shrivelled and was gone. Dr Who writhed in his excitement and his robot knocked against that of Gordon.

"The mandibles, boy," he cried, discretion now gone. "Operate the mandibles and lift those collars from round the necks of your men. I'll do the same. These creatures round us are all hypnotised. If we are quick enough we may bring it off."

His robot angled forward awkwardly and the mandibles, operated by inside levers, went up over the heads of the human prisoners. First one, then two, then three. Gordon by that time having found the right controls, freed the last three. Dr Who could feel the crackling and surging of electric waves as he worked and it seemed obvious that the great Zarbi was fighting them with its only weapons, weapons which, thank heaven, were proving ineffectual against human organisms.

Then the doctor was out of his robot and dragging Gordon out.

"Your guns," he yelled to the released prisoners, still dazed. "That thing up there. Fire anywhere. Empty your magazines. The head, the thorax, the abdomen, anywhere. We don't know where the brain and nerve centres of that thing are—"

Around them the vast hordes of the Zarbi were awakening as the hypnotic control of the giant creature took hold of them. Their trilling sound grew and grew into a crescendo and drowned the noise of the shots as the six crewmen and the doctor emptied their revolvers into the giant form above them. Many of the shots ricochetted from the hard carapace, but many found their way through chinks in that chitinous armour. The doctor saw the creature stagger, its limbs and feelers thrashing about as though in agony. The great expressionless compound eyes brooded downwards over these lilliputian creatures who were intent on thwarting its dreams of world conquest.

It was like a great building falling when at last death came to it. Even above the shrill chirpings of the Zarbi, the crash of that downfall could be heard. It lay still, a fallen hulk of insectile ambition, while all around it surged the myriads of its fellow-creatures which it had dominated.

While they had been attacking it, all eight humans had felt the thrusting limbs and feelers of the Zarbi striving to overcome them, but they had taken no heed but kept on pumping lead into the giant menace above.

Now the Zarbi were leaving them alone and milling about in the haphazard fashion that seemed to be their natural life. The little group stayed in a tight circle, watching with apprehension; but they were not attacked. Dr Who heaved a sigh of relief, and going over to the group of Menoptera prisoners who were still standing motionless, he released them by lifting from their necks the rings which in some odd way must have hypnotised them. Voices began to speak to him. Not human voices, but the soft furry voices of the folk he remembered from his previous meetings on Vortis with the peaceful Menoptera. But he took no notice. He wanted to be with his own kind again.

"Your father, Gordon, how is he?" asked one of the men. "And you, sir, how in heaven's name did you come in the nick of time? We'd given ourselves up for lost. You're from Earth. Where is your ship? When did you land?"

Dr Who chuckled. "One thing at a time, my friend. First, we've got to get out of here, you know. Even with these Zarbi uncontrolled it's going to be hard."

"Zarbi? Zarbi?" said another crewman. "Are these creatures, these bugs, the Zarbi, then? Are they intelligent?"

"They are no more intelligent than their needs demand," came a soft voice and one of the Menoptera stood at their shoulders. "For many years we and the Zarbi shared this world and lived in peace. They were our servants, our workmen and our cattle. We and the Zarbi gave to each other what the other lacked. But, over the generations, evolution has evolved a mighty intelligence in that creature who dominated them and dreamed of world conquest, even of universe conquest. We had no weapons but we are building some and we came as an expedition to see what they were planning and if we could stop them. Look, there are our people emerging from their robots."

All around them from recumbent Zarbi were emerging many of the Menoptera. These were full-grown magnificent specimens, who spread and shook their wings after their confinement. There were many hundreds of them and at once they began to shepherd the now docile Zarbi and leave a path for the exit of the released prisoners. Wonderingly, the humans followed the first Menoptera party, the wingless ones, no doubt elders among them. Their path led upwards through the galleries and passages, out to the world of day.

Gordon's father still lay unconscious but he was breathing better. The rescued men crowded into their ship in great excitement for they had given up all hope of ever seeing it again.

"If you agree, doctor," one of them said. "We can use your ship to ferry us across to Earth to get equipment to repair our ship. In time we could do it ourselves but with Earth being so relatively near—"

"That's what puzzles me about the whole thing," said Dr Who. "By my calculations this planet should be in another galaxy altogether. But Gordon kept telling me about the moons of Jupiter and all such nonsense as that."

"Not nonsense," laughed a crewman. "We found this planet when we were headed for the moons of Jupiter in fact. How it got here and how long it has been here we don't know. How it's been missed by Earth observers beats me."

"The evil Zarbi intelligence devised mighty engines which drove our planet out of its orbit many, many millions of miles away," explained one of the Menoptera. "It was searching for a green, damp world such as yours. We have only just arrived in your skies but before very long we will leave you and will sweep out of your system to find whatever fate has in store for us."

"Not so fast," said one of the men belligerently. "Those engines of the Big Bug we killed will come in mighty handy for humanity, I can tell you. There'll be many things that creature invented that we can use and profit by."

"What profit can be made out of evil?" came the soft voice. "No, we will use the engines to drive our world on a new orbit out of your sky and then we will destroy them and seal them off. It is not given to creatures to do what Zarbi Supremo was trying to do."

"I heartily agree," said Dr Who enthusiastically. "Now, you men must realise that this planet belongs to the Menoptera and the Zarbi, so long as they keep their places, of course. There must be no thought of using the powers that creature developed to dominate other beings."

"You're crazy, old man," said the other coldly. "And what in thunder do you think we're doing exploring the universe? We're looking for just such set-ups as this, inhabited by weak, unintelligent creatures. The natural resources of this world alone, even without the powers that Big Bug down there developed, will put Earth technology millions of years into the future."

There was a stirring of Menoptera wings and the crewman drew his revolver. The doctor was glad to see that the others hung back, while Gordon remained at his father's side in the globular space-ship. He lifted an arm and felt himself clasped by a pair of tiny furry clawlike hands. He was lifted into the air and he saw that all the Menoptera were rising, those wingless ones being lifted by their flying fellows. He looked down. Angrily, the man was firing his empty revolver up at them and then the scene faded from his sight.

Gently and easily they dropped him beside his *Tardis*. "We have legends in our world," said one of the Menoptera, "of you and your strange vessel. We know we have nothing to fear from you, strange immortal human who can flit in and out of all the ages. We will watch those others and will ensure that they bring no harm to us. It was good that you came to our rescue, for how else could Zarbi Supremo have been toppled from his lofty height?"

The doctor beamed at them. Sheer human ingenuity and refusal to admit defeat had won again, he thought, as he turned and went through the great doorway. Activating the controls that would close it, he wondered just what would be the future of the strange world of Vortis.

THE OUTER LIMITS

(United Artists TV, 1963–5 & 1995–)
Starring: Adam West, Rudy Solari & Peter Marko
Directed by Byron Haskin
Story 'The Invisible Enemy' by Jerry Sohl

According to SF historian **John Baxter**, the original Sixties series, *The Outer Limits* "contained the best science fiction ever to be presented on television." This was despite the fact that the series was ill-fated and misunderstood, he says, and although it was loved by teenage audiences, when it was moved to a late evening slot only confused adult audiences with its odd plots and unconventional narrative style which sealed its fate. The *Encyclopedia of Science Fiction* has gone even further and declared it to be 'more imaginative and intelligent than its more famous competitor on CBS, *The Twilight Zone*.' Now, in 1995, the series has returned to the small screen with all the benefits of colour and digital special effects, but the same basic concept brought up to date. Like *The Twilight Zone*, *Outer Limits* also has its own opening address to viewers. "There is nothing wrong with your television set," the disembodied voice of the announcer declares. "Do not attempt to adjust the picture. We are controling transmission. You are about to experience the awe and mystery which reaches from the inner mind to THE OUTER LIMITS." Despite its sad demise, 49 of the fifty-minute episodes of the series have survived and it has been due in no small measure to the successful reshowing of these stories which have gathered a whole new generation of admirers that the series has

Jerry Sohl

at last been revived. The programme was originally created by the playwright Leslie Stevens, but owed much of its originality to producer Joseph Stefano, the man who had written the screenplay for Alfred Hitchcock's most famous movie, *Psycho*. Although Stefano had a tendency to feature monsters as bizarre as anything seen in Doctor Who – and just as likely to terrify viewers – the first series was highlighted by the imagination of its scripts by such fine writers are Harlan Ellison, Jerry Sohl, David Duncan and Meyer Dolinsky, plus the inovative visual style of the major directors, Gerd Oswald, Charles Haas, Leonard Horn and, especially, Byron Haskin the veteran of several famous Hollywood SF movies including *War of the Worlds* (1953), *Conquest of Space* (1955) and *From Earth To The Moon* (1959). The special effects created by the Ray Mercer Company and Projects Unlimited were also way ahead of anything seen on the small screen; as was the bizarre make-up for many of the alien beings which was the handiwork of Wah Chang, Fred Phillips and John Chambers. Once again a number of 'unknown' actors got their early breaks in *Outer Limits* including Robert Culp, Bruce Dern, Martin Landau and David McCallum. The new 1995 series has so far shown itself to be more provocative in its stories, although the quality of the scriptwriting and acting is similarly high. One intriguing episode, 'I, Robot' cleverly linked the past and present by being based on a story by Isaac Asimov and directed by Adam Nimoy, son of the famous Leonard!

Another of the debutants in the original *Outer Limits* was Adam West – two years before he would become famous as TV's Batman – who starred in the chilling drama of 'The Invisible Enemy' about a four-man mission to Mars charged with discovering what has apparently been gobbling up astronauts who land on the planet. The script was by Jerry Sohl (1913–), based on his own short story, and

was yet another example of the ingenious plots that
have been a hallmark of his work as a contributor
to SF magazines, a novelist (*The Transcendent Man*,
1953; *Costigan's Needle*, 1953; *Point Ultimate*, 1955 &
etc.) and writer for television and the movies. Sohl's
teleplays for *The Outer Limits* were certainly amongst
his very best and also contributed substantially to the
programme's enduring legend.

For an hour they had been circling the spot at 25,000
feet while technicians weighed and measured the planet
and electronic fingers probed where no eye could see.

And for an hour Harley Allison had sat in the computer
room accepting the information and recording it on
magnetic tapes and readying them for insertion into
the machine, knowing already what the answer would
be and resenting what the commander was trying to do.

It was quiet in the ship except for the occasional twitter
of a speaker that recited bits of information which Allison
dutifully recorded. It was a relief from the past few days
of alarm bells and alerts and flashing lights and the drone
of the commander's voice over the intercom, even as that
had been a relief from the lethargy and mindlessness that
comes with covering enormous stellar distances, for it
was wonderful to see faces awaken to interest in things
when the star drive went off and to become aware of a
changing direction and the lessening velocity. Then had
eyes turned from books and letters and other faces to the
growing pinpoints of the Hyades on the scanners.

Then had Allison punched the key that had released
the ship from computer control and gave it to manual,
and in the ensuing lull the men of the *Nesbitt* were read
the official orders by Commander William Warrick. Then
they sat down to controls unmanned for so long to seek
out the star among the hundreds in the system, then its
fourth planet and, a few hours ago, the small space ship
that lay on its side on the desert surface of the planet.

* * *

There was laughter and the scrape of feet in the hall and Allison looked up to see Wendell Hallom enter the computer room, followed by several others.

"Well, looks like the rumors were right," Hallom said, eyes squinting up at the live screen above the control panel. The slowly rotating picture showed the half-buried space ship and the four pillars of the force field about it tilted at ridiculous angles. "I suppose you knew all about this, Allison."

"I didn't know any more than you, except we were headed for the Hyades," Allison said. "I just work here, too, you know."

"I wish I was home," Tony Lazzari said, rolling his eyes. "I don't like the looks of that yellow sand. I don't know why I ever joined this man's army."

"It was either join or go to jail," Gordon Bacon said.

"I ought to punch you right in the nose." Lazzari moved toward Bacon who thumbed his nose at him. "In fact, I got a good mind to turn it inside out."

Allison put a big hand on his shoulder, pulled him back. "Not in here you don't. I got enough troubles. That's all I'd need."

"Yeah," Hallom said. "Relax, kid. Save your strength. You're going to need it. See that pretty ship up there with nobody on it?"

"You and the commander," Bacon said. "Why's he got it in for you, Allison?"

"I wouldn't know," Allison said smiling thinly. "I've got a wonderful personality, don't you think?"

Hallom grunted. "Allison's in the Computer Corps, ain't he? The commander thinks that's just like being a passenger along for the ride. And he don't like it."

"That's what happens when you get an old line skipper and try to help him out with a guy with a gadget," Bacon observed.

"It wouldn't be so bad," Homer Petry said at the door, "if it had been tried before."

"Mr Allison," a speaker blared.

"All right, you guys," Allison said. "Clear out." He depressed a toggle. "Yes, Lieutenant?"

"You have everything now, Allison. Might as well run it through."

"The commander can't think of anything else?"

There was a cough. "The commander's standing right here. Shall I ask him?"

"I'll run this right through, Lieutenant."

Commander William Warrick was a fine figure of a man: tall, militant, greying, hatchet-nosed. He was a man who hewed so close to the line that he let little humanity get between, a man who would be perpetually young, for even at fifty there was an absence of paunch, though his eyes held a look of a man who had many things to remember.

He stood for a while at one end of the control room without saying anything, his never-absent map pointer in his right hand, the end of it slapping the open palm of his left hand. His cold eyes surveyed the men who stood crowded shoulder-to-shoulder facing him.

"Men," he said, and his deep voice was resonant in the room, "take a good look at the screen up there." And the eyes of nearly fifty men shifted to the giant screen beside and above him. "That's the *Esther*." The ship was on gyro, circling the spot, and the screen showed a rotation ship on the sand.

"We'll be going down soon and we'll get a better look. But I want you to look at her now because you might be looking at the *Nesbitt* if you're not careful."

The commander turned to look at the ship himself before going on. "The *Esther* is a smaller ship. It had a complement of only eight men. Remember the tense there. *Had.* They disappeared just as the men in the two ships before them did, each carrying eight men

163

– the *Mordite* and the *Halcyon*. All three ships were sent to look for Traveen Abbott and Lew Gesell, two explorers for the Federation who had to their credit successful landings on more than ninety worlds. They were cautious, experienced and wise. Yet this planet swallowed them up. as it did the men of the three ships that followed."

Commander Warrick paused and looked at them severely. "We're fifty men and I think we have a better chance than an eight-man crew, not just because there are more of us but because we have the advantage of knowing we're against something really deadly. In case you haven't deduced our mission, it is simply to find out what it is and destroy it."

The insignia on the commander's collar and sleeve glittered in the light from the ever-changing screen as the ship circled the site of the *Esther*.

"This is a war ship. We are armed with the latest weapons. And—" his eyes caught Allison's "– we even have a man from the Computer Corps with us, if that can be counted as an advantage."

Allison who stood at the rear of the room behind the assembled soldier-technicians, reddened. "The tapes got us here, Commander."

"We could have made it without them," the commander said without ire. "But we're here with or without tape. But just because we are we're not rushing down there. We know the atmosphere is breathable, the gravity is close to Earth's and there are no unusually dangerous bacteria. All this came from the *Esther* prior to the . . . incident, whatever it was. But we checked again just to make sure. The gravity is nine-tenths that of Earth's, there is a day of twenty-four and a half hours, temperature and humidity tropical at this parallel, the atmosphere slightly less rich in oxygen, though not harmfully so – God only knows how a desert planet like this can have any oxygen at all with so little vegetation and no evident animal life. There is no dangerous radiation from the surface or from the sun. Mr Allison has run the assembled data through his machine – would you care to tell the men what the machine had to say, Allison?"

Allison cleared his throat and wondered what the commander was driving at. "The planet could sustain life, if that's what you mean, Commander."

"But what did the machine say about the inhabitants, Mr Allison?"

"There wasn't enough data for an assumption."

"Thank you. You men can get some idea of how the Computer Corps helps out in situations like this."

"That's hardly fair, Commander," Allison protested. "With more data—"

"We'll try to furnish you with armsful of data." The commander smiled broadly. "Perhaps we might let you collect a little data yourself."

There was laughter at this. "So much for the Computer Corps. We could go down now, but we're circling for eighteen more hours for observation. Then we're going down. Slowly."

The ship came out of the deep blue sky in the early morning and the commander was a man of his word. The *Nesbitt* moved down slowly, beginning at sun-up and ending in the sand within a few hundred feet of the *Esther* in an hour.

"You'd think," Lazzari said as the men filed back into the control room for another briefing, "that the commander has an idea he can talk this thing to death."

"I'd rather be talked to death by the commander than by you," Hallom said. "He has a pleasanter voice."

"I just don't like it, all that sand down there and nothing else."

"We passed over a few green places," Allison corrected. "A few rocky places, too. It's not all sand."

"But why do we have to go down in the middle of it?" Lazzari insisted.

"That's where the other ships went down. Whatever it is attacked them on the sand."

"If it was up to me, I'd say: Let the thing be, whatever it is. Live and let live. That's my motto."

"You're just lazy," said Petry, the thin-faced oldster from Chicago. "If we was pickin' apples you'd be askin' why. If you had your way you'd spend the rest of your life in a bunk."

"Lazy, hell!" Lazzari snorted. "I just don't think we should go poking our nose in where somebody's going to bite it off."

"That's not all they'll bite off, Buster," said Gar Caldwell, a radar and sonics man from Tennessee.

Wang Lee, force field expert, raised his thin oriental eyebrows and said, "It is obvious we know more than our commander. We know, for example, *it* bites. It follows then that it has teeth. We ought to report that to the commander."

The commander strode into the room, map pointer under his arm, bearing erect, shoulders back, head high. Someone called attention and every man stiffened but Allison, who leaned against the door. Commander Warrick surveyed them coldly for a moment before putting them at ease.

"We're dividing into five teams," he said. "Four in the field and the command team here. The rosters will be read shortly and duplicate equipment issued. The lieutenants know the plans and they'll explain them to you. Each unit will have a g-car, force field screen, television and radio for constant communication with the command team. There will be a blaster for each man, nuclear bombardment equipment for the weapons man, and so on."

He put his hands on his hips and eyed them all severely. "It's going to be no picnic. It's hot as hell out there. A hundred degrees in the daytime and no shade. It's eighty at night and the humidity's high. But I want you to find out what it is before it finds out what you are. I don't want any missing men. The Federation's lost three small ships and twenty-four men already. And Mr Allison—"

Allison jerked from the wall at the unexpected calling of his name. "Yes, Commander?"

"You understand this is an emergency situation?"

"Well, yes, Commander."

The commander smiled slyly and Allison could read something other than humor behind his eyes.

"Then you must be aware that, under Federation regulations governing ships in space, the commander exercises unusual privileges regarding his crew and civilians who may be aboard."

"I haven't read the regulation, Commander, but I'll take your word for it that it exists."

"Thank you, Mr Allison." The lip curled ever so slightly. "I'd be glad to read it to you in my quarters immediately after this meeting, except there isn't time. For your information in an emergency situation, though you are merely attached to a ship in an advisory capacity, you come under the jurisdiction of the ship's commander. Since we're short of men, I'm afraid I'll have to make use of you."

Allison balled two big, brown hands and put them behind his back. They had told him at Computer Corps school he might meet men like Commander Warrick – men who did not yet trust the maze of computer equipment that only a few months ago had been made mandatory on all ships of the *Nesbitt* class. It was natural that men who had fought through campaigns with the old logistics and slide-rule tactics were not going to feel immediately at home with computers and the men that went with them. It wasn't easy trusting the courses of their ships or questions of attack and defense to magnetized tape.

"I understand, Commander," Allison said. "I'll be glad to help out in whatever way you think best."

"Good of you, I'm sure." The Commander turned to

Jerry Sohl

one of the lieutenants near him. "Lieutenant Cheevers, break out a blaster for Mr Allison, He may need it."

When the great port was opened, the roasting air that rushed in blasted the faces of the men loading the treadwagons. Allison, the unaccustomed weight of the blaster making him conscious of it, went with several of them down the ramp to look out at the yellow sand.

Viewing it from the surface was different from looking at it through a scanner from above. He squinted his eyes as he followed the expanse to the horizon and found there were tiny carpets of vegetation here and there, a few larger grass islands, a wooded area on a rise far away on the right, mountains in the distance on the left. And above it all was a deep blue sky with a blazing white sun. The air had a burned smell.

A tall lieutenant – Cork Rogers who would lead the first contingent – moved down the ramp into the broiling sun and gingerly stepped into the sand. He sank into it up to his ankles. He came back up, shaking his head. "Even the sand's hot."

Allison went down, the sun feeling like a hot iron on his back, bent over and picked up a handful of sand. It was yellower than Earth sand and he was surprised to find it had very little weight. It was more like sawdust, yet it was granular. He looked at several tiny grains closely, saw that they were hollow. They were easily crushed.

"Why was I born?" Lazzari asked no one in particular, his arms loaded with electrical equipment for the wagon. "And since I was, how come I ever got in this lousy outfit?"

"Better save your breath," Allison said, coming up the ramp and wiping his hands on his trousers.

"Yeah, I know. I'm going to need it." He stuck his nose up and sniffed. "They call that air!"

In a few minutes, the first treadwagon loaded with its equipment and men purred down the ramp on its tracks and into the sand. It waited there, its eye tube already

168

revolving slowly high on its mast above the weapons bridge. The soldier on the bridge was at ready, his tinted visor pulled down. He was actually in the small g-car which could be catapulted at an instant's notice.

Not much later there were four treadwagons in the sand and the commander came down the ramp, a faint breeze tugging at his sleeves and collar.

He took the salute of each of the officers in turn – Lieutenant Cork Rogers of Unit North, Lieutenant Vicky Noromak of Unit East, Lieutenant Glen Foster of Unit West and Lieutenant Carl Quartz of Unit South. They raised the green and gold of the Federation flag as he and the command team stood at attention behind him.

Then the commander's hand whipped down and immediately the purrs of the wagons became almost deafening as they veered from one another and started off through the sand, moving gracefully over the rises, churning powder wakes and leaving dusty clouds.

It was quiet and cool in the control room. Commander Warrick watched the four television panels as they showed the terrain in panorama from out-positions a mile in each direction from the ship. On all of them there were these same things: the endless, drifting yellow sand with its frequent carpets of grass, the space ship a mile away, the distant mountain, the green area to the right.

Bacon sat at the controls for the panels, Petry at his side. Once every fifteen seconds a radio message was received from one of the treadwagon units: "Unit West reporting nothing at 12:18:15." The reports droned out over the speaker system with monotonous regularity. Petry checked off the quarter minutes and the units reporting.

Because he had nothing better to do, Allison had been sitting in the control room for four hours and all he had seen were the television panels and all he had heard were the reports – except when Lieutenant Cheevers and three other men returned from an inspection of the *Esther*.

"Pile not taken, eh?" The commander pursed his lips and ran a forefinger along his jaw. "Anything above median level would have taken the pile. I can't see it being ignored."

The lieutenant shook his head. "The *Esther* was relatively new. That would have made her pile pretty valuable."

"I can't figure out why the eight men on the Esther couldn't handle the situation. They had the *Mordite* and the *Halcyon* as object lessons. They must have been taken by surprise. No sign of a struggle, eh, Cheevers?"

"None, sir. We went over everything from stem to stern. Force field was still working, though it had fallen out of line. We turned it off."

"No blood stains? No hair? No bones?"

"No, sir."

"That's odd, don't you think? Where could they have gone?" The commander sighed. "I expect we'll know soon enough. As it is, unless something is done, the *Esther* will sink farther into this sand until she's sunk out of sight with the other two ships." He frowned. "Lieutenant, how would you like to assume command of the *Esther* on our return? It must still be in working order if the pile is there. I'll give you a crew."

"We're not through here yet, sir." Cheevers grinned. "But I'd like it."

"Look good on your service records, eh, Corvin?" The commander then saw Allison sitting at the rear of the room watching the panels. "What do you make of all this, Allison?"

"I hardly know what to think, Commander."

"Why don't you run a tape on it?"

"I wish I could, but with what little we know so far it wouldn't do any good."

"Come, now, Allison, surely a good, man like you – you're a computer man, remember? – surely you could do something. I've heard of the wonders of those little machines. I'll bet you could run that through the machine and it will tell us exactly what we want to know."

"There's not enough data. I'd just get an ID – Insufficient Data – response as I did before."

"It's too bad, Allison, that the computer people haven't considered that angle of it – that someone has to get the data to feed the machine, that the Federation must still rely on guts and horse sense and the average soldier-technician. I'll begin thinking computers are a good thing when they can go out and get their own data."

That had been two hours ago. Two hours for Allison to cool off in. Two hours to convince himself it had been best not to answer the commander. And now they all sat, stony-faced and quiet, watching the never-ending sweep of the eye-tubes that never showed anything different except the changing shadows as the planet's only sun moved across the sky. Yellow sand and carpets of green, the ship, the mountain, the wooded area . . .

It was the same on the next four-hour watch. The eye-tubes turned and the watchers in the ship watched and saw nothing new, and radio reports droned on every fifteen seconds until the men in the room were scarcely conscious of them.

And the sun went down.

Two moons, smaller than Earth's single moon, rode high in the sky, but they didn't help as much, infrared beams from the treadwagons rendered the panel pictures as plain as day. And there was nothing new.

The commander ordered the units moved a mile farther away the second day. When the action was completed, the waiting started all over again.

It would not be fair to say *nothing* was new. There was one thing – tension. Nerves that had been held ready for action began demanding it. And with the ache of taut nerves came impatience and an overexercising of the imagination. The quiet, heat, humidity and monotony of nothing the second day and night erupted in a blast from Unit East early on the morning of the third day. The nuclear weapons man in the g-car had fired at something he saw moving out on the sand.

At the site Technician Gar Caldwell reported by radio while Lieutenant Noromak and another man went through the temporarily damped force field to investigate. There was nothing at the target but some badly burned and fused sand.

Things went back to normal again.

Time dragged through the third day and night, and the hot breezes and high humidity and the waiting grated already raw nerves.

On the morning of the fourth day Homer Petry, who had been checking off the radio reports as they came in, suddenly announced: "No radio report from Unit West at 8:14:45!"

Instantly all eyes went to the Unit West panel.

The screen showed a revolving panorama of shimmering yellow sand and blue sky.

Lieutenant Cheevers opened the switch. "Unit West! Calling Unit West!"

No answer.

"What the hell's the matter with you, Unit West!"

The commander yelled, "Never mind, Lieutenant! Get two men and shoot over there. I'll alert the other units."

Lieutenant Cheevers picked up Allison, who happened to be in the control room at the time, and Hallom, and in a matter of moments the port dropped open and with the lieutenant at the controls and the two men digging their feet in the side stirrups and their hands clasping the rings for this purpose on either side, the small g-car soared out into the sweltering air and screamed toward Unit West.

The terrain rushed by below them as the car picked up still more speed and Allison, not daring to move his head too far from the protective streamlining lest it get caught in the hot airstream, saw the grass-dotted, sun-baked sand blur by.

Then the speed slackened and, raising his head, he saw

the treadwagon and the four force-field pillars they were approaching.

But he saw no men.

The lieutenant put the car in a tight turn and landed it near the wagon. The three grabbed their weapons, jumped from the car and ran with difficulty through the sand to the site.

The force field blocked them.

"What the hell!" Cheevers kicked at the inflexible, impenetrable shield and swore some more.

The treadwagon was there in the middle of the square formed by the force field posts, and there was no one in it. The eye-tube was still rotating slowly and noiselessly, weapons on the bridge beneath still pointed menacingly at the empty desert, the g-car was still in its place, and the Federation flag fluttered in the slight breeze.

But there was nothing living inside the square. The sand was oddly smooth in many places where there should have been footprints and Allison wondered if the slight breeze had already started its work of moving the sand to obliterate them. There were no bodies, no blood, no signs of a struggle.

Since they couldn't get through the barrier, they went back to the g-car and went over it, landing inside the invisible enclosure, still alert for any emergency.

But nothing attacked because there was nothing there. Only the sand, the empty treadwagons, the weapons, the stores.

"Poor Quartz," Cheevers said.

"What, sir?" Hallom asked.

"Lieutenant Quartz. I knew him better than any of the others." He picked up a handful of sand and threw it angrily at the wagon's treads.

Allison saw it hit, watched it fall, then noticed the tread prints were obliterated inside the big square. But as he looked out across the waste to the ship he noticed the tread prints there were quite clear.

He shivered in the hot sun.

The lieutenant reported by the wagon's radio, and after they had collected and packed all the gear, Allison and Hallom drove the treadwagons back to the ship.

"I tell you it's impossible!" The commander's eyes were red-rimmed and bloodshot and he ran sweating hands through wisps of uncombed grey hair. "There must have been *something!*"

"But there wasn't, sir," Cheevers said with anguish. "And nothing was overlooked, believe me."

"But how can that be?" The commander raised his arms angrily, let them fall. "And how will it look in the record? Ten men gone. Just like that." He snapped his fingers. "The Federation won't like it – especially since it is exactly what happened to the others. If only there had been a fight! If there were a chance for reprisal! But this—" he waved an arm to include the whole planet. "It's maddening!"

It was night before the commander could contain himself enough to talk rationally about what had happened and to think creatively of possible action.

"I'm not blaming you, Lieutenant Cheevers, or anybody," he said slouched in his desk chair and idly eyeing the three remaining television screens that revealed an endless, turning desert scene. "I have only myself to blame for what happened." He grunted. "I only wish I knew what happened." He turned to Cheevers, Allison and Hallom, who sat on the other side of the desk. "I've done nothing but think about this thing all day. I don't know what to tell those fellows out there, how they can protect themselves from this. I've examined the facts from every angle, but I always end up where I started." He stared at Cheevers. "Let's hear your idea again, Cheevers."

"It's like I say, sir. The attack could have come from the air."

"Carried away like eagles, eh? You've still got that idea?"

"The sand was smooth, Commander. That would support the idea of wings of birds setting the air in motion so the sand would cover up the footprints."

The commander bit his lower lip, drummed on the desk with his fingers and stared hard at Cheevers. "It *is* possible. Barely possible. But it still doesn't explain why we see no birds, why we saw no birds on the other viewers during the incident, why the other teams saw no birds in flight. We've asked, remember? Nobody has seen a living thing. Where then are we going to get enough birds to carry off ten men? And how does this happen with no bloodshed? Surely one of our men could have got off one shot, could have wounded *one* bird."

"The birds could have been invisible, sir," Hallom said hesitantly.

"Invisible birds!" The commander glared. Then he shrugged. "Hell I suppose anything is possible."

"That's what Allison's machine says."

"I ran the stuff through the computer," Allison said.

"I forgot there was such a thing . . . So that's what came out, eh?"

"Not exactly, Commander." Allison withdrew a roll of facsimile tape. "I sent through what we had. There are quite a few possibilities." He unrolled a little of it. "The men could still exist at the site, though rendered invisible—"

"Nuts!" the commander said. "How the hell—!"

"The data," Allison went on calmly, "was pretty weird itself and the machine lists only the possibilities, taking into consideration everything no matter how absurd. Other possibilities are that we are victims of hypnosis and that we are to see only what *they* – whoever *they* are – want us to see; that the men were surprised and spirited away by something invisible, which would mean none of the other units would have seen or reported it; or that the men themselves would not have seen the – let's say 'invisible birds'; that the men sank into the sand somehow by some change in the composition of the ground itself, or were taken there by something, that there was a change in time or space—"

"That's enough," the commander snapped. He rose, eyes blazing. "I can see we're going to get nothing worthwhile from the Computer Corps. 'Change in Time' hell! I want a straight answer, not a bunch of fancies or something straight from a fairy tale. The only thing you've said so far I'd put any stock in is the idea of the birds. And the lieutenant had that idea first. But as far as their being invisible is concerned, I hardly think that's likely."

"But if it had been just birds," Allison said, putting away the roll of tape, "there would have been resistance and blood would have been spilled somewhere."

Commander Warrick snorted. "If there'd been a fight we'd have seen some evidence of it. It was too quick for a fight, that's all. And I'm warning the other units of birds and of attack without warning."

As a result, the three remaining units altered the mechanism of their eye-tubes to include a sweep of the sky after each 360 degree pan of the horizon.

The fourth night passed and the blazing sun burst forth the morning of the fifth day with the situation unchanged except that anxiety and tension were more in evidence among the men than ever before. The commander ordered sedatives for all men coming off watches so they could sleep.

The fifth night passed without incident.

It was nearly noon on the sixth day when Wang Lee, who was with Lieutenant Glenn Foster's Unit West, reported that one of the men had gone out of his head.

The commander said he'd send over a couple men to get him in a g-car.

But before Petry and Hollam left, Lee was on the radio again. "It's Prince, the man I told you about," he said. "Maybe you can see him in the screen. He's got his blaster out and insists we turn off the force field."

The Invisible Enemy

The television screen showed the sky in a long sweep past the sun down to the sand and around, sweeping past the figure of a man, obviously Prince, as it panned the horizon.

"Lieutenant Foster's got a blaster on him," Lee went on.

"Damn it!" Sweat popped out on the commander's forehead as he looked at the screen. "Not enough trouble without that." He turned to Cheevers. "Tell Foster to blast him before he endangers the whole outfit."

But the words were not swift enough. The screen went black and the speaker emitted a harsh click.

It was late afternoon when the treadwagon from Unit West purred to a stop beside the wagon from Unit South and Petry and Bacon stepped out of it.

"There she is," Cheevers told the commander at his side on the ramp. "Prince blasted her but didn't put her out of commission. Only the radio – you can see the mast has been snapped off. No telling how many men he got in that blast before . . ."

"And now they're all gone. Twenty men." The commander stared dumbly at the wagon and his shoulders slouched a little now. He looked from the wagon to the horizon and followed it along toward the sun, shading his squinting red eyes. "What is it out there, Cheevers? What are we up against?"

"I wish I knew, sir."

They walked down the ramp to the sand and waded through it out to the treadwagon. They examined it from all sides.

"Not a goddam bloodstain anywhere," the commander said, wiping his neck with his handkerchief. "If Prince really blasted the men there ought to be stains and hair and remains and stench and – well, *something*."

"Did Rogers or Noromak report anything while I was gone?"

"Nothing. Not a damned thing . . . Scene look the same as before?"

"Just like before. Smooth sand inside the force field and no traces, though we did find Prince's blaster. At least I think it's his. Found it half-buried in the sand where he was supposed to be standing. We can check his serial number on it."

"Twenty men!" the commander breathed. He stared at the smooth sweep of sand again. "Twenty men swallowed up by nothing again." He looked up at the cloudless sky. "No birds, no life, no nothing. Yet something big enough to . . ." He shook his fist at the nothingness. "Why don't you show yourself, whoever you are – whatever you are! Why do you sneak and steal men!"

"Easy, Commander," Cheevers said, alarmed at the commander's red face, wide eyes and rising voice.

The commander relaxed, turned to the lieutenant with a wry face. "You'll have a command some day, Corvin. Then you'll know how it is."

"I think I know, sir," he said quietly.

"You only think you know. Come on, let's go in and get a drink. I need one. I've got to send in another report."

If it had been up to Allison, he would have called in the two remaining units – Unit East, Lieutenant Noromak's outfit, and Unit North, Lieutenant Rogers' group – because in the face of what had twice proved so undetectable and unpredictable, there was no sense in throwing good men after those who had already gone. He could not bear to think of how the men felt who manned the remaining outposts. Sitting ducks.

But it was not up to him. He could only run the computer and advise. And even his advice need not be heeded by the commanding officer whose will and determination to discover the planet's threat had become something more to pity than admire because he was willing to sacrifice the remaining two units rather than withdraw and consider some other method of attack.

Allison saw a man who no longer looked like a soldier, a man in soiled uniform, unshaven, an irritable man who had spurned eating and sleeping and had come to taking his nourishment from the bottle, a man who now barked his orders in a raucous voice, a man who could stand no sudden noises and, above all, could not tolerate any questions of his decisions. And so he became a lonely man because no one wanted to be near him, and he was left alone to stare with fascination at the two remaining TV panels and listen to the half-minute reports . . . and take a drink once in a while.

Allison was no different from the others. He did not want to face the commander. But he did not want to join the muttering soldiers in crew quarters either. So he kept to the computer room and, for something to do, spliced the tapes he had made from flight technician's information for their homeward flight. It took him more than three hours and when he was finished he put the reels in the flight compartment and, for what he thought surely must have been the hundredth time, took out the tapes he had already made on conditions and factors involved in the current emergency. He rearranged them and fed them into the machine again, then tapped out on the keys a request for a single factor that might emerge and prove helpful.

He watched the last of the tape whip into the machine, heard the gentle hum, the click of relays and watched the current indicators in the three different stages of the machine, knew that inside memory circuits were giving information, exchanging data, that other devices were examining results, probing for other related information, extracting useful bits, adding this to the stream, to be rejected or passed, depending upon whether it fitted the conditions.

At last the delivery section was energized, the soft ding of the response bell and the lighted green bar preceded a moment when the answer facsimile tape whirred out and even as he looked at it he knew, by its length, that it was as evasive and generalized as the information he had asked it to examine.

He had left the door to the computer room open and through it suddenly came the sound of hoarse voices. He jumped to his feet and ran out and down the hall to the control room.

The two television panels showed nothing new, but there was an excited radio voice that he recognized as Lieutenant Rogers'.

"He's violent, Commander, and there's nothing we can do," the lieutenant was saying. "He keeps running and trying to break through the force field – oh, my God!"

"What is it?" the commander cried, getting to his feet.

"He's got his blaster out and he's saying something."

The commander rushed to the microphone and tore it from Cheever's hands. "Don't force him to shoot and don't you shoot, Lieutenant. Remember what happened to Unit West."

"But he's coming up to the wagon now—"

"Don't lose your head, Rogers! Try to knock him out – *but don't use your blaster!*"

"He's entering the wagon now, Commander."

There was a moment's silence.

"He's getting into the g-car, Commander! We can't let him do that!"

"Knock him out!"

"I think we've got him – they're tangling – several men – he's knocked one away – he's got the damned thing going!"

There was a sound of clinking metal, a rasp and scrape and the obvious roar of the little g-car.

"He got away in it! Maybe you can pick it up on the screen . . ."

The TV screen moved slowly across the sky and swept by a g-car that loomed large on it.

"Let him go," the commander said. "We'll send you another. Anybody get hurt?"

"Yes, sir. One of the men got a bad cut. They're still working on him on the sand. Got knocked off the wagon and fell into the sand. I saw his head was pretty bloody a moment ago before the men gathered around him and . . . *my God! No! No!*"

"What!"

"They're coming out of the ground—"

"What?"

There were audible hisses and clanks and screams and . . . and suddenly it was quiet.

"Lieutenant! Lieutenant Rogers!" The commander's face was white. "Answer me, Lieutenant, do you hear? Answer me! You – you can't do this to me!"

But the radio was quiet.

But above, the television screen showed a panorama of endless desert illuminated by infrared and as it swept by one spot Allison caught sight of the horrified face of Tony Lazzari as the g-car soared by.

Allison pushed the shovel deep into the sand, lifted as much of it as he could get in it, deposited it on the conveyor. There were ten of them digging in the soft yellow sand in the early morning sun, sweat rolling off their backs and chins – not because the sand was heavy or that the work was hard but because the day was already unbearable hot – digging a hole that couldn't be dug. The sand kept slipping into the very place they were digging. They had only made a shallow depression two or three feet deep at the most and more than twenty feet wide.

They had found nothing.

Commander Warrick, who stood in the g-car atop Unit North's treadwagon, with Lieutenant Noromak and Lieutenant Cheevers at his side, had first ordered Unit East to return to the ship, which Allison considered the smartest thing he had done in the past five days. Then a group of ten, mostly men who had not been in the field,

181

were dispatched in Unit South's old wagon, with the officers in the g-car accompanying them, to Unit North.

There was no sign of a struggle, just the smooth sand around the wagon, the force field still intact and functioning.

Then the ten men had started digging . . .

"All right," the commander called from the wagon. "Everybody out. We'll blast."

They got out of the hole and on the other side of the wagon while the commander ordered Cheevers to aim at the depression.

The shot was deafening, but when the clouds of sand had settled, the depression was still there with a coating of fused sand covering it.

Later, when the group returned to the ship, three g-car parties were sent out to look for Lazzari. They found him unconscious in the sun in his g-car in the sand. They brought him back to the ship where he was revived.

"What did you see?" the commander asked when Lazzari regained consciousness.

Lazzari just stared.

Allison had seen men like this before. "Commander," he said, "this man's in a catatonic state. He'd better be watched because he can have periods of violence."

The commander glared. "You go punch your goddamn computer, Mr Allison. I'll handle Lazzari."

And as the commander questioned the man, Lazzari suddenly started to cry, then jerked and, wild-eyed, leaped for the commander.

They put Lazzari in a small room.

Allison could have told the commander that was a mistake, too, but he didn't dare.

And, as the commander was planning his next moves against the planet's peril, Lazzari dashed his head against a bulkhead, fractured his skull, and died.

The funeral for Lazzari the commander said, was to be a military one – as military as was possible on a planet revolving around a remote star in the far Hyades. Since rites were not possible for the twenty-nine others of the *Nesbitt* who had vanished, the commander said Lazzari's would make up for the rest.

Then for the first time in a week men had something else to think about besides the nature of things on the planet of the yellow sand that had done away with two explorers, the crews of three ships and twenty-nine Federation soldier-technicians who had come to do battle.

New uniforms were issued, each man showered and shaved, Lieutenant Cheevers read up on the burial service, Gordon Bacon practiced *Taps* on his bugle, Homer Petry gathered some desert flowers in a g-car, and Wendell Hallom washed and prepared Lazzari for the final rites which were to be held within a few hundred feet of the ship.

Though Allison complied with the directives, he felt uneasy about a funeral on the sand. He spent the hour before the afternoon services in the computer room, running tapes through the machine again, seeking the factor responsible for what had occurred.

He reasoned that persons on the sand were safe as long as the onslaught of the *things* out of the ground was not triggered by some action of men in the parties.

He did not know what the Unit South provocation had been – the radio signals had just stopped. He did know the assault on Unit West occurred after Prince's blast at the men on the treadwagon (though the blast in the sand at Unit North had brought nothing to the surface – if one were to believe Lieutenant Roger's final words about *things* coming out of the ground). And the attack at Unit North was fomented by Lazzari's taking off in the g-car and throwing those battling him to the sand.

Allison went so far as to cut new tapes for each incident, adding every possible detail he could think of. Then he inserted these into the machine and tapped out a question of the advisability of men further exposing themselves by holding a burial service for Lazzari in the sand.

In a few moments the response whirred out.

He caught his breath because the message was so short. Printed on the facsimile tape were these words:

Not advised.

Heartened by the brevity of the message and the absence of all the ifs, ands and buts of previous responses, he tapped out another question: Was there danger to life?

Agonizing minutes. Then:

Yes.

Whose life?

All.

Do you know the factor responsible for the deaths?

Yes.

He cursed himself for not realizing the machine knew the factor and wished he had asked for it instead. With his heart tripping like a jackhammer, Allison tapped out: What is the triggering factor?

When the answer came he found it ridiculously simple and wondered why no one had thought of it before. He stood staring at the tape for a long time knowing there could now be no funeral for Tony Lazzari.

He left the computer room, found the commander talking to Lieutenant Cheevers in the control room. Commander Warrick seemed something of his old self, attired in a natty tropical, clean shaven and with a military bearing and a freshness about him that had been missing for days.

"Commander," Allison said. "I don't mean to interrupt, but – we can't have the funeral."

The commander turned to him with a look full of suspicion. Then he said, "Allison, this is the one and only trip you will ever make with me. When we get back it will be either you or me who gets off this ship for the last time. If you want to run a ship you have to go to another school besides the one for Computer Corps men."

"I've known how you feel, Commander," Allison said, "and—"

"The General Staff ought to know that you can't mix army and civilian. I shall make it a point to register my feelings on the matter when we return."

"You can tell them what you wish, Commander, but it so happens that I've found out the factor responsible for all the attacks."

"And it so happens," the commander said icily, "that the lieutenant and I are reviewing the burial rites. A strict military burial has certain formalities which cannot be overlooked, though I don't expect you to understand that. There is too little time to go into any of your fancy theories now."

"This is no theory, Commander. It's a certainty."

"Did your computer have anything to do with it?"

"It had everything to do with it. I'd been feeding the tapes for days—"

"While we're on the subject, Allison, we're not using computer tapes for our home journey. We're going the whole way manually. I'm awaiting orders now to move off this God-forsaken world, in case you want to know. I'm recommending it as out-of-bounds for all ships of the Federation. And I'm also recommending that computer units be removed from the *Nesbitt* and from all other ships."

"You'll never leave this planet if you have the funeral," Allison said heatedly. "It will be death for all of us."

"Is that so?" The commander smiled thinly. "Courtesy of your computer, no doubt. Or is it that you're afraid to go out on the sand again?"

"I'm not afraid of the sand, Commander. I'll go out any time. But it's the others I'm thinking of. I won't go out to see Lazzari buried because of the blood on his head and neither should anyone else. You see, the missing factor – the thing that caused all the attacks – is blood."

"Blood?" The commander laughed, looked at Cheevers,

who was not laughing, then back at Allison. "Sure you feel all right?"

"The blood on Lazzari, Commander. It will trigger another attack."

"What about the blood that's in us, Allison? That should have prevented us from stepping out to the sand without being attacked in the first place. Your reasoning – or rather your computer's reasoning – is ridiculous."

"It's fresh blood. Blood spilled on the sand."

"It seems to me you've got blood on the brain. Lazzari was a friend of yours, wasn't he, Allison?"

"That has nothing to do with it."

The commander looked at him hard and long, then turned to the lieutenant. "Cheevers, Allison doesn't feel very well. I think he'd better be locked up in the computer room until after the funeral."

Allison was stunned. "Commander—!"

"Will you please take him away at once, Lieutenant? I've heard all I want from him."

Sick at heart, Allison watched the commander walk out of the control room.

"You coming along, Allison?" Cheevers asked.

Allison looked at the lieutenant. "Do you know what will happen if you go out there?" But there was no sympathy or understanding in the eyes of the officer. He turned and walked down the hall to the computer room and went in.

"It doesn't make any difference what I think," Cheevers said, his hand on the knob of the door, his face not unkind. "You're not in the service. I am. I have to do what the commander says. Some day I may have a command of my own. Then I'll have a right to my own opinion."

"You'll never have a command of your own . . . after today."

"Think so?" It seemed to Allison that the lieutenant sighed a little. "Goodbye, Allison."

It was an odd way to put it. Allison saw the door close

and click shut. Then he heard the lieutenant walk away. It was quiet.

Anguish in every fiber, Allison clicked on the small screen above the computer, turned a knurled knob until he saw the area of the intended burial. He hated to look at what he was going to see. The eye of the wide, shallow grave stared at him from the viewplate.

In a few minutes he saw Bacon carrying a Federation flag move slowly into view, followed by six men with blasters at raise, then Hallom and his bugle, Lieutenant Cheevers and his book, the stretcher bearing Lazzari with three pall-bearers on either side, and the rest of the men in double ranks, the officers leading them.

Go ahead Commander. Have your military field day because it's one thing you know how to do well. It's men like you who need a computer . . .

The procession approached the depression, Bacon moving to one side, the firing party at the far side of the shallow, Lieutenant Cheevers at the near end, making room for the pallbearers who moved into the depression and deposited their load there. The others moved to either side of the slope in single file.

Make it slick, Commander. By the numbers, straight and strong, because it's the last thing you'll ever do . . .

The men suddenly stiffened to attention, uncovering and holding their dress hats over their left breasts.

Bacon removed the Federation flag from its staff, draped it neatly over Lazzari. Cheevers then moved to the front and conducted the services, which lasted for several minutes.

This is the end, Commander . . .

Allison could see Commander Warrick facing the firing party, saw the blast volleys. But he was more interested in Lazzari. Two soldiers were shoveling the loose sand over him. Hallom raised his bugle to his lips.

Then *they* came.

Large, heavy, white porpoise-like creatures they were, swimming up out of the sand as if it were water, and snatching men in their powerful jaws, rending and tearing – clothes and all – as they rose in a fury of attacks that whipped up sand to nearly hide the scene. There were twenty or more and then more than a hundred rising and sinking and snapping and slashing, sun glistening on their shiny sides, flippers working furiously to stay atop the sand.

This, then, was the sea and these were the fish in it, fish normally disinterested in ordinary sweating men and machines and treadwagons, but hungry for men's blood or anything smeared with it – so hungry that a drop of it on the sand must have been a signal conducted to the depths to attract them all.

And when the men were gone there were still fish-like creatures burrowing into the sand, moving through it swiftly half in and out like sharks, seeking every last vestige of – blood.

Then as suddenly as they had come, the things were gone.

Then there was nothing but smooth sand where before it had been covered by twenty men with bowed heads . . . except one spot which maximum magnification showed to be a bugle half-buried in the sand.

Allison did not know how long he sat there looking at the screen, but it must have been been an hour because when he finally moved he could only do so with effort.

He alone had survived out of fifty men and he – the computer man. He was struck with the wonder of it.

He rose to leave the room. He needed a drink.

Only then did he remember that Cheevers had locked him in.

He tried the door.

It opened!

Cheevers *had* believed him, then. Somehow, this made the whole thing more tragic . . . there might have been others who would have believed, too, if the commander had not stood in the way . . .

The first thing Allison did was close the great port. Then he hunted until he found the bottle he was looking for. He took it to the computer room with him, opened the flight compartment, withdrew the tapes, set them in their proper slots and started them on their way.

Only when he heard the ship tremble alive did he take a drink . . . A long drink.

There would have to be other bottles after this one. There *had* to be. It was going to be a long, lonely ride home.

And there was much to forget.

OUT OF THE UNKNOWN

(BBC TV, 1965–1971)
Starring: Ian Ogilvy, Hamilton Dyce &
Wendy Gifford
Directed by Gerald Blake
Story 'Liar!' by Isaac Asimov

Out of the Unknown was the BBC's answer to the success of Independent Television's *Out of This World*. What both had in common was Irene Shubik as producer, for in the interim she had moved channels with Sydney Newman and in her new role had been allowed to indulge her obvious penchant for SF with a fresh series which also drew on the work of the very best writers in the genre including John Wyndham, Ray Bradbury, Frederick Pohl and Isaac Asimov. On the BBC, however, after two seasons in black and white, the rest of the series was in colour. Once again a Martian story by John Wyndham, 'No Place Like Earth' heralded the start of *Out of the Unknown's* first season in October 1965; but it was to be a group of stories by Isaac Asimov and several contributions from Terry Nation, Leon Griffiths, Hugh Whitemore and Nigel Kneale that would have the biggest impact on audiences. The series was also well served by its team of directors including Peter Sasdy, Alan Bridges and Philip Saville, while working amongst the design team was a young man who would later take Hollywood by storm as the director of *Alien* and *Blade Runner*, Ridley Scott. In all, 49 episodes of *Out of the Unknown* were produced by Irene Shubik and her successor, Alan Bromly, and among the many leading guest actors were stars such as David Hemmings, Warren Mitchell, Rachel Roberts and even George 'Minder' Cole!

For a quite considerable number of viewers the most fascinating episodes were those about robots based on short stories by Isaac Asimov (1920–1992), the prodigeously gifted professor of biochemistry who turned SF writer and is now widely acknowledged as one of the major influences on the genre this century. It was in 1940 that he wrote the first of his robot stories, 'Strange Playfellow', and then a year later followed it with, 'Liar!' which introduced what have been described as the 'Three Laws of Robotics' and once and for all confined the clanking mental monsters of so much earlier SF to oblivion. Of the six Asimov stories that *Out of the Unknown* adapted for television, three were specifically about robots and all featured Dr Susan Calvin, a robot psychologist, with 'Liar!' perhaps the best adaptation of all. From the apprently unexceptional situation of a robot being demonstrated to the press in order to quieten public unrest about possible dangers from the growing number of these machines, director Gerald Blake and his actors – in particular Wendy Gifford as Dr Calvin and Ian Ogilvy as robot RB–34 – produced an engrossing and thought-provoking hour of television which remained remarkably faithful to Asimov's original landmark story. It is reprinted here as a reminder of yet another piece of television's SF history . . .

Alfred Lanning lit his cigar carefully, but the tips of his fingers were trembling slightly. His gray eyebrows hunched low as he spoke between puffs.

"It reads minds all right – damn little doubt about that! But why?" He looked at Mathematician Peter Bogert, "Well?"

Bogert flattened his black hair down with both hands,

"That was the thirty-fourth RB model we've turned out, Lanning. All the others were strictly orthodox."

The third man at the table frowned. Milton Ashe was the youngest officer of U.S. Robot & Mechanical Men, Inc., and proud of his post.

"Listen, Bogert. There wasn't a hitch in the assembly from start to finish. I guarantee that."

Bogert's thick lips spread in a patronizing smile, "Do you? If you can answer for the entire assembly line, I recommend your promotion. By exact count, there are seventy-five thousand, two hundred and thirty-four operations necessary for the manufacture of a single positronic brain, each separate operation depending for successful completion upon any number of factors, from five to a hundred and five. If any one of them goes seriously wrong, the 'brain' is ruined. I quote our own information folder, Ashe."

Milton Ashe flushed, but a fourth voice cut off his reply.

"If we're going to start by trying to fix the blame on one another, I'm leaving." Susan Calvin's hands were folded tightly in her lap, and the little lines about her thin, pale lips deepened, "We've got a mind-reading robot on our hands and it strikes me as rather important that we find out just why it reads minds. We're not going to do that by saying, 'Your fault! My fault!'"

Her cold gray eyes fastened upon Ashe, and he grinned.

Lanning grinned too, and, as always at such times, his long white hair and shrewd little eyes made him the picture of a biblical patriarch. "True for you, Dr Calvin."

His voice became suddenly crisp, "Here's everything in pill-concentrate form. We've produced a positronic brain of supposedly ordinary vintage that's got the remarkable property of being able to tune in on thought waves. It would mark the most important advance in robotics in decades, if we knew how it happened. We don't, and we have to find out. Is that clear?"

"May I make a suggestion?" asked Bogert.

"Go ahead!"

"I'd say that until we do figure out the mess – and as a mathematician I expect it to be a very devil of a mess – we keep the existence of RB-34 a secret. I mean even from the other members of the staff. As heads of the departments, we ought not to find it an insoluble problem, and the fewer know about it—"

"Bogert is right," said Dr Calvin. "Ever since the Interplanetary Code was modified to allow robot models to be tested in the plants before being shipped out to space, anti-robot propaganda has increased. If any word leaks out about a robot being able to read minds before we can announce complete control of the phenomenon, pretty effective capital could be made out of it."

Lanning sucked at his cigar and nodded gravely. He turned to Ashe, "I think you said you were alone when you first stumbled on this thought-reading business."

"I'll say I was alone – I got the scare of my life. RB-34 had just been taken off the assembly table and they sent him down to me. Obermann was off somewheres, so I took him down to the testing rooms myself – at least I started to take him down." Ashe paused, and a tiny smile tugged at his lips, "Say, did any of you ever carry on a thought conversation without knowing it?"

No one bothered to answer, and he continued, "You don't realize it at first, you know. He just spoke to me – as logically and sensibly as you can imagine – and it was only when I was most of the way down to the testing rooms that I realized that I hadn't said anything. Sure, I thought lots, but that isn't the same thing, is it? I locked that thing up and ran for Lanning. Having it walking beside me, calmly peering into my thoughts and picking and choosing among them gave me the willies."

"I imagine it would," said Susan Calvin thoughtfully. Her eyes fixed themselves upon Ashe in an oddly intent manner. "We are so accustomed to considering our own thoughts private."

Lanning broke in impatiently, "Then only the four of us know. All right! We've got to go about this systematically. Ashe, I want you to check over the assembly line from beginning to end everything. You're to eliminate all operations in which there was no possible chance of an error, and list all those where there were, together with its nature and possible magnitude."

"Tall order," grunted Ashe.

"Naturally! Of course, you're to put the men under you to work on this – every single one if you have to, and I don't care if we go behind schedule, either. But they're not to know why, you understand."

"Hm-m-m, yes!" The young technician grinned wryly. "It's still a lulu of a job."

Lanning swiveled about in his chair and faced Calvin, "You'll have to tackle the job from the other direction. You're the robopsychologist of the plant, so you're to study the robot itself and work backward. Try to find out how he ticks. See what else is tied up with his telepathic powers, how far they extend, how they warp his outlook, and just exactly what harm it has done to his ordinary RB properties. You've got that?"

Lanning didn't wait for Dr Calvin to answer.

"I'll co-ordinate the work and interpret the findings mathematically." He puffed violently at his cigar and mumbled the rest through the smoke, "Bogert will help me there, of course."

Bogert polished the nails of one pudgy hand with the other and said blandly, "I dare say. I know a little in the line."

"Well! I'll get started." Ashe shoved his chair back and rose. His pleasantly youthful face crinkled in a grin, "I've got the darnedest job of any of us, so I'm getting out of here and to work."

He left with a slurred, "B' seein' ye!"

Susan Calvin answered with a barely perceptible nod,

but her eyes followed him out of sight and she did not answer when Lanning grunted and said, "Do you want to go up and see RB-34 now, Dr Calvin?"

RB-34's photoelectric eyes lifted from the book at the muffled sound of hinges turning and he was upon his feet when Susan Calvin entered.

She paused to readjust the huge 'No Entrance' sign upon the door and then approached the robot.

"I've brought you the texts upon hyperatomic motors, Herbie – a few anyway. Would you care to look at them?"

RB-34 – otherwise known as Herbie – lifted the three heavy books from her arms and opened to the title page of one:

"Hm-m-m! 'Theory of Hyperatomics.'" He mumbled inarticulately to himself as he flipped the pages and then spoke with an abstracted air, "Sit down, Dr Calvin! This will take me a few minutes."

The psychologist seated herself and watched Herbie narrowly as he took a chair at the other side of the table and went through the three books systematically.

At the end of half an hour, he put them down, "Of course, I know why you brought these."

The corner of Dr Calvin's lip twitched, "I was afraid you would. It's difficult to work with you, Herbie. You're always a step ahead of me."

"It's the same with these books, you know, as with the others. They just don't interest me. There's nothing to your textbooks. Your science is just a mass of collected data plastered together by make-shift theory – and all so incredibly simple, that it's scarcely worth bothering about.

"It's your fiction that interests me. Your studies of the interplay of human motives and emotions" – his mighty hand gestured vaguely as he sought the proper words.

Dr Calvin whispered, "I think I understand."

"I see into minds, you see," the robot continued, "and

you have no idea how complicated they are. I can't begin to understand everything because my own mind has so little in common with them – but I try, and your novels help."

"Yes, but I'm afraid that after going through some of the harrowing emotional experiences of our present-day sentimental novel" – there was a tinge of bitterness in her voice – "you find real minds like ours dull and colorless."

"But I don't!"

The sudden energy in the response brought the other to her feet. She felt herself reddening, and thought wildly, "He must know!"

Herbie subsided suddenly, and muttered in a low voice from which the metallic timbre departed almost entirely. "But, of course, I know about it, Dr Calvin. You think of it always, so how can I help but know?"

Her face was hard. "Have you – told anyone?"

"Of course not!" This, with genuine surprise. "No one has asked me."

"Well, then," she flung out, "I suppose you think I am a fool."

"No! It is a normal emotion."

"Perhaps that is why it is so foolish." The wistfulness in her voice drowned out everything else. Some of the woman peered through the layer of doctorhood. "I am not what you would call – attractive."

"If you are referring to mere physical attraction, I couldn't judge. But I know, in any case, that there are other types of attraction."

"Nor young." Dr Calvin had scarcely heard the robot.

"You are not yet forty." An anxious insistence had crept into Herbie's voice.

"Thirty-eight as you count the years; a shriveled sixty as far as my emotional outlook on life is concerned. Am I a psychologist for nothing?"

She drove on with bitter breathlessness, "And he's barely thirty-five and looks and acts younger. Do you

suppose he ever sees me as anything but . . . but what
I am?"

"You are wrong!" Herbie's steel fist struck the plastic-
topped table with a strident clang. "Listen to me—"

But Susan Calvin whirled on him now and the hunted
pain in her eyes became a blaze, "Why should I? What
do you know about it all, anyway, you . . . you machine.
I'm just a specimen to you; an interesting bug with
a peculiar mind spread-eagled for inspection. It's a
wonderful example of frustration, isn't it? Almost as
good as your books." Her voice, emerging in dry sobs,
choked into silence.

The robot cowered at the outburst. He shook his head
pleadingly. "Won't you listen to me, please? I could help
you if you would let me."

"How?" Her lips curled. "By giving me good advice?"

"No, not that. It's just that I know what other people
think – Milton Ashe, for instance."

There was a long silence, and Susan Calvin's eyes
dropped. "I don't want to know what he thinks," she
gasped. "Keep quiet."

"I think you would want to know what he thinks."

Her head remained bent, but her breath came more
quickly. "You are talking nonsense," she whispered.

"Why should I? I am trying to help. Milton Ashe's
thoughts of you—" he paused.

And then the psychologist raised her head, "Well?"

The robot said quietly, "He loves you."

For a full minute, Dr Calvin did not speak. She merely
stared. Then, "You are mistaken! You must be. Why
should he?"

"But he does. A thing like that cannot be hidden, not
from me."

"But I am so . . . so—" she stammered to a halt.

"He looks deeper than the skin, and admires intellect
in others. Milton Ashe is not the type to marry a head of
hair and a pair of eyes."

Susan Calvin found herself blinking rapidly and waited

before speaking. Even then her voice trembled, "Yet he certainly never in any way indicated—"

"Have you ever given him a chance?"

"How could I? I never thought that—"

"Exactly!"

The psychologist paused in thought and then looked up suddenly. "A girl visited him here at the plant half a year ago. She was pretty, I suppose – blond and slim. And, of course, could scarcely add two and two. He spent all day puffing out his chest, trying to explain how a robot was put together." The hardness had returned, "Not that she understood! Who was she?"

Herbie answered without hesitation, "I know the person you are referring to. She is his first cousin, and there is no romantic interest there, I assure you."

Susan Calvin rose to her feet with a vivacity almost girlish. "Now isn't that strange? That's exactly what I used to pretend to myself sometimes, though I never really thought so. Then it all must be true."

She ran to Herbie and seized his cold, heavy hand in both hers. "Thank you, Herbie." Her voice was an urgent, husky whisper. "Don't tell anyone about this. Let it be our secret – and thank you again." With that, and a convulsive squeeze of Herbie's unresponsive metal fingers, she left.

Herbie turned slowly to his neglected novel, but there was no one to read *his* thoughts.

Milton Ashe stretched slowly and magnificently, to the tune of cracking joints and a chorus of grunts, and then glared at Peter Bogert, Ph.D.

"Say," he said, "I've been at this for a week now with just about no sleep. How long do I have to keep it up? I thought you said the positronic bombardment in Vac Chamber D was the solution."

Bogert yawned delicately and regarded his white hands with interest. "It is. I'm on the track."

"I know what *that* means when a mathematician says it. How near the end are you?"

Liar!

"It all depends."

"On what?" Ashe dropped into a chair and stretched his long legs out before him.

"On Lanning. The old fellow disagrees with me." He sighed, "A bit behind the times, that's the trouble with him. He clings to matrix mechanics as the all in all, and this problem calls for more powerful mathematical tools. He's so stubborn."

Ashe muttered sleepily, "Why not ask Herbie and settle the whole affair?"

"Ask the robot?" Bogert's eyebrows climbed.

"Why not? Didn't the old girl tell you?"

"You mean Calvin?"

"Yeah! Susie herself. That robot's a mathematical wiz. He knows all about everything plus a bit on the side. He does triple integrals in his head and eats up tensor analysis for dessert."

The mathematician stared skeptically, "Are you serious?"

"So help me! The catch is that the dope doesn't like math. He would rather read slushy novels. Honest! You should see the tripe Susie keeps feeding him: 'Purple Passion' and 'Love in Space.'"

"Dr Calvin hasn't said a word of this to us."

"Well, she hasn't finished studying him. You know how she is. She likes to have everything just so before letting out the big secret."

"She's told *you*."

"We sort of got to talking. I have been seeing a lot of her lately." He opened his eyes wide and frowned, "Say, Bogie, have you been noticing anything queer about the lady lately?"

Bogert relaxed into an undignified grin, "She's using lipstick, if that's what you mean."

"Hell, I know that. Rouge, powder and eye shadow, too. She's a sight. But it's not that. I can't put my finger on it. It's the way she talks – as if she were happy about something." He thought a little, and then shrugged.

The other allowed himself a leer, which, for a scientist past fifty, was not a bad job, "Maybe she's in love."

Ashe allowed his eyes to close again, "You're nuts, Bogie. You go speak to Herbie; I want to stay here and go to sleep."

"Right! Not that I particularly like having a robot tell me my job, nor that I think he can do it!"

A soft snore was his only answer.

Herbie listened carefully as Peter Bogert, hands in pockets, spoke with elaborate indifference.

"So there you are. I've been told you understand these things, and I am asking you more in curiosity than anything else. My line of reasoning, as I have outlined it, involves a few doubtful steps, I admit, which Dr Lanning refuses to accept, and the picture is still rather incomplete."

The robot didn't answer, and Bogert said, "Well?"

"I see no mistake," Herbie studied the scribbled figures.

"I don't suppose you can go any further than that?"

"I daren't try. You are a better mathematician than I, and – well, I'd hate to commit myself."

There was a shade of complacency in Bogert's smile, "I rather thought that would be the case. It is deep. We'll forget it." He crumpled the sheets, tossed them down the waste shaft, turned to leave, and then thought better of it.

"By the way—"

The robot waited.

Bogert seemed to have difficulty. "There is something – that is, perhaps you can—" He stopped.

Herbie spoke quietly. "Your thoughts are confused, but there is no doubt at all that they concern Dr Lanning. It is silly to hesitate, for as soon as you compose yourself, I'll know what it is you want to ask."

The mathematician's hand went to his sleek hair in the familiar smoothing gesture. "Lanning is nudging seventy," he said, as if that explained everything.

"I know that."

"And he's been director of the plant for almost thirty years." Herbie nodded.

"Well, now," Bogert's voice became ingratiating, "you would know whether . . . whether he's thinking of resigning. Health, perhaps, or some other—"

"Quite," said Herbie, and that was all.

"Well, do you know?"

"Certainly."

"Then – uh – could you tell me?"

"Since you ask, yes." The robot was quite matter-of-fact about it. "He has already resigned!"

"What!" The exclamation was an explosive, almost inarticulate, sound. The scientist's large head hunched forward, "Say that again!"

"He has already resigned," came the quiet repetition, "but it has not yet taken effect. He is waiting, you see, to solve the problem of – er – myself. That finished, he is quite ready to turn the office of director over to his successor."

Bogert expelled his breath sharply, "And this successor? Who is he?" He was quite close to Herbie now, eyes fixed fascinatedly on those unreadable dull-red photoelectric cells that were the robot's eyes.

Words came slowly, "You are the next director."

And Bogert relaxed into a tight smile, "This is good to know. I've been hoping and waiting for this. Thanks, Herbie."

Peter Bogert was at his desk until five that morning and he was back at nine. The shelf just over the desk emptied of its row of reference books and tables, as he referred to one after the other. The pages of calculations before him increased microscopically and the crumpled sheets at his feet mounted into a hill of scribbled paper.

At precisely noon, he stared at the final page, rubbed a blood-shot eye, yawned and shrugged. "This is getting worse each minute. Damn!"

Isaac Asimov

He turned at the sound of the opening door and nodded at Lanning, who entered, cracking the knuckles of one gnarled hand with the other.

The director took in the disorder of the room and his eyebrows furrowed together.

"New lead?" he asked.

"No," came the defiant answer. "What's wrong with the old one?"

Lanning did not trouble to answer, nor to do more than bestow a single cursory glance at the top sheet upon Bogert's desk. He spoke through the flare of a match as he lit a cigar.

"Has Calvin told you about the robot? It's a mathematical genius. Really remarkable."

The other snorted loudly, "So I've heard. But Calvin had better stick to robopsychology. I've checked Herbie on math, and he can scarcely struggle through calculus."

"Calvin didn't find it so."

"She's crazy."

"And I don't find it so." The director's eyes narrowed dangerously.

"You!" Bogert's voice hardened. "What are you talking about?"

"I've been putting Herbie through his paces all morning, and he can do tricks you never heard of."

"Is that so?"

"You sound skeptical!" Lanning flipped a sheet of paper out of his vest pocket and unfolded it. "That's not my handwriting, is it?"

Bogert studied the large angular notation covering the sheet, "Herbie did this?"

"Right! And if you'll notice, he's been working on your time integration of Equation 22. It comes" – Lanning tapped a yellow fingernail upon the last step – "to the identical conclusion I did, and in a quarter the time. You had no right to neglect the Linger Effect in positronic bombardment."

202

"I didn't neglect it. For Heaven's sake, Lanning, get it through your head that it would cancel out—"

"Oh, sure, you explained that. You used the Mitchell Translation Equation, didn't you? Well – it doesn't apply."

"Why not?"

"Because you've been using hyper-imaginaries, for one thing."

"What's that to do with?"

"Mitchell's Equation won't hold when—"

"Are you crazy? If you'll reread Mitchell's original paper in the *Transactions of the Far*—"

"I don't have to. I told you in the beginning that I didn't like his reasoning, and Herbie backs me in that."

"Well, then," Bogert shouted, "let that clockwork contraption solve the entire problem for you. Why bother with nonessentials?"

"That's exactly the point. Herbie can't solve the problem. And if he can't, we can't – alone. I'm submitting the entire question to the National Board. It's gotten beyond us."

Bogert's chair went over backward as he jumped up a-snarl, face crimson. "You're doing nothing of the sort."

Lanning flushed in his turn, "Are you telling me what I can't do?"

"Exactly," was the gritted response. "I've got the problem beaten and you're not to take it out of my hands, understand? Don't think I don't see through you, you desiccated fossil. You'd cut your own nose off before you'd let me get the credit for solving robotic telepathy."

"You're a damned idiot, Bogert, and in one second I'll have you suspended for insubordination" – Lanning's lower lip trembled with passion.

"Which is one thing you won't do, Lanning. You haven't any secrets with a mind-reading robot around, so don't forget that I know all about your resignation."

The ash on Lanning's cigar trembled and fell, and the cigar itself followed, "What . . . what—"

Bogert chuckled nastily, "And I'm the new director, be it understood. I'm very aware of that; don't think I'm not. Damn your eyes, Lanning, I'm going to give the orders about here or there will be the sweetest mess that you've ever been in."

Lanning found his voice and let it out with a roar. "You're suspended, d'ye hear? You're relieved of all duties. You're broken, do you understand?"

The smile on the other's face broadened, "Now, what's the use of that? You're getting nowhere. I'm holding the trumps. I know you've resigned. Herbie told me, and he got it straight from you."

Lanning forced himself to speak quietly. He looked an old, old man, with tired eyes peering from a face in which the red had disappeared, leaving the pasty yellow of age behind, "I want to speak to Herbie. He can't have told you anything of the sort. You're playing a deep game, Bogert, but I'm calling your bluff. Come with me."

Bogert shrugged, "To see Herbie? Good! Damned good!"

It was also precisely at noon that Milton Ashe looked up from his clumsy sketch and said, "You get the idea? I'm not too good at getting this down, but that's about how it looks. It's a honey of a house, and I can get it for next to nothing."

Susan Calvin gazed across at him with melting eyes. "It's really beautiful," she sighed. "I've often thought that I'd like to—" Her voice trailed away.

"Of course," Ashe continued briskly, putting away his pencil, "I've got to wait for my vacation. It's only two weeks off, but this Herbie business has everything up in the air." His eyes dropped to his fingernails, "Besides, there's another point – but it's a secret."

"Then don't tell me."

"Oh, I'd just as soon, I'm just busting to tell someone

– and you're just about the best – er – confidante I could find here." He grinned sheepishly.

Susan Calvin's heart bounded, but she did not trust herself to speak.

"Frankly," Ashe scraped his chair closer and lowered his voice into a confidential whisper, "the house isn't to be only for myself. I'm getting married!"

And then he jumped out of his seat, "What's the matter?"

"Nothing!" The horrible spinning sensation had vanished, but it was hard to get words out. "Married? You mean—"

"Why, sure! About time, isn't it? You remember that girl who was here last summer. That's she! But you *are* sick. You—"

"Headache!" Susan Calvin motioned him away weakly. "I've . . . I've been subject to them lately. I want to . . . to congratulate you, of course. I'm very glad—" The inexpertly applied rouge made a pair of nasty red splotches upon her chalk-white face. Things had begun spinning again. "Pardon me – please—"

The words were a mumble, as she stumbled blindly out the door. It had happened with the sudden catastrophe of a dream – and with all the unreal horror of a dream.

But how could it be? Herbie had said—

And Herbie knew! He could see into minds!

She found herself leaning breathlessly against the door jamb, staring into Herbie's metal face. She must have climbed the two flights of stairs, but she had no memory of it. The distance had been covered in an instant, as in a dream.

As in a dream!

And still Herbie's unblinking eyes stared into hers and their dull red seemed to expand into dimly shining nightmarish globes.

He was speaking, and she felt the cold glass pressing against her lips. She swallowed and shuddered into a certain awareness of her surroundings.

Still Herbie spoke, and there was agitation in his voice
– as if he were hurt and frightened and pleading.

The words were beginning to make sense. "This is
a dream," he was saying, "and you mustn't believe in
it. You'll wake into the real world soon and laugh at
yourself. He loves you, I tell you. He does, he does! But
not here! Not now! This is an illusion."

Susan Calvin nodded, her voice a whisper, "Yes! Yes!"
She was clutching Herbie's arm, clinging to it, repeating
over and over, "It isn't true, is it? It isn't, is it?"

Just how she came to her senses, she never knew – but
it was like passing from a world of misty unreality to one
of harsh sunlight. She pushed him away from her, pushed
hard against that steely arm, and her eyes were wide.

"What are you trying to do?" Her voice rose to a harsh
scream. "What are you trying to do?"

Herbie backed away, "I want to help."

The psychologist stared, "Help? By telling me this is
a dream? By trying to push me into schizophrenia?" A
hysterical tenseness seized her, "This is no dream! I wish
it were!"

She drew her breath sharply, "Wait! Why . . . why, I
understand. Merciful Heavens, it's so obvious."

There was horror in the robot's voice, "I had to!"

"And I believed you! I never thought—"

Loud voices outside the door brought her to a halt.
She turned away, fists clenching spasmodically, and
when Bogert and Lanning entered, she was at the far
window. Neither of the men paid her the slightest
attention.

They approached Herbie simultaneously; Lanning angry
and impatient, Bogert, coolly sardonic. The director
spoke first.

"Here now, Herbie. Listen to me!"

The robot brought his eyes sharply down upon the aged
director, "Yes, Dr Lanning."

"Have you discussed me with Dr Bogert?"

Liar!

"No, sir." The answer came slowly, and the smile on Bogert's face flashed off.

"What's that?" Bogert shoved in ahead of his superior and straddled the ground before the robot. "Repeat what you told me yesterday."

"I said that—" Herbie fell silent. Deep within him his metallic diaphragm vibrated in soft discords.

"Didn't you say he had resigned?" roared Bogert. "Answer me!"

Bogert raised his arm frantically, but Lanning pushed him aside, "Are you trying to bully him into lying?"

"You heard him, Lanning. He began to say 'Yes' and stopped. Get out of my way! I want the truth out of him, understand!"

"I'll ask him!" Lanning turned to the robot. "All right, Herbie, take it easy. Have I resigned?"

Herbie stared, and Lanning repeated anxiously, "Have I resigned?" There was the faintest trace of a negative shake of the robot's head. A long wait produced nothing further.

The two men looked at each other and the hostility in their eyes was all but tangible.

"What the devil," blurted Bogert, "has the robot gone mute? Can't you speak, you monstrosity?"

"I can speak," came the ready answer.

"Then answer the question. Didn't you tell me Lanning had resigned? Hasn't he resigned?"

And again there was nothing but dull silence, until from the end of the room, Susan Calvin's laugh rang out suddenly, high-pitched and semi-hysterical.

The two mathematicians jumped, and Bogert's eyes narrowed, "You here? What's so funny?"

"Nothing's funny." Her voice was not quite natural. "It's just that I'm not the only one that's been caught. There's irony in three of the greatest experts in robotics in the world falling into the same elementary trap, isn't there?" Her voice faded, and she put a pale hand to her forehead, "But it isn't funny!"

This time the look that passed between the two men

Isaac Asimov

was one of raised eyebrows. "What trap are you talking about?" asked Lanning stiffly. "Is something wrong with Herbie?"

"No," she approached them slowly, "nothing is wrong with him – only with us." She whirled suddenly and shrieked at the robot, "Get away from me! Go to the other end of the room and don't let me look at you."

Herbie cringed before the fury of her eyes and stumbled away in a clattering trot.

Lanning's voice was hostile, "What is all this, Dr Calvin?"

She faced them and spoke sarcastically, "Surely you know the fundamental First Law of Robotics."

The other two nodded together. "Certainly," said Bogert, irritably, "a robot may not injure a human being or, through inaction, allow him to come to harm."

"How nicely put," sneered Calvin. "But what kind of harm?"

"Why – any kind."

"Exactly! Any kind! But what about hurt feelings? What about deflation of one's ego? What about the blasting of one's hopes? Is that injury?"

Lanning frowned, "What would a robot know about—" And then he caught himself with a gasp.

"You've caught on, have you? *This* robot reads minds. Do you suppose it doesn't know everything about mental injury? Do you suppose that if asked a question, it wouldn't give exactly that answer that one wants to hear? Wouldn't any other answer hurt us, and wouldn't Herbie know that?"

"Good Heavens!" muttered Bogert.

The psychologist cast a sardonic glance at him, "I take it you asked him whether Lanning had resigned. You wanted to hear that he had resigned and so that's what Herbie told you."

"And I suppose that is why," said Lanning, tonelessly, "it would not answer a little while ago. It couldn't answer either way without hurting one of us."

Liar!

There was a short pause in which the men looked thoughtfully across the room at the robot, crouching in the chair by the bookcase, head resting in one hand.

Susan Calvin stared steadfastly at the floor, "He knew of all this. That . . . that devil knows everything – including what went wrong in his assembly." Her eyes were dark and brooding.

Lanning looked up, "You're wrong there, Dr Calvin. He doesn't know what went wrong. I asked him."

"What does that mean?" cried Calvin. "Only that you didn't want him to give you the solution. It would puncture your ego to have a machine do what you couldn't. Did you ask him?" she shot at Bogert.

"In a way." Bogert coughed and reddened. "He told me he knew very little about mathematics."

Lanning laughed, not very loudly and the psychologist smiled caustically. She said, "I'll ask him! A solution by him won't hurt my ego." She raised her voice into a cold, imperative, "Come here!"

Herbie rose and approached with hesitant steps.

"You know, I suppose," she continued, "just exactly at what point in the assembly an extraneous factor was introduced or an essential one left out."

"Yes," said Herbie, in tones barely heard.

"Hold on," broke in Bogert angrily. "That's not necessarily true. You want to hear that, that's all."

"Don't be a fool," replied Calvin. "He certainly knows as much math as you and Lanning together, since he can read minds. Give him his chance."

The mathematician subsided, and Calvin continued, "All right, then, Herbie, give! We're waiting." And in an aside, "Get pencils and paper, gentlemen."

But Herbie remained silent, and there was triumph in the psychologist's voice, "Why don't you answer, Herbie?"

The robot blurted out suddenly, "I cannot. You know I cannot! Dr Bogert and Dr Lanning don't want me to."

"They want the solution."

"But not from me."

Lanning broke in, speaking slowly and distinctly, "Don't be foolish, Herbie. We do want you to tell us."

Bogert nodded curtly.

Herbie's voice rose to wild heights, "What's the use of saying that? Don't you suppose that I can see past the superficial skin of your mind? Down below, you don't want me to. I'm a machine, given the imitation of life only by virtue of the positronic interplay in my brain – which is man's device. You can't lose face to me without being hurt. That is deep in your mind and won't be erased. I can't give the solution."

"We'll leave," said Dr Lanning. "Tell Calvin."

"That would make no difference," cried Herbie, "since you would know anyway that it was I that was supplying the answer."

Calvin resumed, "But you understand, Herbie, that despite that, Drs Lanning and Bogert want that solution."

"By their own efforts!" insisted Herbie.

"But they want it, and the fact that you have it and won't give it hurts them. You see that, don't you?"

"Yes! Yes!"

"And if you tell them that will hurt them, too."

"Yes! Yes!" Herbie was retreating slowly, and step by step Susan Calvin advanced. The two men watched in frozen bewilderment.

"You can't tell them," droned the psychologist slowly, "because that would hurt and you mustn't hurt. But if you don't tell them, you hurt, so you must tell them. And if you do, you will hurt and you mustn't, so you can't tell them; but if you don't, you hurt, so you must; but if you do, you hurt, so you mustn't; but if you don't, you hurt, so you must; but if you do, you—"

Herbie was up against the wall, and here he dropped to his knees. "Stop!" he shrieked. "Close your mind! It is full of pain and frustration and hate! I didn't mean it,

Liar!

I tell you! I tried to help! I told you what you wanted to hear. I had to!"

The psychologist paid no attention. "You must tell them, but if you do, you hurt, so you mustn't; but if you don't, you hurt, so you must; but—"

And Herbie screamed!

It was like the whistling of a piccolo many times magnified – shrill and shriller till it keened with the terror of a lost soul and filled the room with the piercingness of itself.

And when it died into nothingness, Herbie collapsed into a huddled heap of motionless metal.

Bogert's face was bloodless, "He's dead!"

"No!" Susan Calvin burst into body-racking gusts of wild laughter, "not dead – merely insane. I confronted him with the insoluble dilemma, and he broke down. You can scrap him now – because he'll never speak again."

Lanning was on his knees beside the thing that had been Herbie. His fingers touched the cold, unresponsive metal face and he shuddered. "You did that on purpose." He rose and faced her, face contorted.

"What if I did? You can't help it now." And in a sudden access of bitterness, "He deserved it."

The director seized the paralysed, motionless Bogert by the wrist, "What's the difference. Come, Peter." He sighed, "A thinking robot of this type is worthless anyway." His eyes were old and tired, and he repeated, "Come, Peter!"

It was minutes after the two scientists left that Dr Susan Calvin regained part of her mental equilibrium. Slowly, her eyes turned to the living-dead Herbie and the tightness returned to her face. Long she stared while the triumph faded and the helpless frustration returned – and of all her turbulent thoughts only one infinitely bitter word passed her lips.

"*Liar!*"

*   *   *

That finished it for then, naturally. I knew I couldn't get any more out of her after that. She just sat there behind her desk, her white face cold and – remembering.

I said, "Thank you, Dr Calvin!" but she didn't answer. It was two days before I could get to see her again.

THE MARTIAN CHRONICLES

> (BBC TV, 1980)
> Starring: Rock Hudson, Gayle Hunnicutt &
> Roddy McDowall
> Directed by Michael Anderson
> Story 'I'll Not Look For Wine' by Ray Bradbury

The Martian Chronicles **has, to date, been the most ambitious and faithful adaptation of one of Ray Bradbury's stories for television. Ray, who is one of the most respected names in contempory SF, has had a considerable number of his tales brought to the small screen during the past forty years ever since Alfred Hitchcock first used his story 'Touched With Fire' (retitled 'Shopping For Death') on his CBS show** *Alfred Hitchcock Presents* **in January 1956. Bradbury's highly individual work has also been seen on other anthology shows including Jane Wyman's Fireside Theatre ('The Marked Bullet', 1956), Rendezvous ('The Wonderful Ice Cream Suit', 1958), The Twilight Zone ('I Sing The Body Electric', 1962), Movie of the Week ('The Screaming Woman', 1972) and so on almost** *ad infinitum.* **But it is his famous novel about the experiences of the first astronauts on an alien planet,** *The Martian Chronicles* **(1950), which was adapted as a big budget, three part special in 1980 which remains the most memorable.**

Ray Bradbury (1920–) was a science fiction fan – producing his own magazine, *Futuria Fantasia* **– before becoming a published writer in the pages of the legendary pulp magazine,** *Weird Tales,* **in the early Forties. Always fascinated by the cinema, two of his**

early SF stories were adapted for the screen – *It Came From Outer Space* (1953) and *The Beast From 20,000 Fathoms* (1953) – before he made his break-through as a scriptwriter when John Houston took him to Ireland in 1956 to work on his epic version of *Moby Dick*, starring Gregory Peck. Although the series of stories which make up *The Martian Chronicles* were among some of the earliest written by Ray, the gestation of the film was one of the longest on record. "The book had been optioned time and time again over thirty years, but never actually made it to the screen until 1980," Ray recalls. "John Houseman, Kirk Douglas, Alan Pakula and Robert Mulligan were all seriously interested in putting the *Chronicles* on either film or television. I actually spent a year off and on writing a script for Pakula and Mulligan, and then when I finished it was the summer we first circumnavigated Mars and photographed the surface. There obviously wasn't anything there, or supposedly there wasn't, and all the studios said, 'Oh, my god, there's no life on Mars – we don't want to make *that* film!'" It was, however, at the time of the Viking landing on Mars that Ray was approached for the rights once again by producer Charles Fried who said he was particularly keen to be faithful to Ray's story of man's intrusion onto an alien planet. Now, with considerably more optimism, Ray gave his blessing. The all-star cast, headed by Rock Hudson as the leader of the Zeus III Mars Expedition, was well-served by the special effects department – but especially by the acting of James Faulkner, as the humanoid-like Martian, Mr K, and his wife, Ylla, played by Maggie Wright. Their subtle and elegant portrayal of two planet dwellers waiting fearfully for the impact of men in silver rockets was a particular delight to Ray because this part of the drama was based on one of his favourite short stories, 'I'll Not Look For Wine': first published in the Canadian magazine, *Maclean's* in January, 1950

and later retitled 'Ylla' for book publication. It is this magical tale which represents another landmark of SF on TV . . .

They had a house of crystal pillars on the planet Mars by the edge of an empty sea, and every morning you could see Mrs K eating the golden fruits that grew from the crystal walls, or cleaning the house with handfuls of magnetic dust which, taking all dirt with it, blew away on the hot wind. Afternoons, when the fossil sea was warm and motionless, and the wine trees stood stiff in the yard, and the little distant Martian bone town was all enclosed, and no one drifted out their doors, you could see Mr K himself in his room, reading from a metal book with raised hieroglyphs over which he brushed his hand, as one might play a harp. And from the book, as his fingers stroked, a voice sang, a soft ancient voice, which told tales of when the sea was red steam on the shore and ancient men had carried clouds of metal insects and electric spiders into battle.

Mr and Mrs K had lived by the dead sea for twenty years, and their ancestors had lived in the same house, which turned and followed the sun, flower-like, for ten centuries.

Mr and Mrs K were not old. They had the fair, brownish skin of the true Martian, the yellow coin eyes, the soft musical voices. Once they had liked painting pictures with chemical fire, swimming in the canals in the seasons when the wine trees filled them with green liquors, and talking into the dawn together by the blue phosphorous portraits in the speaking-room.

They were not happy now.

This morning Mrs K stood between the pillars, listening to the desert sands heat, melt into yellow wax, and seemingly run on the horizon.

Something was going to happen.

She waited.

Ray Bradbury

She watched the blue sky of Mars as if it might at any moment grip in on itself, contract, and expel a shining miracle down upon the sand.

Nothing happened.

Tired of waiting, she walked through the misting pillars. A gentle rain sprang from the fluted pillar-tops, cooling the scorched air, falling gently on her. On hot days it was like walking in a creek. The floors of the house glittered with cool streams. In the distance she heard her husband playing his book steadily, his fingers never tired of the old songs. Quietly she wished he might one day again spend as much time holding and touching her like a little harp as he did his incredible books.

But no. She shook her head, an imperceptible, forgiving shrug. Her eyelids closed softly down upon her golden eyes. Marriage made people old and familiar, while still young.

She lay back in a chair that moved to take her shape even as she moved. She closed her eyes tightly and nervously.

The dream occurred.

Her brown fingers trembled, came up, grasped at the air. A moment later she sat up, startled, gasping.

She glanced about swiftly, as if expecting someone there before her. She seemed disappointed; the space between the pillars was empty.

Her husband appeared in a triangular door. "Did you call?" he asked irritably.

"No!" she cried.

"I thought I heard you cry out."

"Did I? I was almost asleep and had a dream!"

"In the daytime? You don't often do that."

She sat as if struck in the face by the dream. "How strange, how very strange," she murmured. "The dream."

"Oh?" He evidently wished to return to his book.

"I dreamed about a man."

"A man?"

"A tall man, six feet one inch tall."

216

"How absurd; a giant, a misshapen giant."

"Somehow" – she tried the words – "he looked all right. In spite of being tall. And he had – oh, I know you'll think it silly – he had *blue* eyes!"

"Blue eyes! Gods!" cried Mr K. "What'll you dream next? I suppose he had *black* hair?"

"How did you *guess*?" She was excited.

"I picked the most unlikely colour," he replied coldly.

"Well, black it was!" she cried. "And he had a very white skin; oh, he was *most* unusual! He was dressed in a strange uniform and he came down out of the sky and spoke pleasantly to me." She smiled.

"Out of the sky; what nonsense!"

"He came in a metal thing that glittered in the sun," she remembered. She closed her eyes to shape it again. "I dreamed there was the sky and something sparkled like a coin thrown into the air, and suddenly it grew large and fell down softly to land, a long silver craft, round and alien. And a door opened in the side of the silver object and this tall man stepped out."

"If you worked harder you wouldn't have these silly dreams."

"I rather enjoyed it," she replied, lying back. "I never suspected myself of such an imagination. Black hair, blue eyes, and white skin! What a strange man, and yet – quite handsome."

"Wishful thinking."

"You're unkind. I didn't think him up on purpose; he just came in my mind while I drowsed. It wasn't like a dream. It was so unexpected and different. He looked at me and he said, 'I've come from the third planet in my ship. My name is Nathaniel York—'"

"A stupid name; it's no name at all," objected the husband.

"Of course it's stupid, because it's a dream," she explained softly. "And he said, 'This is the first trip across space. There are only two of us in our ship, myself and my friend Bert.'"

"*Another* stupid name."

"And he said, 'We're from a city on *Earth*; that's the name of our planet,'" continued Mrs K. "That's what he said. 'Earth' was the name he spoke. And he used another language. Somehow I understood him. With my mind. Telepathy, I suppose."

Mr K turned away. She stopped him with a word. "Yll?" she called quietly. "Do you ever wonder if – well, if there *are* people living on the third planet?"

"The third planet is incapable of supporting life," stated the husband patiently. "Our scientists have said there's far too much oxygen in their atmosphere."

"But wouldn't it be fascinating if there were people? And they travelled through space in some sort of ship?"

"Really, Ylla, you know how I hate this emotional wailing. Let's get on with our work."

It was late in the day when she began singing the song as she moved among the whispering pillars of rain. She sang it over and over again.

"What's that song?" snapped her husband at last, walking in to sit at the fire table.

"I don't know." She looked up, surprised at herself. She put her hand to her mouth, unbelieving. The sun was setting. The house was closing itself in, like a giant flower, with the passing of light. A wind blew among the pillars; the fire table bubbled its fierce pool of silver lava. The wind stirred her russet hair, crooning softly in her ears. She stood silently looking out into the great sallow distances of sea bottom, as if recalling something, her yellow eyes soft and moist. "'Drink to me only with thine eyes, and I will pledge with mine,'" she sang, softly, quietly, slowly. "'Or leave a kiss but in the cup, and I'll not look for wine.'" She hummed now, moving her hands in the wind ever so lightly, her eyes shut. She finished the song.

It was very beautiful.

"Never heard that song before. Did you compose it?" he inquired, his eyes sharp.

"No. Yes. No, I don't know, really!" She hesitated wildly. "I don't even know what the words are; they're another language!"

"What language?"

She dropped portions of meat numbly into the simmering lava. "I don't know." She drew the meat forth a moment later, cooked, served on a plate for him. "It's just a crazy thing I made up, I guess. I don't know why."

He said nothing. He watched her drown meats in the hissing fire pool. The sun was gone. Slowly, slowly the night came in to fill the room, swallowing the pillars and both of them, like a dark wine poured to the ceiling. Only the silver lava's glow lit their faces.

She hummed the strange song again.

Instantly he leaped from his chair and stalked angrily from the room.

Later, in isolation, he finished supper.

When he arose he stretched, glanced at her, and suggested, yawning, "Let's take the flame birds to town tonight to see an entertainment."

"You don't *mean* it?" she said. "Are you feeling well?"

"What's so strange about that?"

"But we haven't gone for an entertainment in six months!"

"I think it's a good idea."

"Suddenly you're so solicitous," she said.

"Don't talk that way," he replied peevishly. "Do you or do you not want to go?"

She looked out at the pale desert. The twin white moons were rising. Cool water ran softly about her toes. She began to tremble just the least bit. She wanted very much to sit quietly here, soundless, not moving until this thing occurred, this thing expected all day, this thing that could not occur but might. A drift of song brushed through her mind.

"I—"

"Do you good," he urged. "Come along now."

"I'm tired," she said. "Some other night."

"Here's your scarf." He handed her a phial. "We haven't gone anywhere in months."

"Except you, twice a week to Xi City." She wouldn't look at him.

"Business," he said.

"Oh?" She whispered to herself.

From the phial a liquid poured, turned to blue mist, settled about her neck, quivering.

The flame birds waited, like a bed of coals, glowing on the cool smooth sands. The white canopy ballooned on the night wind, flapping softly, tied by a thousand green ribbons to the birds.

Ylla laid herself back in the canopy and, at a word from her husband, the birds leaped, burning, towards the dark sky. The ribbons tautened, the canopy lifted. The sand slid whining under; the blue hills drifted by, drifted by, leaving their home behind, the raining pillars, the caged flowers, the singing books, the whispering floor creeks. She did not look at her husband. She heard him crying out to the birds as they rose higher, like ten thousand hot sparkles, so many red-yellow fireworks in the heavens, tugging the canopy like a flower petal, burning through the wind.

She didn't watch the dead, ancient bone-chess cities slide under, or the old canals filled with emptiness and dreams. Past dry rivers and dry lakes they flew, like a shadow of the moon, like a torch burning.

She watched only the sky.

The husband spoke.

She watched the sky.

"Did you hear what I said?"

"What?"

He exhaled. "You might pay attention."

"I was thinking."

"I never thought you were a nature-lover, but you're certainly interested in the sky tonight," he said.

"It's very beautiful."

"I was figuring," said the husband slowly. "I thought I'd call Hulle tonight. I'd like to talk to him about us spending some time, oh, only a week or so, in the Blue Mountains. It's just an idea—"

"The Blue Mountains!" She held to the canopy rim with one hand, turning swiftly towards him.

"Oh, it's just a suggestion."

"When do you want to go?" she asked, trembling.

"I thought we might leave tomorrow morning. You know, an early start and all that," he said very casually.

"But we *never* go this early in the year!"

"Just this once, I thought—" He smiled. "Do us good to get away. Some peace and quiet. You know. You haven't anything *else* planned? We'll go, won't we?"

She took a breath, waited, and then replied, "No."

"What?" His cry startled the birds. The canopy jerked.

"No," she said firmly. "It's settled. I won't go."

He looked at her. They did not speak after that. She turned away.

The birds flew on, ten thousand firebrands down the wind.

In the dawn the sun, through the crystal pillars, melted the fog that supported Ylla as she slept. All night she had hung above the floor, buoyed by the soft carpeting of mist that poured from the walls when she lay down to rest. All night she had slept on this silent river, like a boat upon a soundless tide. Now the fog burned away, the mist level lowered until she was deposited upon the shore of wakening.

She opened her eyes.

Her husband stood over her. He looked as if he had stood there for hours, watching. She did not know why, but she could not look him in the face.

"You've been dreaming again!" he said. "You spoke out and kept me awake. I *really* think you should see a doctor."

"I'll be all right."

"You talked a lot in your sleep!"

"Did I?" She started up.

Dawn was cold in the room. A grey light filled her as she lay there.

"What was your dream?"

She had to think a moment to remember. "The ship. It came from the sky again, landed, and the tall man stepped out and talked with me, telling me little jokes, laughing, and it was pleasant."

Mr K touched a pillar. Founts of warm water leaped up, steaming; the chill vanished from the room. Mr K's face was impassive.

"And then," she said, "this man, who said his strange name was Nathaniel York, told me I was beautiful and – and kissed me."

"Ha!" cried the husband, turning violently away, his jaw working.

"It's only a dream." She was amused.

"Keep your silly, feminine dreams to yourself!"

"You're acting like a child." She lapsed back upon the few remaining remnants of chemical mist. After a moment she laughed softly. "I thought of some *more* of the dream," she confessed.

"Well, what is it, what *is* it?" he shouted.

"Yll, you're so bad-tempered."

"Tell me!" he demanded. "You can't keep secrets from me!" His face was dark and rigid as he stood over her.

"I've never seen you this way," she replied, half shocked, half entertained. "All that happened was this Nathaniel York person told me – well, he told me that he'd take me away into his ship, into the sky with him, and take me back to his planet with him. It's really quite ridiculous."

"Ridiculous, is it!" he almost screamed. "You should

have heard yourself, fawning on him, talking to him, singing with him, oh gods, all night; you should have *heard* yourself!"

"Yll!"

"When's he landing? Where's he coming down with his damned ship?"

"Yll, lower your voice."

"Voice be damned!" He bent stiffly over her. "And *in* this dream" – he seized her wrist – "didn't the ship land over in Green Valley, *didn't* it? Answer me!"

"Why, yes—"

"And it landed this afternoon, didn't it?" he kept at her.

"Yes, yes, I think so, yes, but only in a dream!"

"Well" – he flung her hand away stiffly – "it's good you're truthful! I heard every word you said in your sleep. You mentioned the valley and the time." Breathing hard, he walked between the pillars like a man blinded by a lightning bolt. Slowly his breath returned. She watched him as if he were quite insane. She arose finally and went to him. "Yll," she whispered.

"I'm all right."

"You're sick."

"No." He forced a tired smile. "Just childish. Forgive me, darling." He gave her a rough pat. "Too much work lately. I'm sorry. I think I'll lie down awhile—"

"You were so excited."

"I'm all right now. Fine." He exhaled. "Let's forget it. Say, I heard a joke about Uel yesterday, I meant to tell you. What do you say you fix breakfast, I'll tell the joke, and let's not talk about all this."

"It was only a dream."

"Of course." He kissed her cheek mechanically. "Only a dream."

At noon the sun was high and hot and the hills shimmered in the light.

"Aren't you going to town?" asked Ylla.

"Town?" He raised his brows faintly.

"This is the day you *always* go." She adjusted a flowercage on its pedestal. The flowers stirred, opening their hungry yellow mouths.

He closed his book. "No. It's too hot, and it's late."

"Oh." She finished her task and moved towards the door. "Well, I'll be back soon."

"Wait a minute! Where are you going?"

She was in the door swiftly. "Over to Pao's. She invited me!"

"Today?"

"I haven't seen her in a long time. It's only a little way."

"Over in Green Valley, isn't it?"

"Yes, just a walk, not far, I thought I'd—" She hurried.

"I'm sorry, really sorry," he said, running to fetch her back, looking very concerned about his forgetfulness. "It slipped my mind. I invited Dr Nlle out this afternoon."

"Dr Nlle!" She edged towards the door.

He caught her elbow and drew her steadily in. "Yes."

"But Pao—"

"Pao can wait, Ylla. We must entertain Nlle."

"Just for a few minutes—"

"No, Ylla."

"No?"

He shook his head. "No. Besides, it's a terribly long walk to Pao's. All the way over through Green Valley and then past the big canal and down, isn't it? And it'll be very, very hot, and Dr Nlle would be delighted to see you. Well?"

She did not answer. She wanted to break and run. She wanted to cry out. But she only sat in the chair, turning her fingers over slowly, staring at them expressionlessly, trapped.

"Ylla?" he murmured. "You *will* be here, won't you?"

"Yes," she said after a long time. "I'll be here."

"All afternoon?"

Her voice was dull. "All afternoon."

Late in the day Dr Nlle had not put in an appearance. Ylla's husband did not seem overly surprised. When it was quite late he murmured something, went to a closet, and drew forth an evil weapon, a long yellowish tube ending in a bellows and a trigger. He turned, and upon his face was a mask, hammered from silver metal, expressionless, the mask that he always wore when he wished to hide his feelings, the mask which curved and hollowed so exquisitely to his thin cheeks and chin and brow. The mask glinted, and he held the evil weapon in his hands, considering it. It hummed constantly, an insect hum. From it hordes of golden bees could be flung out with a high shriek. Golden, horrid bees that stung, poisoned, and fell lifeless, like seeds on the sand.

"Where are you going?" she asked.

"What?" He listened to the bellows, to the evil hum. "If Dr Nlle is late, I'll be damned if I'll wait. I'm going out to hunt a bit. I'll be back. You be sure to stay right here now, won't you?" The silver mask glimmered.

"Yes."

"And tell Dr Nlle I'll return. Just hunting."

The triangular door closed. His footsteps faded down the hill.

She watched him walking through the sunlight until he was gone. Then she resumed her tasks with the magnetic dusts and the new fruits to be plucked from the crystal walls. She worked with energy and dispatch, but on occasion a numbness took hold of her and she caught herself singing that odd and memorable song and looking out beyond the crystal pillars at the sky.

She held her breath and stood very still, waiting.

It was coming nearer.

At any moment it might happen.

It was like those days when you heard a thunderstorm coming and there was the waiting silence and then the faintest pressure of the atmosphere as the climate blew over the land in shifts and shadows and vapours. And the change pressed at your ears and you were suspended in the waiting time of the coming storm. You began to tremble. The sky was stained and coloured; the clouds were thickened; the mountains took on an iron taint. The caged flowers blew with faint sighs of warning. You felt your hair stir softly. Somewhere in the house the voice-clock sang. "Time, time, time, time . . ." ever so gently, no more than water tapping on velvet.

And then the storm. The electric illumination, the engulfments of dark wash and sounding black fell down, shutting in, forever.

That's how it was now. A storm gathered, yet the sky was clear. Lightning was expected, yet there was no cloud.

Ylla moved through the breathless summer-house. Lightning would strike from the sky any instant; there would be a thunder-clap, a boll of smoke, a silence, footsteps on the path, a rap on the crystalline door, and her *running* to answer . . .

Crazy Ylla! she scoffed. Why think these wild things with your idle mind?

And then it happened.

There was a warmth as of a great fire passing in the air. A whirling, rushing sound. A gleam in the sky, of metal.

Ylla cried out.

Running through the pillars, she flung wide a door. She faced the hills. But by this time there was nothing.

She was about to race down the hill when she stopped herself. She was supposed to stay here, go nowhere. The doctor was coming to visit, and her husband would be angry if she ran off.

She waited in the door, breathing rapidly, her hand out.

She strained to see over towards Green Valley, but saw nothing.

Silly woman. She went inside. You and your imagination, she thought. That was nothing but a bird, a leaf, the wind, or a fish in the canal. Sit down. Rest.

She sat down.

A shot sounded.

Very clearly, sharply, the sound of the evil insect weapon.

Her body jerked with it.

It came from a long way off. One shot. The swift humming distant bees. One shot. And then a second shot, precise and cold, and far away.

Her body winced again and for some reason she started up, screaming, and screaming, and never wanting to stop screaming. She ran violently through the house and once more threw wide the door.

The echoes were dying away, away.

Gone.

She waited in the yard, her face pale, for five minutes.

Finally, with slow steps, her head down, she wandered about the pillared rooms, laying her hand to things, her lips quivering, until finally she sat alone in the darkening wine-room, waiting. She began to wipe an amber glass with the hem of her scarf.

And then, from far off, the sound of footsteps crunching on the thin, small rocks.

She rose up to stand in the centre of the quiet room. The glass fell from her fingers, smashing to bits.

The footsteps hesitated outside the door.

Should she speak? Should she cry out, "Come in, oh, come in"?

She went forward a few paces.

The footsteps walked up the ramp. A hand twisted the door latch.

She smiled at the door.

The door opened. She stopped smiling.

It was her husband. His silver mask glowed dully.

He entered the room and looked at her for only a

moment. Then he snapped the weapon bellows open, cracked out two dead bees, heard them spat on the floor as they fell, stepped on them, and placed the empty bellows-gun in the corner of the room as Ylla bent down and tried, over and over, with no success, to pick up the pieces of the shattered glass. "What were you doing?" she asked.

"Nothing," he said with his back turned. He removed the mask.

"But the gun – I heard you fire it. Twice."

"Just hunting. Once in a while you like to hunt. Did Dr Nlle arrive?"

"No."

"Wait a minute." He snapped his fingers disgustedly. "Why, I remember now. He was supposed to visit us *tomorrow* afternoon. How stupid of me."

They sat down to eat. She looked at her food and did not move her hands. "What's wrong?" he asked, not looking up from dipping his meat in the bubbling lava.

"I don't know. I'm not hungry," she said.

"Why not?"

"I don't know; I'm just not."

The wind was rising across the sky; the sun was going down. The room was small and suddenly cold.

"I've been trying to remember," she said in the silent room, across from her cold, erect, golden-eyed husband.

"Remember what?" He sipped his wine.

"That song. That fine and beautiful song." She closed her eyes and hummed, but it was not the song. "I've forgotten it. And, somehow, I don't want to forget it. It's something I want always to remember." She moved her hands as if the rhythm might help her to remember all of it. Then she lay back in her chair. "I can't remember." She began to cry.

"Why are you crying?" he asked.

"I don't know, I don't know, but I can't help it. I'm sad and I don't know why, I cry and I don't know why, but I'm crying."

Her head was in her hands; her shoulders moved again and again.

"You'll be all right tomorrow," he said.

She did not look up at him; she looked only at the empty desert and the very bright stars coming out now on the black sky, and far away there was a sound of wind rising and canal waters stirring cold in the long canals. She shut her eyes, trembling.

"Yes," she said. "I'll be all right tomorrow."

DISCWORLD

(Granada TV, 1996)
Produced by Andy Harries
Story 'Final Reward' by Terry Pratchett

The comic fantasy novels by Terry Pratchett have become a phenomenonal success story, earning the author lavish praise in the press – *The Mail on Sunday* declaring him to be, 'This country's greatest living novelist . . . the Dickens of the 20th Century.' Such praise leaves the bearded, unassuming Terry rather amused, although he takes considerable pride at having reached such a vast and appreciative readership: his famous series of Discworld novels alone have already sold more than 4 million copies in the UK. And having conquered the literary world – each new novel from his pen invariably reaches the top of the best seller lists – Terry has already had two of his other stories made into television programmes: *Truckers* (1991) an animated film about a family of tiny Nomes stowed away on a truck, which was filmed by Cosgrove Hall; and *Johnny and the Dead* (1995) featuring a schoolboy (Andrew Falvey) who can walk through a cemetery and talk to the occupants – even resurecting some of them for a chat including a Victorian worthy (George Baker), an old Communist (Brian Blessed) and a sufragette (Jane Lapotaire). Now Granada TV have bought the rights to the Discworld books – stories of a world dominated by magic travelling through space on the back of a giant turtle being slowly turned by four elephants – and producer Andy Harries is planning an ambitious two-hour pilot film to be followed by a series of hour long episodes. The project has already been described, somewhat tongue-in-cheek, by one TV critic as 'Star Trek meets Monty Python'.

Terry Pratchett (1948–), who was born in Beaconsfield, has admitted that the Kenneth Grahame classic, *Wind in the Willows*, was one of his earliest influences, and such was his natural skill as a storyteller that he sold his first story, 'The Hades Business' to *Science Fantasy Magazine* when he was just 13 years old. After leaving school, Terry became a reporter on the *Bucks Free Press* and, working in his spare time, wrote his first novel for children, *The Carpet People* in 1971. Later he became a press officer with the Central Electricity Generating Board and in 1976 published his first adult novel, *The Dark Side of the Sun*, which some critics have seen as a 'stepping stone' to the Discworld series which was launched seven years later with *The Colour of Magic*. The elements of fantasy mixed with satirical wit that have made the subsequent 18 books in the series so successful was evident from the very start, as the US trade magazine *Publishers Weekly* spotted in its review: 'Heroic barbarians, chthonic monsters, beautiful princesses and fiery dragons; they're all here, but none of them is doing business as usual.' Hereunder is one of Terry's rare short stories about an equally out-of-the-ordinary barbarian hero which he wrote for *Games Magazine* in 1988. It is appearing in book form for the first time and will no doubt be as welcome to Terry's huge army of fans as the thought of his mad and magical world becoming the latest in the continuing series of space movies on television . . .

Final Reward

Dogger answered the door when he was still in his dressing gown. Something unbelievable was on the doorstep.

Terry Pratchett

"There's a simple explanation," thought Dogger, "I've gone mad."

This seemed a satisfactory enough rationalisation at seven o'clock in the morning. He shut the door again and shuffled down the passage, while outside the kitchen window the Northern Line rattled with carriages full of people who weren't mad, despite appearances.

There is a blissful period of existence which the Yen Buddhists* call *plinki*. It is defined quite precisely as that interval between waking up and being hit on the back of the head by all the problems that kept you awake the night before; it ends when you realise that this was the morning everything was going to look better in, and it doesn't.

He remembered the row with Nicky. Well, not exactly *row*. More a kind of angry silence on her part, and an increasingly exasperated burbling on his, and he wasn't quite sure how it had started anyway. He recalled saying something about some of her friends looking as though they wove their own bread and baked their own goats, and then it has escalated to the level where he'd probably said things like *Since you ask, I do think green 2CVs have the anti-nuclear sticker laminated into their rear window before they leave the factory*. If he had been on the usual form he achieved after a pint of white wine he'd probably passed a remark about dungarees on women, too. It had been one of those rows where every jocular attempt to extract himself had opened another chasm under his feet.

And then she'd broken, no, shattered the silence with all those comments about Erdan *macho wish-fulfillment for adolescents*, and there'd been comments about Rambo, and then he'd found himself arguing the case for people who, in cold sobriety, he detested as much as she did.

And then he'd come home and written the last chapter of *Erdan and the Serpent of the Rim*, and out of pique, alcohol and rebellion he'd killed his hero off on the

* Like Zen Buddish only bigger begging bowls.

232

last page. Crushed under an avalanche. The fans were going to hate him, but he'd felt better afterwards, freed of something that had held him back all these years. And had made him quite rich, incidentally. That was because of computers, because half the fans he met now worked in computers, and of course in computers they gave you a wheelbarrow to take your wages home; science fiction fans might break out in pointy ears from time to time, but they bought books by the shovelful and read them round the clock.

Now he'd have to think of something else for them, write proper science fiction, learn about black holes and quantums . . .

There was another point nagging his mind as he yawned his way back to the kitchen.

Oh, yes. Erdan the Barbarian had been standing on his doorstep.

Funny, that.

This time the hammering made small bits of plaster detach themselves from the wall around the door, which was an unusual special effect in a hallucination. Dogger opened the door again.

Erdan was standing patiently next to his milk. The milk was white, and in bottles. Erdan was seven feet tall and in a tiny chain mail loincloth; his torso looked like a sack full of footballs. In one hand he held what Dogger knew for certainty was Skung, the Sword of the Ice Gods.

Dogger was certain about this because he had described it thousands of times. But he wasn't going to describe it again.

Erdan broke the silence.

"I have come," he said, "to meet my Maker."

"Pardon?"

"I have come," said the barbarian hero, "to receive my Final Reward." He peered down Dogger's hall expectantly and rippled his torso.

"You're a fan, right?" said Dogger. "Pretty good costume . . ."

233

"What," said Erdan, "is fan?"

"I want to drink your blood," said Skung, conversationally.

Over the giant's shoulder – metaphorically speaking, although under his massive armpit in real life – Dogger saw the postman coming up the path. The man walked around Erdan, humming, pushed a couple of bills into Dogger's unresisting hand, opined against all the evidence that it looked like being a nice day, and strolled back down the path.

"I want to drink his blood, too," said Skung.

Erdan stood impassively, making it quite clear that he was going to stay there until the Snow Mammoths of Hy-Kooli came home.

History records a great many foolish comments, such as "It looks perfectly safe", or "Indians? What Indians?" and Dogger added to the list with an old favourite which has caused more encyclopedias and life insurance policies to be sold than you would have thought possible.

"I suppose," he said, "that you'd better come in."

No one could look that much like Erdan. His leather jerkin looked as though it had been stored in a compost heap. His fingernails were purple, his hands calloused, his chest a trelliswork of scars. Something with a mouth the size of an armchair appeared to had got a grip on his arm at some time, but couldn't have liked the taste.

What it is, Dogger said, is I'm externalising my fantasies. Or I'm probably still asleep. The important thing is to act natural.

"Well, well," he said.

Erdan ducked into what Dogger liked to call his study, which was just like any other living room but had his wordprocessor on the table, and sat down in the armchair. The springs gave a threatening creak.

Then he gave Dogger an expectant look.

Of course, Dogger told himself, he may just be your everyday homicidal maniac.

"Your final reward?" he said weakly.

Erdan nodded.

"Er. What form does this take, exactly?"

Erdan shrugged. Several muscles had to move out of the way to allow the huge shoulders to rise and fall.

"It is said," he said, "that those who die in combat will feast and carouse in your hall forever."

"Oh." Dogger hovered uncertainly in the doorway. "My hall?"

Erdan nodded again. Dogger look around him. What with the telephone and the coatrack it was already pretty crowded. Opportunities for carouse looked limited.

"And, er," he said, "how long is forever, exactly?"

"Until the stars die and the Great Ice covers the world," said Erdan.

"Ah. I thought it might be something like that."

Cobham's voice crackled in the earpiece.

"You've what?" it said.

"I said I've given him a lager and a chicken leg and put him in the front of the television," said Dogger. "You know what? It was the fridge that really impressed him. He says I've got the next Ice Age shut in a prison, what do you think of that? And the TV is how I spy on the world, he says. He's watching *Neighbours* and he's laughing."

"Well, what do you expect me to do about it?"

"Look, no one could act that much like Erdan! It'd take weeks just to get the stink right! I mean, it's him. Really him. Just as I always imagined him. And he's sitting in my study watching soaps! You're my agent, what do I do next?"

"Just calm down." Cobham's voice sounded soothing. "Erdan is your creation. You've lived with him for years."

"Years is okay! Years was in my head. It's right now in my house that's on my mind!"

". . . and he's very popular and it's only to be expected that, when you take a big step like killing him off . . ."

"You know I had to do it! I mean, twenty-six books!"

The sound of Erdan's laughter boomed through the wall.

"Okay, so it's preyed on your mind. I can tell. He's not really there. You said the milkman couldn't see him.

"The postman. Yes, but he walked around him! Ron, I created him! He thinks I'm God! And now I've killed him off, he's come to meet me!"

"Kevin?"

"Yes? What?"

"Take a few tablets or something. He's bound to go away. These things do."

Dogger put the phone down carefully.

"Thanks a lot," he said bitterly.

In fact, he gave it a try. He went down to the hypermarket and pretended that the hulking figure that followed him wasn't really there.

It wasn't that Erdan was invisible to other people. Their eyes saw him all right, but somehow their brains seemed to edit him out before he impinged on any higher centres.

That is, they could walk around him and even apologised automatically if they bumped into him, but afterwards they would be at loss to explain what they had walked around and who they had apologised to.

Dogger left him behind in the maze of shelves, working on a desperate theory that if Erdan was out of his sight for a while he might evaporate, like smoke. He grabbed a few items, scurried through a blessed clear checkout, and was back on the pavement before a cheerful shout made him stiffen and turn around slowly, as though on castors.

Erdan had mastered shopping trolleys. Of course, he was really quite bright. He'd worked out the Maze of the Mad God in a matter of hours, after all, so a wire box on wheels was a doddle.

He'd even come to terms with the freezer cabinets. Of course, Dogger thought. *Erdan and the Top of the World*,

Chapter Four: he'd survived on 10,000 year old woolly mammoth, fortuitously discovered in the frozen tundra. Dogger had actually done some research about that. It had told him it wasn't in fact possible, but what the hell. As far as Erdan was concerned, the wizard Tesco had simply prepared these mammoths in handy portion packs.

"I watch everyone," said Erdan proudly. "I like being dead."

Dogger crept up to the trolley. "But it's not yours!"

Erdan looked puzzled.

"It is now," he said. "I took it. Much easy. No fighting. I have drink, I have meat, I have My-Name-Is-TRACEY-How-May-I-Help-You, I have small nuts in bag."

Dogger pulled aside most of a cow in small polystyrene boxes and Tracey's mad, terrified eyes looked up at him from the depths of the trolley. She extended a sticker gun in both hands, like Dirty Harry about to have his made, and priced his nose at 98p a lb. "Soap," said Dogger. "It's called soap. Not like *Neighbours*, this one is useful. You wash with it." He sighed. "Vigorous movements of the wet flannel over parts of your body," he went on, "It's a novel idea, I know."

"And this is the bath," he added. "And this is the sink. And this is called a lavatory. I explained about it before."

"It is smaller than the bath," Erdan complained mildly.

"Yes. *Nevertheless*. And these are towels, to dry you. And this is a toothbrush, and this is a razor." He hesitated. "You remember," he said, "When I put you in the seraglio of the Emir of the White Mountain? I'm pretty certain you had a wash and shave then. This is just like that."

"Where are the houris?"

"There are no houris. You have to do it yourself."

A train screamed past, rattling the scrubbing brush into the washbasin. Erdan growled.

"It's just a train," said Dogger. "A box to travel in. It won't hurt you. Just don't try to kill one."

Ten minutes later Dogger sat listening to Erdan singing, although that in itself wasn't the problem; it was a sound you could imagine floating across sunset taiga. Water dripped off the light fitting, but that wasn't the problem.

The problem was Nicky. It usually was. He was going to meet her after work at the House of Tofu. He was horribly afraid that Erdan would come with him. This was not likely to be good news. His stock with Nicky was bumping on the bottom even before last night, owing to an ill-chosen remark about black stockings last week, when he was still on probation for what he said ought to be done with mime-artists. Nicky liked New Men, although the term was probably out of date now. Jesus, he'd taken the *Guardian* to keep up with her and got another black mark when he said its children's page read exactly like someone would write if they set out to do a spoof *Guardian* children's page . . . Erdan wasn't a New Man. She was bound to notice him. She had a sort of radar for things like that.

He had to find a way to sent him back.

"I want to drink your blood," said Skung, from behind the sofa.

"Oh, shut up."

He tried some positive thinking again.

It is absolutely impossible that a fictional character I created is having a bath upstairs. It's overwork, caused by hallucinations. Of course I don't feel mad, but I wouldn't, would I? He's . . . he's a projection. That's right. I've, I've being going through a bad patch lately, basically since I was about ten, and Erdan is just a projection of the sort of macho thingy I secretly want to be. Nicky said I wrote the books because of that, she said. I can't cope with the real world, so I turned all the problems into monsters and invented a character that could handle them. Erdan is how I cope with the world. I never realised it myself. So all I need do be positive, and he won't exist.

He eyed the pile of manuscript on the table.

I wonder if Conan Doyle had this sort of problem?

Perhaps he was just sitting down to tea when Sherlock Holmes knocked at the door, still dripping wet from the Richtofen Falls or whatever, and then started hanging around the house making clever remarks until Doyle trapped him between pages again.

He half rose from his chair. That was it. All he had to do was rewrite the . . .

Erdan pushed open the door.

"Ho!" he said, and then stuck his little, relatively little finger in one wet ear and made a noise like a cork coming out of a bottle. He was wearing a bath towel. Somehow he looked neat, less scared. Amazing what hot water could do, Dogger decided.

"All my clothes they prickle," he said cheerfully.

"Did you try washing them?" said Dogger weakly.

"They dry all solid like wood," said Erdan. "I pray for clothes like gods, mighty Kevin."

"None of mine would fit," said Dogger. He looked at Erdan's shoulders. "None of mine would half fit," he added, "Anyway, you're not going anywhere. I give in. I'll rewrite the last chapter. You can go home."

He beamed. This was exactly the right way. By taking the madness seriously he could make it consume itself. All he need do was change the last page, he didn't even need to write another Erdan book, all he needed to do was to make it clear that Erdan was still alive somewhere.

"I'll write you some new clothes, too," he said. "Silly, isn't it," he went on, "A big lad like you dying in an avalanche! You've survived much worse."

He pulled the manuscript towards him.

"I mean," he burbled happily, "Don't you remember when you had to cross the Grebor Desert without water, and you . . ."

A hand like closed over his wrist, gently but firmly. Dogger remembered one of those science films which had showed an industrial robot, capable of putting two tons of pressure on a point an eighth of an inch across, gently picking up an egg. Now his wrist knew how the egg felt.

"I like it here," said Erdan.

He made him leave Skung behind. Skung was a sword of few words, and none of them would go down well in a wholefood restaurant where even the beansprouts were free-range. Erdan wasn't going to be left behind, though. Where does a seven foot barbarian hero go? Dogger thought. Wherever he likes.

He also tried writing Erdan a new suit of clothes. It was only partially successful. Erdan was not cut out by nature, by him, to wear a sports jacket. He ended up looking as Dogger had always pictured him, like a large and over-enthusiastic Motorhead fan.

Erdan seemed to be becoming more obvious. Maybe whatever kind of mental antibodies prevented people from seeing him wore away after a while. He certainly got a few odd looks.

"Who is tofu?" said Erdan, as they walked to the bus-stop.

"Ah. Not a who, an it. It's a sort of food and tiling grout combined. It's . . . it's something like . . . well, sometimes it's green, other times it isn't," said Dogger. This didn't help much. "Well," he said, "remember when you went to fight for help Doge of Tenitti? I was pretty sure I wrote you eating pasta."

"Yes."

"Compared to tofu, pasta is a taste explosion. Two to the centre please," Dogger added, to the conductor.

The man squinted at Erdan. "Rock concert on, is there? he said.

"And you carouse in this tofu?" said Erdan, as they alighted.

"You can't carouse organically. My girl . . . a young lady I know works there. She believes in things. And, look, I don't want you spoiling it, okay? My romantic life isn't exactly straightforward at the moment." A thought struck him. "And don't let's have any advice from you about how to straighten it. Throwing women over your pommel and riding off into the night isn't approved around here. It's probably an ism," he added gloomily.

"It works for me," said Erdan.

"Yes," muttered Dogger. "It always did. Funny, that. You never had any trouble, I saw to that. Twenty-six books without a change of clothes and no girl ever said she was washing her hair."

"Not my fault, they just throw . . ."

"I'm not saying it was. I'm just saying a chap has only got so much of it, and I gave mine to you."

Erdan's brow wrinkled mightily with the effort of thought. His lips moved as he repeated the sentence to himself, once or twice. Then he appeared to reach a conclusion.

"What?" he said.

"And you go back in the morning."

"I like it here. You have picture television, sweet food, soft seats."

"You enjoyed it in Chimera! The snowfields, the bracing wind, the endless taiga . . ."

Erdan gave him a sidelong glance.

"Didn't you?" said Dogger, uncertainly.

"If you say so," said Erdan.

"And you watch too much far-seeing box."

"Television," corrected Erdan. "Can I take it back?"

"What, to Chimera?"

"It get lonely on the endless taiga between books."

"You found the Channel Four button, I see." Dogger turned the idea over in his mind. It had certain charm. Erdan the Barbarian with his blood-drinking sword, chain-mail kilt, portable television and thermal blanket.

No, it wouldn't work. It wasn't as if there were many channels in Chimera, and probably one of the few things you couldn't buy in the mysterious souks of Ak-Terezical was a set of decent ni-cads.

He shivered. What was he thinking about? He really was going mad. The fans would kill him.

And he knew he'd never been able to send Erdan

back. Not now. Something had changed, he'd never be able to do it again. He'd enjoyed creating Chimera. He only had to close his eyes and he could see the Shemark mountains, every lofty peak trailing its pennant of snow. He knew the Prades delta like the back of his hand. *Better*. And now it was all going, ebbing like the tide. Leaving Erdan.

Who was evolving.

"Here it say 'House of Tofu'," said Erdan.

Who had learnt to read.

Whose clothes somehow looked less hairy, whose walk was less of a shamble.

And Dogger knew that, when they walked through that door, Erdan and Nicky would hit it off. She'd see him all right. She always seemed to look right through Dogger, but she'd see Erdan.

His hair was shorter. His clothes looked merely stylish. Erdan had achieved in a short walk from the bus-stop what it had taken most barbarians ten thousand years to accomplish. Logical, really. After all, Erdan was basically your total hero type. Put him in any environment and he'd change to fit. Two hours with Nicky and he'd be torpedoing whaling ships and shutting down nuclear power stations single-handedly.

"You go on in," he said.

"Problems?" said Erdan.

"Just got something to sort out. I'll join you later. Remember, though. I made you what you are."

"Thank you," said Erdan.

"Here's the spare key to the flat in case I'm not back. You know. Get held up or something."

Erdan took it gravely.

"You go ahead. Don't worry, I won't send you back to Chimera."

Erdan gave him a look in which surprise was leavened with just the hint of amusement.

"Chimera?" he said.

*   *   *

The wordprocessor clicked into life.

And the monitor was without form, and void, and darkness was upon the screen, with of course the exception of the beckoning flicker of the cursor.

Dogger's hand moved upon the face of the keyboard.

It ought to work both ways. If belief was the engine of it all, it ought to be possible to hitch a ride if you really were mad enough to try it.

Where to start?

A short story would be enough, just to create the character. Chimera already existed, in a little bubble of fractal reality created by these ten fingers.

He began to type, hesitantly at first, and then speeding up as the ideas began to crystallise out.

After a little while he opened the kitchen window. Behind him, in the darkness, the printer started up.

The key turned in the lock.

The cursor pulsed gently as the two of them came in, talked, made coffee, talked again in the body language of people finding they really have a lot in common. Words like "holistic approach" floated past its uncritical beacon.

"He's always doing things like this," she said. "It's the drinking and smoking. It's not a healthy life. He doesn't know how to look after himself."

Erdan paused. He found the printed output cascading down the table, and now he put down the short MS half read. Outside a siren wailed, dopplered closer, shut off.

"I'm sorry?" he said.

"I said he doesn't look after himself."

"I think he may have to learn," he said. He picked up a pencil, regarded the end of it thoughtfully until the necessary skills clicked precisely in his head, and made a few insertions. The idiot hadn't even specified what kind of clothing he was wearing. If you're really going to write first person, you might as well keep warm. It got damn cold out on the steppes.

"You've known him a long time, then?"

"Years."

"You don't look like most of his friends."

"We were quite close at one time. I expect I'd better see to the place until he comes back." He pencilled in *but the welcoming firelight of a Skryling encampment showed through the freezing trees.* Skrylings were okay, they considered that crazy people were great shamen, Kevin should be all right there.

Nicky stood up. "Well, I'd better be going," she said. The tone and pitch of her voice turned tumblers in his head.

"You needn't," he said. "It's entirely up to you, of course."

There was a long pause. She walked up behind him and looked over his shoulder, her manner a little awkward.

"What's this?" she said, in an attempt to turn the conversation away from its logical conclusions.

"Just a story of his. I'd better mail it in the morning."

"Oh. Are you a writer, too?"

Erdan glanced at the wordprocessor. Compared to the Bronze Hordes of Merkle it didn't look too fearsome. A whole new life was waiting for him, he could feel it, he could flow out into it. And change to suit.

"Just breaking into it," he said.

"I mean, I quite like Kevin," she said quickly. "He just never seemed to relate to the real world." She turned away to hide her embarrassment, and peered out of the window.

"There's a lot of blue lights down on the railway line," she said.

Erdan made a few more alterations. "Are there?" he said.

"And there's people milling about."

"Oh." Erdan changed the title to *The Traveller of the*

Falconsong. What was needed was more development, he could see that. He'd write about what he knew.

After a bit of thought he added *Book One in the Chronicles of Kevin the Bardsinger*.

It was the least he could do.